FINAL EDITION

THE THIRD LINDSAY GORDON MYSTERY

VAL McDERMID

First published by The Women's Press Ltd, 1991
A member of the Namara Group
34 Great Sutton Street, London EC1V ODX

Reprinted 1993

This edition 1998

British Library Cataloguing-in-Publication Data
A catalogue record for this book is available from the
British Library.

ISBN 0 7043 4593 5

Typeset by AKM Associates (UK) Ltd, Southall, London
Printed and bound in Great Britain by Cox & Wyman Ltd,
Reading, Berkshire

Acknowledgments

I'd like to thank Linzi Moody for her much-tried patience, her support and for the constant flow of ideas and suggestions that have made this a better book than it would otherwise have been; Christine Hamilton, Mary Timlin and Jennifer Young for helpful suggestions and for bearing with me while we trawled the delights of the City of Culture; my journalistic colleagues who couldn't be more different from the heartless hacks I sometimes portray; Simon Travers, who explained the myth of fingerprints; and last but not least, my agents, Jane Gregory and Lisanne Radice whose unfailing good humour and encouragement help to keep me sane.

Prologue

Glasgow, Scotland, December 1989

Jackie Mitchell stared down at the murdered body of Alison Maxwell, fear and horror mingling in equal measure. Alison was sprawled on the familiar bedroom carpet, limbs crooked, blonde hair spread round her head in a jagged halo. The ravages of strangulation had left her face barely recognisable. The scarf that was wound into a tight ligature round her neck was, however, only too easily identifiable. Jackie would know her own distinctive yellow tartan muffler anywhere. Slowly, with an enormous effort of will, she forced herself to look up.

Jackie gazed round the crowded courtroom, only too aware of the accusing eyes that had already made their judgment about her guilt. The photograph she clutched in her sweating hands was her first sight of Alison Maxwell's corpse. But she knew that the number of people in the stuffy courtroom who genuinely believed that could be counted on the fingers of one hand. Certainly the fifteen members of the jury, who were flicking through the prosecution's photograph album with looks of shock, horror and disgust that mirrored her own emotions, were not among them.

The wiry figure of Duncan Leslie, the Advocate-Depute charged with presenting the prosecution case against her, paced to and fro across the wood-panelled courtroom as he gently drew every last scrap of damning information from the pathologist in the witness box. 'And in your opinion,'

1

Leslie probed in his soft Borders accent, 'are the features of this case consistent with strangulation by a male or a female?'

The pathologist paused momentarily, glancing towards the dock, refusing to meet Jackie's pale green eyes. His mouth tightened in disapproval. 'In my view,' he said in a clipped voice, 'I would say that this method of killing would suggest either a woman, or a man who was not very strong.'

'Would you explain that opinion to the court?'

'Well, strangulation with a ligature like this scarf requires considerable strength. But the need for brute force is avoided by using a lever with the ligature. In this case, as you can see from Photograph Number Five, the killer used the handle of a strong hairbrush to twist the ligature tighter. That implies to me that the strangler was not sufficiently strong to perform the act manually, thus suggesting either a woman or a weak male.'

Another nail in my coffin, thought Jackie in despair, her hands involuntarily gripping the wooden rail of the dock. As the evidence droned on around her, she looked despondently round the courtroom. In her seventeen years as a journalist, she'd had little experience of the courts. While she'd been a young trainee on a weekly paper in Ayrshire, she'd occasionally covered routine cases in the Sheriff Court. But after that, she had become a feature writer and had never even crossed the threshold of the imposing High Court building by the Clyde.

It wasn't an environment she felt comfortable with, unlike the crowd of news reporters crammed into the press bench. All men, for crime reporting was still a male preserve in Glasgow. They sat there, hour after hour, like eager jackals, taking down every detail in their meticulous shorthand. And tomorrow, she knew, the bricks of evidence that were slowly building a wall round her would be reassembled to provide the foundations of sensational stories that would strip all her privacy from her. She knew most of these men. That was the hardest part of all. For ten years, she had been a leading freelance feature writer in the city, working for all the major newspapers and magazines. These were men she'd laughed with, gossiped with, drunk with. Now, as she studied them intent on their task, they looked like strangers. Familiar features seemed to have shifted, hardened, changed somehow. She wasn't their pal Jackie any more. She was a brutal bitch, an animal with a perverted sexuality who had killed one of their number. In life, Alison Maxwell had been a talented Scottish *Daily Clarion* feature writer with a dubious personal reputation. In death, she had been promoted to the Blessed Martyr of Fleet Street.

When she could no longer bear to look at her former colleagues, Jackie turned her eyes to the jury. Nine men, six women. A spread of ages from early twenties to middle fifties. They looked for the most part like solid, respectable citizens. The sort of people for whom her first crime was being a lesbian, a state from which any other crime might naturally flow. When she'd been led into the dock on the first morning, they had looked at her curiously, weighing her up as if calculating the likelihood of her guilt. But as the prosecution had steadily built its case, they had shown an increasing reluctance to look at her, contenting themselves with furtive glances. She began to wonder if she'd been right to listen to her solicitor's advice about her clothes. The series of smart, feminine suits and dresses she'd chosen for the trial made her look too normal, she feared. Almost as if she were one of them. Perhaps they'd have been more open-minded about the evidence placed before them if she hadn't disturbed them with that subtle threat. Maybe they'd have been less unnerved by her if she was standing there with her copper hair cropped short, wearing a Glad to Be Gay sweatshirt. Then they could have treated her more like Exhibit A.

Wearily she sighed, and tried to raise her spirits with a glance at the one person she could be certain still believed in her innocence. In the front row of the public benches, her fine, white-blonde hair falling round her head like a gleaming helmet, Claire Ogilvie sat taking notes. Her neat, small features, dwarfed by the huge glasses she wore, were fixed in concentration, except when she looked up at Jackie. Then she would give a small, encouraging smile, which against all odds and logic kept a flicker of hope alive in Jackie's heart. In the five years they'd been together, she'd never had to rely so much on Claire. Whatever happened at the end of the trial, she'd never be able to repay that debt.

As soon as the police had arrived that October evening to arrest Jackie, Claire had been on the phone to one of Glasgow's top criminal lawyers, who had responded to the call of a fellow solicitor with a speed astonishing to anyone familiar with the procrastinations of his breed. Jim Carstairs had actually been waiting at the Maryhill Police Station when they'd brought her in to charge her with the murder of Alison Maxwell. Although Claire Ogilvie's flourishing commercial law practice never dealt with criminal law, she always sent any of her clients who needed a good trial lawyer to Macari, Stevenson and Carstairs, so Jim had pulled out all the stops for Jackie. But it had made little difference. Because of the gravity of the charge, bail had been refused, and she'd spent the last eight weeks on remand in the women's prison near Stirling. In spite of the demands of her clients, Claire had somehow contrived to visit her almost every day. It had been the only thing that had kept Jackie going when she felt the walls closing in and heard the voices of madness in her head. There had been times when she'd even begun to wonder herself if she'd killed Alison in a moment of insanity that she could no longer recall.

But through it all, Claire had been there, practical, indomitable, supportive. Although Claire concentrated on commercial and contract law herself, she had many friends with criminal practices, and she knew only too well the costs of mounting a first-class defence. So, the morning after the bail hearing, she'd put their fashionable three-bedroomed first-floor flat on the market. Because of its size and its position on a sunny corner near the University, it had been sold within days, thanks to the efficient processes of the Scottish property laws. Claire had dutifully paid half the proceeds into Jackie's bank account to fund her lover's defence. She had promptly bought herself a new home, free from all past associations, in a newly renovated block in the heart of the Merchant City, the yuppified district in the city centre where property developers were busily cashing in on the aspirations of the suddenly rich. Claire told herself she had no doubts about Jackie's innocence; but she was nobody's fool when it came to the law. She'd had enough discussion with Jim Carstairs to realise that Jackie's chances of walking away from this murder indictment were so slim as to be negligible. Although Jackie was unaware of it, the ever-practical Claire Ogilvie had already started to rebuild her life.

Part of that rebuilding took the shape of the attractive, dark-haired woman who sat next to her during the trial. As far as Jackie was concerned, Cordelia Brown was simply a friend who had done her best to help the defence in the build-up to the trial. In her despair at ever clearing her name of the charge, Jackie had dredged up the name of one person that she believed might be able to find out the truth. When Claire had gone looking for Lindsay Gordon she had quickly discovered that Cordelia was their only hope of finding her. But their efforts had been fruitless. Like everything else that had happened to Jackie since her last visit to Alison's flat, things hadn't worked out according to plan. But for Claire, it was a very different story.

Duncan Leslie got to his feet and slowly surveyed the jury. The trial was almost over, and he was filled with a quiet confidence. He had spun his web around Jackie Mitchell. Now, all he had to do was to draw the threads together to present her to the jury as a tightly wrapped cocoon with no prospect of escape.

'Ladies and gentlemen of the jury,' he began, pacing slowly backwards and forwards in front of the jury box. 'This has not been a pleasant case for any of us. A woman has been brutally killed in the one place where she could reasonably hope to be safe – in the bedroom of her own flat, in the arms of her lover. The defence have tried to cloud your judgment with tawdry allegations about the victim of this particularly horrific crime. But I'd like to remind you that it is not Alison Maxwell who is on trial here today – it is her killer, Jackie Mitchell.

'You have heard how, on the afternoon of 16 October, Jackie Mitchell visited Alison Maxwell in her flat, thus betraying her own live-in lover. The two women went to bed together and had sex. A quarrel followed. Jackie Mitchell then left the flat. Within minutes of her departure, Alison Maxwell's strangled body was discovered, still warm. None of these facts is in dispute.' Leslie stopped walking to and fro and turned to face the jury, fixing them one by one with an unblinking stare that, more effectively than any histrionics, gave force to his words.

'My colleague for the defence is asking you to believe that in those few short moments, a third party managed to enter a block of flats protected by security entryphones and contrived to get into Alison Maxwell's flat, leaving no signs of any break-in. Then this unknown assailant strangled her with Jackie Mitchell's own scarf – a method of killing, incidentally, which does not lend itself to speed. This mysterious murderer then managed to make a clean getaway. And during all this, our killer was never seen, never heard.

'If you believe that, ladies and gentlemen of the jury, then I expect you will also believe that the moon is made of green cheese.

'The truth is far, far simpler.' Leslie turned away from the jury and stared at Jackie. At the end of his dramatic pause, he turned back to the jury, who looked mesmerised by a performance that was outshining every courtroom drama they'd ever watched on television. 'Forget the mysterious stranger. Alison Maxwell's killer is sitting before you now, ladies and gentlemen.

'Jackie Mitchell wanted to end her affair with Alison Maxwell. Now, Alison's sexual preferences might be alien to most people, but her emotional responses were identical to ours. She didn't want Jackie to depart from her life. Like most of us, faced with losing someone we care about, she used emotional blackmail in a bid to hold on to her lover. What she didn't realise was that she was trying to blackmail a killer. The threat of losing the things that mattered to her drove Jackie Mitchell over the edge.

6

'Jackie Mitchell was the only other person in that flat on the afternoon of 16 October. Jackie Mitchell was overheard quarrelling angrily with Alison Maxwell. And Jackie Mitchell's scarf was the weapon that choked the life out of Alison Maxwell. Ladies and gentlemen of the jury, this is an open and shut case. On the basis of the evidence before you, the only possible verdict you can bring in this case is guilty.'

The defence advocate did his best. But his emotive pleas clearly had less effect on the jury than the short, measured address of Duncan Leslie. As the judge summed up, Jackie felt as if a door had been slammed in her face. There was no escape, she realised. Her worst fears were about to become her new reality. She could feel the eyes of everyone in the room fixed on her, but she could meet none of them. She stared straight ahead at a point on the wall above the judge's head, a creeping numbness filling her. She felt cold sweat trickling uncomfortably down her spine, and she suddenly became aware that the simple act of breathing needed conscious effort. As the jury filed out, the slow shuffle of their feet reminded her of the prison sounds that had filled her ears for the last weeks, and would now be part of her life for as long as she could imagine. It was all over.

The verdict came as no surprise to Claire. Her faith in the ability of the legal system to achieve justice had diminished as the circumstantial evidence had piled up against Jackie. Nevertheless, she felt tension grip her chest, forcing the breath from her, as the foreman of the jury got to his feet, carefully looking only at the judge, and delivered the inevitable sentence. 'We find the panel guilty.'

The judge's voice seemed to be coming from a great distance. The words 'life imprisonment' boomed hollowly in Claire's ears. Her notepad fell to the floor with a soft rustle and her head dropped into her hands.

Cordelia immediately put her arm round Claire, comforting her, a complicated mixture of emotions bringing her close to tears. She glanced up to the dock, where Jackie was being led away to begin her sentence. Then she turned back to Claire and murmured softly, 'It's all over.'

Claire raised her head. There were no tears, just a coldness in her eyes that had not been there before. She gazed over at the empty dock and slowly said, 'No, Cordelia. It's only just begun.'

1

Death would be a welcome release. That was her first conscious thought. Behind her eyes, a dull pain throbbed. It seemed as if an iron band constricting her forehead were being slowly, continuously tightened. Her throat was so dry that it felt as though she were forcing down a lump of cold potato each time she swallowed. The last time her stomach had been as bad as this was on a long ferry crossing in a force ten gale. A sheen of sweat covered her body. She stirred tentatively and wished she hadn't. Her limbs were stiff and aching; her legs and feet in particular protested. Bloody grappa, she thought. Bloody, bloody grappa.

She forced herself out of the camper van's double berth and stumbled to the stove. The coffee pot was sitting ready. She had known before she went out the previous evening exactly how she'd feel now and had taken precautions. She turned on the gas and headed straight for the van's shower compartment. Under the stream of warm water, she gradually began to feel less like the living dead. Two mugs of coffee later, her body began to feel restored. She pulled on a pair of sweat pants, a sweatshirt and a pair of trainers and emerged into the daylight.

New Year's Day had brought a watery sun to the grassy grove quartered by pine trees that had been her home for the last eight months. For most of the year it was a thriving campsite, choked with the caravans and tents of northern Europeans determined to extract the maximum return from the delights of the Veneto and the Adriatic. But now, in the off-season, the only vehicle left was the one from which she carried out her limited tasks as on-site watchdog and caretaker. She jogged slowly round the ten-hectare site, checking that all the toilet blocks, shops and restaurants were still properly locked up and shuttered.

She carried on to the site's private beach, part of the shoreline that curls round like a crescent moon from Trieste to Venice. She slowed down as she made her way through the heavy sand to the water's margin then, turning her back on the tower block hotels of Lido di Jesolo, she started to run the hangover out of her system. It had been a hell of a party.

The family who owned the site, the Maciocias, had accepted her for no better reason than that her hairdresser in the UK was their niece. When she had turned up with her life in shreds, looking for a place to hide and heal, they had asked no questions. Instead, they had persuaded her to occupy her time by working for them. In the summer months, she'd been the ideal candidate for dealing with the English families whose Italian never seemed to encompass more than 'Arrivederci Roma', and whose demands caused constant chaos at Reception. And when the end of the season arrived, she had decided to stay on, living in her van, earning a few thousand lire a day for keeping an eye on things.

Last night's New Year celebration should have reinforced her decision. The Maciocias had taken over a trattoria owned by someone's brother-in-law, and she couldn't remember ever having been at a party like it. The food had been lavish, delicious and deeply traditional. Cousin Bartolomeo had brought his dance band along and the singing and dancing had enveloped her like summer sunlight. The kindness of these strangers who had become her surrogate family meant her glass was never allowed to become empty. It had taken the full resources of her Italian, her diplomacy and her determination to persuade all the male relatives that she'd be safe to return to her van without an escort. But as she walked home alone with the desperate concentration of the mortally drunk, she had been overwhelmed with homesickness.

She knew beyond the shadow of a doubt what she had longed for as soon as midnight struck. The mellow taste of good malt soaked up by shortbread, oatcakes and caboc. The hysterical, ordered chaos of 'Strip the Willow'. The sound of accordion, bass and drums. The voice of her father singing 'The Road And The Miles To Dundee'. The contented smile of her mother as she listened. The welcoming warmth in Cordelia's deep, grey eyes. For too long, Lindsay thought sadly, she'd been looking into brown eyes. At the time, she had forced the thoughts away, telling herself she was maudlin and sentimental. Back at the van, a final tumbler of fiery grappa had brought a welcome oblivion.

But this morning, as she jogged back along the beach, she forced herself to examine her life in the hungover light of day. She'd left Britain in a state of panic, and all her actions since then had been governed by the lurking fear that she might lose her liberty or even her life. When she'd been unwillingly caught up in a murder investigation at a women's peace camp, she'd had no idea what she'd uncover. The last thing she'd expected was to find herself embroiled in the cover-up of a spy scandal.

The knowledge she'd ended up with was the sort of thing it was only safe to know if you were inside the charmed circle of the secret society. For her, a dedicated anti-establishment journalist, it had nearly sealed her death warrant. So she'd fled, but had refused to keep silence. After her story had been published by a German magazine, she knew she couldn't go home till long after the dust had settled. And that had meant not only leaving Cordelia behind, but keeping her in ignorance of her whereabouts. She had left a long letter to explain her absence, and she'd sent a card to Cordelia to reassure her that she was alive and well, but she hadn't been able to bring herself to reveal where she was. The card had been mailed in a sealed envelope to an old friend in New York, with instructions to address it to Cordelia care of her literary agent and to post it on to

London from there. A more direct route might have brought the full weight of the Special Branch down on Cordelia. She'd even been afraid to phone in case the line was tapped and they could trace the call.

While she was still a marked woman as far as the British security services were concerned, Lindsay wasn't prepared to do anything that might expose Cordelia to more trouble than she'd already been through on her account. And that meant not giving her any information that might provide them with a reason to lean on her. If her lover had known where to find her, she'd have been out on the next plane, no doubt with a team of heavies on her trail. The irony of keeping silent was that she now had no way of knowing if the heat had died down. Maybe she'd been wrong not to trust Cordelia to act responsibly, but the fear had gnawed too deep into Lindsay for her to feel able to take even the smallest chance.

But she couldn't run forever. Minding an Italian campsite wasn't part of her life-plan, in so far as she had one. It was time to face up to the truth. She had been in hiding for long enough. Some of the questions she had been trying to answer were resolved. Others never would be, she suspected. But at least she had the strength now to face the consequences she had run away to avoid. The time had come for Lindsay Gordon to go home.

The confirmation of that decision came only two days later on her weekly trip into Venice. As usual, she caught the early steamer from Punta Sabbione and huddled against the window in the saloon as the boat chugged across the Venetian lagoon. Half an hour later, she was walking down the wide quay of the Riva Schiavoni, past the Bridge of Sighs and the Doge's Palace, and into the Piazza San Marco, the domes of the basilica lost in the January mist that swirled around the sinking city. Lindsay had never particularly cared for the huge square. As a tourist attraction, it lived up to its promise, but precisely because it was a tourist attraction, it repelled her. It was never free from the souvenir vendors, the gaping crowds and the hordes of pigeons, encouraged by the food the tourists bought from the stall holders. The white smears of their droppings were everywhere, ruining the vista that Napoleon had called 'the finest drawing room in Europe'.

Lindsay much preferred the other Venice, that maze of twisting alleys, canals and bridges where she could escape the crowds and wander alone, savouring the sights, smells and sounds of the real life that lurked behind the picture postcard facades. She loved watching the Venetians display the skills that living on the water had forced them to develop. On that particular January morning, after collecting her subscription copy of the *Sunday Times* from the central post office at the far end of the Piazza San Marco, she made her way through the narrow alleys to a wooden landing stage on the Grand Canal, pausing only to watch a builder with a heavy hod of bricks climbing a ladder precariously balanced in a motor boat. After a few minutes wait, the *traghetto*, one of the long gondolas that ferry passengers across the canal for a few hundred lire, crossed back to her side and she climbed aboard. The gondolier looked cold and miserable, a sharp contrast to the carefree image he would present to the summer tourists. On the other side of the canal, she plunged into a labyrinth of passages, following a familiar route to a small café near the Frari church.

The man behind the counter greeted Lindsay with a nod as she sat at a small table by the door, and busied himself with the espresso machine. He brought her usual cappuccino over to the table, exchanged a few pleasantries about the New Year, and left her to her paper. Lindsay tore open the wrapper and unfolded the paper. Before she could take in the headlines, her eye was caught by a box on the side of the page trailing the attractions in the rest of the paper. 'Cordelia Brown: Booker Prize this time?'

Lindsay's stomach churned and she reached instinctively for a cigarette. She hardly smoked at all these days, but this wasn't something she could face nicotine-free. With trembling fingers, she turned to the review section. The whole of the front page was devoted to an interview with her . . . how should she describe Cordelia these days? Her lover? Her former lover? Her lover-in-abeyance?

13

At first, Lindsay had been too busy covering her tracks and establishing a safe routine to miss Cordelia. Because their relationship had hit a rough patch before Lindsay left, she'd stopped noticing all the ways in which she had relied on Cordelia. Now she was alone in a foreign country, she had begun to realise how much she had depended on her lover. The problems they'd had had all been external – the unpredictable pressures of Lindsay's job as a national newspaper journalist, the paralysing writer's block that had gripped Cordelia. Deep down, Lindsay had slowly come to understand, their relationship had been founded on solid ground. Knowing she had walked away from that because of her stubborn adherence to principle was the hardest thing Lindsay had had to deal with since her arrival in Italy.

But now she'd decided to go home, she also began to see how they could start to rebuild their life together. There was no way she wanted to go back into national newspaper journalism, even supposing anyone would have her. Whatever else she chose to do would provide a more straight-forward life. No more shift working, late nights and unpredictable overnight stays away from home. And, judging by this article that she was deliberately postponing reading, Cordelia had cured her writer's block.

Lindsay gulped a mouthful of hot coffee and stubbed out her cigarette. Taking a deep breath, she plunged into the words. 'Eighteen months ago, Cordelia Brown feared she'd never write another novel,' she read. Too true, Lindsay remembered with a sweet sadness. She had been the one caged in that beautiful London house with Cordelia while she paced the floor restlessly, ranting about her vanished talent. In vain Lindsay had tried to reasssure her, pointing to her successes as a television scriptwriter. 'Pap and crap,' Cordelia had spat back at her before storming out of the room to spend yet more hours motionless in front of the blank screen of her word processor.

But something had obviously happened to change all that. And it must have happened fast. For her to have a new book out now, she must have written it in a flurry of energy. It was nine months since Lindsay had left. Making a few quick mental calculations, she worked out that Cordelia must have written the first draft in the space of eight weeks at the very most. She never managed to work like that when she was with me, Lindsay thought painfully. Lighting another cigarette, she read on.

With four successful novels, a film script and three television series under her belt, the 36-year-old writer suffered a crippling failure of imagination. 'I was in a state of blind panic,' she revealed. 'I felt as if I had used myself up.'

Then a friend told her the moving story of a Black South African woman who had died in police custody after battling to uncover the truth about the death of her lover. The tragic events struck a deep chord in Cordelia, who sat down the following day and wrote *Ikhaya Lamaqhawe* in a record six weeks.

It's being hailed as her masterpiece, and although the Booker Prize ceremony is still ten months away, book trade insiders consider *Ikhaya Lamaqhawe* is certain to be a strong contender. A moving *tour de force* of controlled emotion, the book has astonished the literary world by its penetrating insights into the life of Black people under apartheid.

Ikhaya Lamaqhawe – which means Home Of The Heroes – tells the story of Alice Nbala, a teacher in a Black township. Her lover, Joseph Bukolo, is a mildly political student who is caught in a spiral of circumstances that leads to his disappearance. When his horribly mutilated body is found, Alice sets out to discover what happened to him. As she slowly realises that he has been a victim of the security forces, the net begins to close round her too.

Cordelia, who has never visited South Africa, admitted, 'I was terrified that I wouldn't get it right. I was aware of the sensitivities around this issue, and I didn't want to be seen as another white liberal trying to hijack a subject I knew nothing about from personal experience. But although I haven't gone through the traumas myself, I could relate very strongly to the emotions and the responses of the characters. I knew a lot about South Africa from reading and talking to Black people who had escaped from the regime, and I drew heavily on what they'd told me.'

News to me, thought Lindsay self-critically. She couldn't remember Cordelia ever showing more than the general interest expected of a right-on feminist in the whole issue of racial oppression. Had she really known so little about what was going on in her lover's mind?

With another deep sigh, she read on.

> Not only has Cordelia got it right, she's won plaudits from a wide spectrum of Black activists and writers, who privately have expressed their astonishment that a white writer could have written so passionate and accurate an exposé of the grim truth of life in the RSA.

Lindsay signalled for another cappuccino and quickly read on to the end of the article. To her relief, there was no mention of her and the spy scandal that had led to her exile. It would have been an obvious point for the interviewer to pick up on, given its tenuous parallels with Cordelia's plot. Maybe it really had been the nine-day wonder Cordelia had predicted. If that was the case, then there truly was no reason why she shouldn't go home. Or maybe it was simply that Cordelia had excised her so thoroughly from her life that she had insisted on no mention of Lindsay's name. After all, what right had Lindsay to assume that Cordelia would want her back?

There was only one way to find out. Lindsay carefully folded up her paper, got to her feet and took the first step on the road home.

2

Glasgow, Scotland, February 1990

'I always maintained that Glasgow was the only truly European city in Britain,' Lindsay stated smugly as she stared out of the taxi window at the rows of sandblasted tenements glowing yellow in the streetlights. 'But I didn't realise till now how right I was.'

'Listen to it,' muttered her companion. 'Nine months in Italy and suddenly she's an expert on European culture.' Eight years of friendship had given Sophie Hartley the right to snipe at Lindsay's occasional pomposity and she never hesitated.

'Listen,' Lindsay argued. 'Nothing you've told me about this wine bar we're heading for sounds British to me. A place where writers, actors, lawyers and politicians go to drink good wine, eat serious food and put the world to rights sounds like café society in Paris or Vienna or Berlin, not bloody Glasgow. I know it's three years since I lived here, but it seems to me that everything's changed.'

Sophie smiled. 'It's got yuppified, if that's what you mean. Every other car a BMW. Don't forget, it's the European City of Culture now,' she teased.

'As if I could,' Lindsay replied ironically. 'Every corner shop has got posters up advertising some cultural beanfeast. Everything from opera to open days, from puppets to psychodrama. I don't even recognise the streets any more. Where there used to be nice wee bakeries selling cream doughnuts and every other sort of cholesterol-packed traditional Scottish goody, there are wholefood cafés. I tell you, Soph, I felt less of a stranger in Venice than I feel in Glasgow these days,' she added with a sigh.

'Well, you shouldn't have stayed away from us so long, should you?' said Sophie mercilessly, choosing to ignore the fact that she had been Lindsay's first port of call after her duty visit to her parents in the Highlands.

'I didn't have much of a choice. I never wanted to be a bloody hero. All I wanted was to be the best journalist I could be.'

'Don't be so melodramatic, Lindsay. If those mad bastards in the secret service had really wanted you, they'd have come and got you, wherever you were. Spy scandals are ten a penny these days. A couple of months after you broke the story, your average 007 would have been hard pressed even to remember your name, never mind what lid you had lifted.'

'Thanks for the vote of confidence,' Lindsay said gloomily. 'You make it all seem worthwhile.'

Sophie laughed. 'Come on, Lindsay, you're still in one piece, and you've got the satisfaction of knowing you did the right thing. Stop feeling sorry for yourself.'

Before Lindsay could reply, the cab driver pushed back his glass partition. 'Youse gonny sit there blethering all night while the meter runs?' he enquired pleasantly.

'Sorry,' Sophie said, pushing Lindsay out of the cab and paying the driver. Lindsay watched her as she searched her bag for her wallet. Time was being kind to Sophie, she thought. Now she had passed thirty, she seemed to have grown into her bones. In her twenties, her high cheekbones, straight nose and strong jaw had given her face a raw, unfinished look. But age had softened the impression, producing a striking image of humour and strength of character. Her curly brown hair was shot with grey now, giving an effect that other women paid their hairdressers fortunes for. Tonight, she was wearing a silky cobalt-blue jogging suit under a padded ski jacket, and Lindsay envied her style.

Sophie turned round and caught Lindsay's scrutiny. One eyebrow twitched upwards in amusement. 'You look like you're sizing me up for the kill,' she remarked wryly. 'Come on, this is it,' she said, pointing down an alley between the tall, Victorian buildings. A large square sign swinging in the evening air proclaimed 'Soutar Johnnie's' above a painting of a cobbler working at his last. 'We'll have a drink and something to eat here before we meet Helen and Rosalind at the Tron Bar after their Labour Party meeting. Let's just hope my radiopager doesn't go off,' she added as she led the way down the alley.

'You're not on call tonight, are you?' Lindsay asked.

'Technically, no. But if one of my patients goes into labour, they'll probably call me in. The price of being a specialist.' Sophie was a consultant gynaecologist at Stobhill Hospital, where she was in the vanguard of those treating the city's growing numbers of HIV-positive women, mainly prostitutes and drug addicts.

Sophie pushed open the polished wooden door of the bar and Lindsay followed her in. She stopped on the threshold, taken aback. There had been nowhere quite like this when she had been a struggling freelance journalist in the city, and it was a shock to a system accustomed to the functional, masculine atmosphere of the old-fashioned city-centre pubs. The bar was well lit, with square tables and comfy looking chairs scattered around. Food was being eaten at several tables, and even at first glance it looked completely different from the old pub staple of pie and peas. And, to Lindsay's astonishment, quite a few of the patrons appeared to be drinking coffee rather than alcohol. Very Continental, she thought wryly as she followed Sophie to the horseshoe shaped mahogany bar.

Lindsay joined Sophie and studied the long list of wines scrawled on the blackboard behind the bar. Her astonishment grew as she read it. Not a single Liebfraumilch or Lambrusco to be seen! The wine list was as varied and interesting as the clientele, who ranged from a few long-haired hippies who looked like reluctant refugees from the sixties, to well-barbered young men in double-breasted suits.

Sophie meanwhile had caught the attention of the barman, a huge bull of a man with a mop of thick black curls and a black patch over one eye. 'Hi, Cosmo,' Sophie said as he approached. 'Give us a bottle of the Australian Chardonnay and two glasses, please.'

'Coming up, Sophie,' he replied, opening a tall glass-fronted fridge. 'What's all this, then? Buying classy bottles of wine for strange women? Good gossip! Wait till the Sisters of Treachery get to hear about this!'

Sophie grinned as she paid for the wine and picked it up. 'If they do, I'll know who told them, Cosmo,' she replied. 'This is an old friend of mine, Lindsay Gordon. Lindsay, meet Cosmo Mackay. He owns this disreputable dive.'

'Pleased to meet you, Lindsay. Any friend of Sophie's stands a good chance of becoming one of my best customers. She's never introduced me to a teetotaller yet! Are you eating tonight, by the way?' he asked.

'You bet,' said Sophie.

Cosmo handed her a menu. 'I'll take your order in a minute. There's plenty of tables in the back room.' He turned away to serve another customer.

'What was all that about?' Lindsay demanded. 'Who in God's name are the Sisters of Treachery?'

'It's a little political joke. Cosmo's a member of the same Constituency Labour Party as Helen and Rosalind. The party's been split over lots of issues lately, so there's been a lot of intriguing going on. One of the right-wingers was having a go at Helen and Rosalind one night and he called them the Sisters of Treachery. The pair of them thought it was hysterical, and the name became a sort of in-joke among the left,' Sophie explained. 'Now, what do you want to eat?'

Lindsay studied the menu with delight. There were all the traditional favourites like black pudding with scrambled eggs, mutton stovies and haggis. But there were also vegetarian dishes, and new variations on old themes, like spiced chicken stovies – a mixture of potatoes, onions and spiced chicken pieces. Just reading the list made her mouth water. What a change from pasta and pizza, she thought happily. Eventually she settled on haggis with mashed potatoes and turnips.

While they were waiting for Cosmo to return, Sophie turned to Lindsay and asked, 'Have you given any more thought to what you're going to do for a living?'

Lindsay shrugged. 'Not really. I don't think I can go back to being a journo, though, even if they wanted me. My heart just isn't in it any more.'

'You could always become a private detective. After all, you've solved two murders so far. I can just see you with the snap-brimmed trilby and the bottle of Jack Daniels in the desk drawer. And just think of the perks! All those beautiful blondes falling at your feet,' Sophie teased.

Lindsay pulled a face and shook her head. 'No thanks. I'm looking for a quiet life these days.'

'You came to the wrong place, then,' Cosmo interrupted. 'What can I get you ladies – sorry, women – to eat?'

Having given their order to Cosmo, Sophie steered a path through the crowded bar towards a doorway at the rear. Lindsay followed her into a remarkable room. The far wall and the sloping roof were made of glass, and the other walls were covered from floor to ceiling with plants trained over trellises. Chattering groups of people sat on white garden furniture with brightly, coloured cushions. Before she had a chance to take it all in, she cannoned into Sophie who had stopped dead.

Sophie turned on her heel and tried to usher Lindsay out of the room. But she was too late. Lindsay had already spotted the reason for her abrupt, awkward halt. Sitting at a table on the far side of the room were two women, deeply engrossed in conversation. It was obvious to the most casual observer that they were a couple. She had never seen the slender blonde before. But the woman sitting opposite her was as familiar to Lindsay as her own face in the mirror. She felt her stomach lurch and fought the desperate urge to be sick. Without even realising she was doing it, she shrugged off Sophie's restraining arm and purposefully crossed the room.

Neither of the two women registered her presence till she

was only feet from their table. Even then, it was the blonde who looked up first. When she saw Lindsay, a series of reactions flashed across her face in a moment. Curiosity was overtaken by bewilderment, bewilderment by shock, and shock by a strange mixture of relief and amusement. Her companion was slower to realise they had company, since Lindsay had approached from behind her. She turned in her chair and her eyes widened. 'Lindsay!' she gasped, pushing her chair back and getting to her feet. She gave a nervous half-smile, apparently incapable of further speech.

'Hello, Cordelia. Fancy meeting you here. That explains why I couldn't find you in London,' Lindsay said with ice in her voice.

The blonde woman got to her feet and extended a slim hand. 'Hello, Lindsay. We've never met before, but I've heard a lot about you . . .'

'I bet you have,' Lindsay interrupted savagely, ignoring the outstretched hand.

Undaunted, the other continued. 'I'm Claire Ogilvie. Jackie – Jackie Mitchell, that is, told me a lot about you. That's how I came to meet Cordelia.'

'How fascinating,' Lindsay said with heavy sarcasm, mentally slotting Claire into place. Jackie's girlfriend, the lawyer. Portia with a Porsche. Cordelia had obviously had her fill of working-class heroes and reverted to type, Lindsay thought furiously. In a cold voice she said, 'Well, don't let us interrupt your intimate little tête-à-tête. Come on, Sophie,' she added, turning away. 'We'll find somewhere more congenial to eat.'

'No, wait,' said Cordelia, finally finding her tongue. 'Don't go, Lindsay.'

'Why not? You've obviously not been counting the minutes till I got back, have you?'

'I think you're being a little unfair, Lindsay,' Claire said. 'Why don't you calm down and sit down and we can discuss this like adults?'

'Discuss what?' Lindsay demanded, her voice rising. 'Discuss your relationship with the woman I have just discovered is my ex-lover?'

'Lindsay,' Sophie said in the soothing but firm voice she'd developed years ago to deal with drunks in casualty. 'Cool it. Either let's go now, or else sit down and have a drink.'

Lindsay, struggling with a mixture of anger, disappointment and hurt, abruptly sat down, followed by the other three.

'When did you get back? And where have you been?' Cordelia asked. Even to herself, her questions sounded empty and irrelevant. But she didn't know what else to say. Seeing Lindsay again so unexpectedly had left her floundering in a welter of emotions that she could neither separate nor identify.

'I got back a week ago,' Lindsay replied in weary tones. 'I tried to phone a couple of times *en route*, but I kept getting the answering machine, and it didn't seem the appropriate way to break the silence. When I got to London, I went straight to the house, but you weren't there. I rang your mother, but she didn't seem to know where you were. Your agent said you'd gone away for a couple of weeks, she wasn't sure where either, so rather than hang about in London on the off-chance that you'd be back, I drove up to Yorkshire, gave Deborah her van back and collected my MG. Then I went to see my parents and came back to Glasgow. I've been in Italy. By myself, which is more than I can say for you,' she added bitterly.

'My God, you've got a nerve,' Cordelia said. 'You vanish off the face of the earth for nine bloody months and you expect to come home like the prodigal daughter and find everything exactly the way it was?'

'Obviously I was wrong, wasn't I? You knew exactly why I went to ground. For God's sake, I left a letter explaining what the hell was going on. And I sent you a card to let you know I was safe.'

'One poxy card in nine months! I could recite it from memory. "Weather stunning. Natives friendly. Hope to get over to London to see you soon, but life is hectic right now. Be patient!" ' Cordelia flashed back sarcastically.

'I was trying to protect you. I didn't want them leaning on you to turn me in,' Lindsay replied defensively.

'How noble!' Cordelia retorted, grey eyes cloudy with anger, generous mouth uncharacteristically pursed.

'I did what I thought was right. I didn't expect you to jump into bed with someone else the minute my back was turned,' Lindsay accused.

'What the hell was I supposed to do? Answer me that! How long was I supposed to wait before I started to put my life back together again? Have you any idea how much time, energy and money I spent trying to find you? I rang everyone I could think of, I went everywhere I thought you might be. I even went to bloody New York!'

'And how long did it take you to steal Jackie's girlfriend?'

Both Claire and Cordelia looked shocked by Lindsay's question. But it was Claire who collected herself first and said in conciliatory tones, 'It wasn't like that. I was looking for you, and a mutual friend introduced me to Cordelia, who was in Glasgow at the time, also trying to get a lead on your whereabouts. So we joined forces and spent a lot of time trying to track you down. But you made a good job of your disappearing act.'

'And what the hell business of yours was it where I was?' Lindsay snapped, stalling while she took in what Claire had said.

'Jackie asked me to find you.'

'So why couldn't she look for me herself if she was so desperate?' said Lindsay defiantly. She remembered Jackie Mitchell well – a hard-working, hard-bitten journalist, well capable of fighting her own battles. If Jackie had wanted to find her, she wouldn't have delegated her mission to this toffee-nosed yuppie.

'It's a bit hard to scour the world for someone when you're behind bars,' Claire replied ironically.

'Behind bars? You mean . . . in prison?' Lindsay asked, confused.

'That's right. She's serving life for the murder of Alison Maxwell.'

Lindsay stared at Claire, unbelieving. 'This has got to be some kind of sick joke,' she muttered. Lindsay turned to Sophie. 'Tell me she's making this up.'

Sophie shook her head. 'She's telling you the truth. The trial was just before Christmas. I'm sorry, I didn't think to tell you.'

'Jesus,' Lindsay sighed, dragging out the syllables. 'Alison? What the hell happened?'

Claire took over in businesslike fashion, perhaps because she sensed that Cordelia was too shaken to deal with Lindsay. 'Alison was found strangled in her flat. Jackie had been there with her shortly before she was killed, and in the absence of any other obvious candidate, the police chose her. Unfortunately, the jury agreed with them. Shortly after her arrest, Jackie asked me to see if I could find you. She knew you'd been involved with a couple of murder investigations before, and she was very impressed with your courage over the Brownlow Common spy scandal. And of course, because you're gay, she thought you'd be more sympathetic. She believed that if anyone could prove her innocence, it was you. While I was searching for you, I met Cordelia. I'm sorry if our relationship outrages you, but you can hardly have expected Cordelia to take a vow of chastity till you deigned to show up.'

Lindsay stared miserably at Cordelia. It was all too much to take in. She had lost the one woman with whom she had ever formed an equal relationship; a former lover was dead; and a former colleague was in prison for her murder. Once she could have turned to Cordelia for the love and support to carry her through those moments when the roof caved in on her life. But it was too late for that now. She gradually became aware that Claire was talking to her. 'I'm sorry,' Lindsay said. 'I didn't catch what you said.'

'I said I'd like to discuss with you the possibility of trying to clear Jackie's name. It's not too late for an appeal if we can dig up some fresh evidence. I'm not asking you to make any decision now – I realise this has been rather a traumatic evening. But I'd appreciate it if you'd call me tomorrow when you've had time to think it over.' Claire fished in the inevitable filofax and produced a card. 'My home and my business numbers are both there.'

Lindsay stared numbly at the card lying on the table. She

couldn't remember the last time she'd encountered someone with Claire's thick-skinned audacity. Her nerve was breathtaking, a sharp contrast to the way Lindsay herself was feeling. She couldn't believe this was happening to her. Coming home was supposed to feel good. But she couldn't remember the last time she'd felt so bad.

3

Lindsay sat staring at the cigarette in her hand, watching the smoke spiral up to join the thick layer that hung below the ceiling in the crowded bar of the Tron Theatre. The noisy chatter of the literary wing of Glasgow's renaissance could not distract her from the bleakness that filled her. She was shaken from her reverie by Sophie's return from the bar with two spritzers, condensation already dripping down the glasses. 'Drink up, doctor's orders,' Sophie said sympathetically as she sat down.

'Thanks,' Lindsay muttered. 'Sorry to spoil your evening.'

'Don't be daft,' Sophie replied. 'I haven't seen a cabaret as good as that since last year's Edinburgh Festival. I'd forgotten what a drama queen you can be. I'll be dining out on it for months.' In spite of herself, Lindsay smiled. 'So, what are you going to do about it?' Sophie added.

'About Cordelia or about Jackie?'

'Both.'

Lindsay sighed. 'There doesn't seem to be a whole lot I can do about Cordelia, does there? She's got herself a class act to cuddle up to. Much more her speed than a toerag like me, don't you think?'

'More fool Cordelia, then,' said Sophie consolingly. Privately, she thought Lindsay's reaction to Cordelia's new relationship was completely unreasonable, but she was too fond of her to say so yet. There would be plenty of time to thrash it out when Lindsay was feeling less raw. She tried to take her mind off the débâcle in Soutar Johnnie's, saying,

'But what about Jackie?'

Lindsay shrugged. 'I don't know. The fact that I've managed to dig out the truth a couple of times in the past doesn't mean I'm some kind of private eye. You know, Sophie, I can't seem to take it in that Alison's dead. I mean, when I was having my own little fling with her, God knows I felt like strangling her often enough; but the difference between feeling like that and actually doing it . . . I can't imagine what makes that possible. I suppose I feel like I've got a score to settle on Alison's account, never mind Jackie. But I'm in such a mess about myself and my future that I don't know how much use I'd be.'

Sophie ran a hand through her curly hair, a gesture Lindsay recognised from the days when the brown hadn't been streaked with grey. 'I know what you mean,' she said with feeling. 'But you're not committed to anything else right now, are you? And in spite of the way you've been putting yourself down ever since you saw Claire and Cordelia together, you've got a pretty good track record when it comes to discovering things that the police have missed or ignored. And there is one other aspect of it you might not have considered. If you can get Jackie released, it might well be enough to drive a wedge between Cordelia and Claire. That would at least give you the chance to find out if the two of you have still got a future together.'

Before Lindsay could reply, a booming Liverpool accent rang across the room. 'Bloody skinflint, Hartley. Where's the bottle? I suppose we'll have to buy our own drinks?'

Lindsay swung round in her seat to see Helen Christie waving from the bar, her unmistakable mane of carrot-red hair glinting under the lights. Behind her, paying for a carafe of wine, was her fellow Sister of Treachery, Rosalind Campbell. As they came over to the table, Lindsay thought it was no wonder that they struck terror into their political opponents. They looked like a pair of Valkyries striding across the bar.

'My God,' Helen groaned as she subsided into a chair, after planting a cursory kiss on the top of Sophie's head. 'What a night we've had! That lot couldn't organise an explosion in a fireworks factory!'

Lindsay watched fondly as Helen and Rosalind launched into a double-act recitation of the evening's meeting. No matter how down Lindsay felt, Helen had always had the power to make her laugh. They'd met at Oxford, the only working-class students reading English at St Mary's College. They'd instantly formed an alliance whose main weapon had been satire, a desperate wit born of their never-admitted feelings of inferiority. After university, their ways had parted, Lindsay choosing journalism, Helen arts administration. Now, she ran her own television and film casting agency, and, with what was left from her boundless supply of energy, she had thrown herself into local politics.

But the two women had stayed in touch, and even when Helen and Sophie had set up home together eight years earlier, there had been no diminution of the close friendship that still bound Lindsay and Helen. In fact, Lindsay had gained a friend in Sophie. When Helen and Sophie had split up eighteen months before, Lindsay had feared that she would be forced to choose between her two friends. But to her amazement, the ending of their love affair had been remarkably without rancour, and they had remained the closest of friends. The only real change, as far as Lindsay could see, was that they now lived separately. Neither had formed any lasting relationship with anyone else, although, according to Sophie, Helen had recently been spending time with a young actress she'd spotted in a pub theatre group and placed in a new television series.

Lindsay suddenly became aware that Helen was looking enquiringly at her. She pulled herself back into the painful present. 'I'm sorry,' she confessed, 'I didn't catch what you said.'

'Pearls before swine,' Helen sighed. 'Here am I, bringing you despatches from the front line of British politics, and you're daydreaming about some leggy blonde, no doubt. I said, what kind of evening have you had, Lindsay?'

'Ask Sophie,' Lindsay replied wryly. 'She's already told me it's given her enough ammo to sing for her supper for months to come. You might as well practise on the experts, Soph.'

Sophie pulled a face, then launched into a detailed account of their earlier encounter at Soutar Johnnie's. Before she could finish, Helen had exploded. 'My God, what a complete shit for you, Lindsay!' she exclaimed. 'I had no idea she was still around, did you, Sophie? We saw her a couple of times after you first left, Lindsay. She was desperate to get in touch with you and thought you might have been in contact with one or other of us. But I thought she'd gone back to London. Poor you!'

With her usual detachment, Rosalind had been listening. As Helen paused for breath, she cut in. 'You will take it on, though, won't you? I can't imagine you sitting back and letting Jackie rot.'

Reluctantly, Lindsay nodded. 'I don't suppose I've got much choice.'

'Well at least Claire can afford it,' Rosalind said.

'Afford what?' Helen demanded.

'Afford Lindsay,' Rosalind replied.

'What do you mean, afford me?' Lindsay asked, puzzled.

'You've got to be realistic about it,' Rosalind said patiently. 'You've got no job and no prospect of one, if I understand you correctly. If you refuse to help and Claire wants to pursue this, she's going to have to go to a private detective. There is no reason on God's earth why you should be prepared to do it for free. And Claire Ogilvie can certainly afford to pay.'

Lindsay looked stunned. 'I'm not taking money from that bloody designer dyke,' she replied angrily. 'What do you take me for?'

'Ros is right,' Sophie said quietly. 'If Claire wants you to do a job, she should be prepared to pay the going rate.'

'It feels like taking money under false pretences,' said Lindsay stubbornly. 'I'm hardly Philip Marlowe, am I?'

'You've got skills and specialist knowledge,' Rosalind argued. 'It's unprofessional not to charge her for exercising them. I can't imagine Claire dishing out free professional advice, can you?'

'But I don't know where to start,' Lindsay said weakly, knowing she had been outflanked by Rosalind. And, given the tenacity of her friends, she knew she'd actually have to go through with the business of charging Claire for her services.

'I might just be able to help you there,' Rosalind said with a slow smile.

Lindsay rang off and threw the cordless phone to the other end of the sofa. Burned my boats now, she thought with a scowl. 'Why do I let myself get talked into these things?' she muttered as she walked through to the big, airy kitchen of Sophie's tenement flat. Lindsay poured herself a cup of coffee and sat down to think. She had agreed to meet Claire in an hour's time, and she wanted to get everything straight in her head before then.

Recalling Alison Maxwell wasn't difficult. They had met the first time Lindsay had been hired to do a shift on the Scottish *Daily Clarion*. Lindsay had been standing at the library counter waiting for a packet of cuttings. She turned to find herself faced with a woman who seemed to have stepped out of her most secret fantasies, the ones she guiltily felt shouldn't inhabit the mind of a politically aware feminist. The vision had sandy blonde hair, and an almost Scandinavian cast to her high-cheekboned features. She was a couple of inches taller than Lindsay, with slim hips, and a cleavage that was impossible to ignore. 'Hi,' she said in a rich, cultivated Kelvinside accent. 'I'm Alison Maxwell. Features department.'

Lindsay had fallen head over heels in lust. 'Pleased to meet you,' she croaked, feeling gauche and adolescent. 'I'm Lindsay Gordon. I'm doing a shift for the newsdesk.'

'Ah,' said Alison. 'Pity you're not a photographer, then I could call you Flash Gordon.'

'If I get the front page tonight, then you can call me Splash Gordon instead.'

Lindsay hadn't made the front page splash that night, but she'd still been Splash from then on to Alison. To Lindsay's surprise, the feature writer seemed determined to include Lindsay in her busy social life, inviting her out to dinner, to parties and to her flat for drinks. It wasn't long before they became lovers. But it was Alison who made the first move. If it had been up to Lindsay, they would never have got beyond a peck on the cheek when they parted. Lindsay would have been happy to leave Alison on her pedestal, having no confidence at all in her own power to attract a woman so different from her previous lovers.

At first, Lindsay was in a daze of lust fulfilled by exotic and imaginative sex. But once the initial infatuation wore off, she began to see Alison more clearly, and she grew to dislike and distrust what she saw. Lindsay gradually came to understand that Alison Maxwell was a woman who was incapable of simple human relationships. She was too in love with power to have love left over for people. That power was usually exercised through the nuggets of information she'd acquired in the bedroom. It took only a matter of days for Lindsay to discover that she was far from being Alison's only lover. In a matter of weeks, she had reached the bitter conclusion that Alison was sexually omnivorous.

Faced with this, Lindsay had made up her mind to end their relationship. That was when she had discovered the cruellest streak in Alison. For Alison was a woman who only let go when *she* was ready. She had to have control over every situation, and that included the ending of her sexual relationships. When Lindsay had announced her intention to sever their connection, Alison had wept and raged, and finally threatened. She would claim that Lindsay had got her drunk and seduced her. She would make sure everyone knew what a twisted little dyke Lindsay was. And she'd make sure that Lindsay never did another day's work at the *Clarion*. Her venom had unnerved Lindsay, and she had allowed herself to be swallowed up in the passion of their reconciliation.

The following day, ashamed of having given in to Alison's blackmail, Lindsay had left town for a few days, making the excuse of a feature she wanted to research in Aberdeen. By the time she had returned, Alison had been absorbed in someone new, and had lost all interest in Lindsay, much to her relief. Being dropped from Alison's social circle had left a gap at first, but Lindsay was grateful to have survived relatively unscathed. As the months passed and she observed her former lover wreaking havoc in other people's lives, Lindsay vowed never to let her fantasies run away with her again.

Since she'd moved away from Glasgow, Alison had been no more than a distant memory. But the news of her death had brought these memories to life. There had been so much life in Alison. It might not have been a desirable vivacity, but nevertheless, Lindsay felt herself diminished by Alison's death. They had hit the heights together, after all. And she'd been a bloody good journalist. The same skills that she used to wind her lovers round her little finger were invaluable when it came to persuading interviewees to open up to her. Alison might have been a bitch, thought Lindsay sadly, but she didn't deserve to die like that. And however hard she tried, Lindsay couldn't picture Jackie Mitchell as her killer. Jackie had been a hard-nosed journalist, but underneath, like so many of them, she was soft-centred and weak. Nothing Lindsay had learned about the murder seemed to fit her image of Jackie.

Rosalind had provided a surprising amount of information about Alison Maxwell's murder. Surprising, that is, until Lindsay had remembered that Rosalind's compact modern flat was in the same block as the dead woman's apartment. As a result, Rosalind had taken a keen interest in the progress of the investigation and trial. The training and experience she'd acquired over her years in the civil service had stood her in good stead when it came to reporting her version of events to Lindsay. She had run through everything she knew in a crisp, factual way, making Lindsay feel like a Scottish Office Minister on the receiving end of some vital briefing. No wonder politicians felt inferior to their senior civil servants! And no wonder Rosalind had climbed to the rank of Principal Officer.

All the evidence against Jackie had been circumstantial, Rosalind had reported. She had never denied that she had been in Alison's flat on the afternoon of the murder. She had never denied that they had been to bed together. She had—

never denied her ownership of the scarf that had strangled Alison. But from the moment of her arrest till now, convicted and sentenced, she had vigorously denied killing her. The point at issue, according to Rosalind, was whether Jackie was telling the truth about the time of her departure.

'Jackie was seen by Alison's mother leaving the building by the side door at five minutes to six. Mrs Maxwell was trying to gain admittance to the block. We have security entryphones, and there was no response from Alison's flat. Mrs Maxwell had to wait another fifteen minutes before someone arrived who could let her into the building. They went up in the lift together. Mrs Maxwell went straight to Alison's flat, where the front door was ajar. She walked as far as the bedroom door, saw her daughter and started screaming,' Rosalind explained.

'Jackie maintained at the time, and later, that she had left the flat nearly half an hour before the body was discovered. She had walked down the fire escape stairs rather than take the lift, and stopped to have a cigarette and a think. The police took the not unreasonable view that this was scarcely normal behaviour. And of course, once they had Jackie in custody, and had satisfied the Procurator Fiscal that the case against her covered all the eventualities, the investigation stopped dead.'

It didn't leave too many avenues for exploring, Lindsay thought to herself as she finished her coffee. But Rosalind had been able to give her a spare set of keys to the building and her flat. Later this afternoon, Lindsay would take advantage of that to have a good look around and refresh her memory about the layout of the block that had once been almost as familiar as her own tenement. But first, she had to face Claire.

She glanced in the full-length mirror in the hall as she reached for her heavy sheepskin jacket. If Cordelia was going to be at Claire's, Lindsay wanted to look her best. All the exercise and healthy eating in Italy had left her nearly a stone lighter, and her tight Levis emphasised the fact. But her thick Aran sweater did her no favours. Impatiently, Lindsay pulled it off and surveyed herself in the loose but flattering scarlet polo shirt she was wearing underneath. She'd probably freeze to death, but at least she was looking pretty good. She shrugged into her jacket, determined to show Cordelia exactly what she was missing!

4

Lindsay managed to find a free parking meter by the river, a couple of streets away from Claire's flat. She set the alarm on her ancient MGB roadster then strode briskly through the misty winter air, casting a jaundiced eye on the cold grey waters of the Clyde. Not an improvement on the blue of the Adriatic, she thought. At times like this, she wished she'd never left Italy. Fancy thinking coming home would solve anything.

Following Claire's detailed instructions, she turned into a narrow alleyway which opened out into a small courtyard with several staircases leading off it. Originally, these had been the semi-slum homes of the ill-paid clerks who had tended the fortunes of the Victorian merchants and shipping magnates who had once made the city great. Over the years, the properties had deteriorated, till they were precariously balanced on the edge of demolition. But in the nick of time, a new prosperity had arrived in Glasgow and the property developers had snapped up the almost derelict slums and renovated them. Now, there were luxury flats with steel doors and closed circuit video security systems where once there had been open staircases that rang with the sounds of too many families crammed into too small a space. Lindsay surveyed the clean, sandblasted courtyard with an ironic smile, before pressing the buzzer for Claire's flat and glowering at the camera lens three feet above her head.

The speaker at her ear crackled, and she could just make out Claire's voice. 'It's Lindsay,' she said, and was rewarded by the angry buzz of the door release. Lindsay mounted the stairs to the third landing, where Claire stood by her open front door. Lindsay took in the details of her appearance that she had been too upset to notice the night before. The most striking thing about her was her height. She was nearly six feet tall, and her body had all the willowy sinuousness of a model. Her fine white-blonde hair was beautifully cut, like the severely tailored grey herringbone woollen suit she wore. She looked like a recruitment poster for law graduates.

'Come in,' Claire greeted her. 'You're very punctual.'

Lindsay bit back a sarcastic retort and followed her through a spacious hallway furnished with a small Turkish carpet and several pale wood bookcases. In an alcove, behind glass doors, was a collection of Oriental porcelain. Claire showed her into a huge square room with two bay windows which overlooked the river. The room must originally have been the living rooms of two separate flats, Lindsay thought to herself. Two families would have occupied the space now filled with Claire's Scandinavian pine furniture and colourful wall hangings. Even the stereo system and the CD collection were housed in tailor-made glass-fronted pine units. It could have come straight from the pages of the kind of glossy magazine Lindsay couldn't imagine wanting to write for. Cordelia would feel right at home here, she thought bitterly, taking in the Cartier briefcase standing beside the sofa. The room's designer consumerism epitomised everything that had disturbed Lindsay about their life together. But Cordelia had never shared her discomfort.

'Can I get you a drink?' Claire asked.

'No thanks,' Lindsay replied. She might have to take Claire's money, but she was damned if she would accept anything that fell outside the ambit of a purely professional relationship. At least Cordelia wasn't here to churn up her emotions again, she thought with a mixture of relief and regret. 'So, you said that Jackie wants my help,' she added, perching on the edge of a pine-framed armchair.

Claire pushed her glasses up her nose in a nervous gesture. 'That's right,' she said. 'Look, before we start, I just wanted to apologise for last night. I realise it must have been something of a shock for you, and I'm sorry if I was less than helpful.'

Lindsay shrugged. 'What exactly did Jackie want me to do?'

Claire was clearly unsettled by Lindsay's ungracious response to her apology, and walked over to the window to stare out at the mist-shrouded water. 'She thought you could establish her innocence.'

'But why? What made her think I could succeed where the police and her own lawyers had failed? Surely if there had been anything to go on you would have hired a private detective before the trial.'

Having recovered her poise, Claire turned back and sat down on the edge of the sofa. Lindsay couldn't help picturing Cordelia curled up there beside her, watching television or just talking. She pushed the bitter thought aside and forced herself to listen to Claire. 'We didn't go to a conventional private detective because Jackie didn't believe that we'd find one who would genuinely be on our side. I have to say that in my experience professionally with the breed, I wouldn't expect to find one who was sympathetic to a gay woman. Jackie thought you'd believe her. And she thought you'd have a vested interest in finding out the truth. She knew about your own affair with Alison, knew you'd understand what she'd been put through.'

Lindsay lit a cigarette without her usual courtesy of asking permission first. Claire leapt to her feet, saying, 'I'll get you an ashtray.' She disappeared through another door and returned moments later with an ostentatiously large crystal ashtray. Lindsay felt that using it would be like shouting in a museum. Claire placed it on the occasional table next to Lindsay's chair and said, 'Well, will you help? She didn't do it, you know.' There was a note of desperation in her voice that touched Lindsay in spite of herself.

Wearily, Lindsay nodded. 'I'll do what I can,' she said. 'My daily rate is £100 plus expenses. I'd expect a week's payment in advance, as a retainer,' she added quickly, amazed at how easily it came out.

Claire's eyebrows rose. 'Cordelia didn't seem to think you'd expect to be paid,' she said coolly. 'But I'm used to paying for professional services. In return, I expect full reports on what you are doing.' Claire opened her briefcase and swiftly wrote a cheque for £700. She handed it to Lindsay with a look of contempt.

'That goes without saying,' Lindsay replied. She glanced at the cheque and noted it was drawn on the JM Defence Account. Claire might be happy to splash out on maintaining her own high-flying image, but clearly a private detective wasn't considered a designer accessory, Lindsay thought with a spurt of anger. She took a deep breath before she spoke. 'Now, before we go any further, I want you to tell me everything you know about the events leading up to the murder.' Lindsay took a notebook out of her shoulder bag to take down Claire's words in her rusty shorthand.

Claire took a deep breath and went back to her vantage point at the window. 'We'd been having a difficult time. We'd been together just over five years, and I suppose we'd started taking each other for granted. I had only recently been made a partner in my firm, and I was bringing a lot of work home. And Jackie was busier than ever. So many new magazines have been launched in the last couple of years, and they're all hungry for strong, well-written features. But I was too absorbed in my own problems to notice the strain she was under. I suppose that was Alison's appeal for her. Alison was in the same business, and they could talk shop together. I know Jackie had a lot of professional respect for Alison.' Claire sighed deeply and walked across to a tray with a decanter and glasses. She poured herself a careful inch of Scotch, turning to Lindsay and saying, 'Sure you won't have one?'

Lindsay shook her head. 'Go on,' she probed.

Claire paced the floor. 'It was the old, old story. I was the last to know. It had apparently been going on for about two months when I found out.'

'How did you find out?' Lindsay asked gently. She couldn't help herself. Even with a woman she instinctively disliked so much, she still slipped straight into the persona of the professionally sympathetic interviewer.

'I usually went to bed before Jackie. One night, I couldn't sleep, so I got up to make myself a cup of cocoa. I came through from the bedroom and I could hear Jackie's voice. It wasn't that I was eavesdropping, I just couldn't help overhearing. She was clearly having an intimate conversation with someone . . .' Claire's voice tailed off, and she traced the pattern on the crystal glass with one long fingernail.

'What made you think it was the sort of intimate conversation you have with lovers?' Lindsay probed.

'For want of a better way of putting it, she was talking dirty to someone,' Claire said with a look of distaste. 'I was completely stunned. The idea of her having a lover had never once crossed my mind, can you believe it?'

'Oh, I can believe it all right,' Lindsay said, pushing the thought of Cordelia away again. 'But how did you find out it was Alison? Did you confront Jackie then and there?'

'I didn't know what to do, so I crept back to bed. When she finally came through, I waited till she'd fallen asleep, then I got up and pressed the last number redial button on the phone. I got Alison Maxwell's answering machine. The following evening, I confronted Jackie with it, and she admitted it immediately. It was almost as if it was a relief to her.' Claire took off her glasses and rubbed her eyes. 'We had a very traumatic evening. A lot of tears, a lot of talking. At the end of it, we decided that there was still too much between us to finish it. Jackie agreed that she would stop seeing Alison. And as far as I was concerned, that was the end of it. Two days later, I came home to find Jackie in tears. She told me she'd been to see Alison to break it off, but that Alison had been completely unreasonable. She had threatened to tell me all sorts of lies about what they had done together, and to destroy Jackie's career. Jackie was in a hell of a state. Before we could sort anything out between us, the police arrived and arrested her.' Claire stopped pacing and stared at Lindsay in mute misery. The cool lawyer's façade had vanished completely. 'It was only later that I discovered that Alison and Jackie had been to bed together that afternoon. I know it sounds absurd, but I was more upset over her lying to me about that than I was about her being accused of the murder.'

'So instead of pledging yourself to wait for her, you jumped into bed with Cordelia. Very supportive,' Lindsay said, fighting the sympathy she was beginning to feel for Claire with her anger at Cordelia.

'That's not fair,' Claire protested angrily. 'It wasn't like that. Neither of us planned what happened.'

Lindsay ignored Claire's response and asked, 'Is there anything more you can tell me that might shed some light? Did Jackie mention anyone else in connection with Alison?'

Claire shook her head. 'No. You'll need to ask Jackie all the details of what actually happened that afternoon,' she grimaced. 'Ever the lawyer, you see, I'm not giving you any hearsay evidence. I'll also speak to Jackie's lawyer, Jim Carstairs, so you can have access to all the legal papers. Remember – what I'm interested in is getting Jackie freed. To do that, you don't have to provide definitive proof against any individual. You simply have to come up with enough new evidence to cast reasonable doubt on the conviction.'

'I might not have a law degree, but I do have a qualification in Scots law for journalists, Claire. I'm well aware of the standard of proof required by the courts,' Lindsay retorted, feeling patronised by Claire's spelling out of the situation.

Claire flushed. 'Very well. What do you plan to do next?'

'I want to see Jackie as soon as that can be arranged. In the meantime, I'm going to take a look at the flats where Alison lived. I've borrowed a set of keys from a friend of mine who lives in the block. I want to refresh my memory on the layout. I'll ring Jim Carstairs and arrange a time to see the papers. And I'll look up a few contacts from my *Clarion* days. I'll call you tomorrow evening and let you know how I'm going on.'

'Where can I reach you?' Claire asked. 'Cordelia told me you rented your flat out when you moved to London three years ago.'

'Yes. Unfortunately, the students who are in it now have a lease that doesn't run out till July. So I'm staying with a friend.' Lindsay scribbled down Sophie's number on a sheet from her notebook. She got to her feet. 'Goodbye, Claire. I'll see myself out.'

Lindsay drove out of the city centre with a sour taste in her mouth. How could Cordelia have fallen for a pretentious yuppie like Claire Ogilvie? To distract herself, she studied Great Western Road as she drove out towards Alison's flat in Hyndland. There had been a few changes here in recent years. It all looked smarter, somehow, the last-ditch hippy emporia of the seventies having finally vanished, overtaken by bookshops, up-market restaurants and interesting food shops. I like being back, she thought with surprise as she swung left off the main road and headed for Caird House. The flats were a ten-storey modern block, built by a housing association in the late seventies. Alison's flat was on the sixth floor, two below Rosalind's.

Lindsay left her car in one of the visitors' parking bays, then walked down the ramp and past the barrier into the residents' underground car park. It was almost empty in the late afternoon. Like Claire's Merchant City eyrie, these were flats for single professionals, or couples without children. At this time of day, they would all be at work. Lindsay crossed the garage and examined the door. Unlike the ground floor entrances, this one had no entryphone, just the same seven-lever mortice lock as the other outside doors. Presumably only residents were expected to come in from the garage. Lindsay tried the key that Rosalind had given her and entered the block.

She noticed the two lifts, but ignored them and headed for the fire escape stairs. She climbed up one level and emerged through a heavy swing door into the foyer. There were two outside exits, one on either side of the block, each leading to a small landscaped parking area. Through the far door, she could just see the nose of her own car. There were no flats on the ground floor, merely boxroom storage areas and the collection area where the rubbish chutes deposited their contents. Lindsay pushed the fire door open again and climbed the stairs. She'd always used the lifts before, and wanted to see for herself how likely it was that Jackie might have been spotted from the outside as she'd sat on the stairs smoking. Small frosted glass windows provided the only daylight, killing that possibility. Overhead, fluorescent strips hummed. At the sixth floor, Lindsay emerged on to a familiar landing.

There were four flats on each landing, one at each corner of the central core. Two had one bedroom, the others had two, she remembered. Ahead of her lay Alison's front door. 6A. How many times had she stood here in a fever of anticipation, desperate for the satisfaction she knew she'd find on the other side of that cherry-red door?

Lindsay turned away, aware for the first time of the depth of her sorrow for Alison. She examined the landing more carefully. Beside the lifts was another door. Curious, she opened it. Inside, there was just room for a person to stand. In the wall was a large, square hole with a sign above it saying 'Rubbish Chute'. Cautiously, Lindsay stuck her head into the gap. It was pitch black. Presumably this was the chute that carried bin bags from the flats down to the huge bins in the ground floor storeroom.

Lindsay withdrew and thoughtfully returned to the landing. She pressed the lift button and waited a few seconds for it to arrive. The double doors slid back, revealing a woman standing in the cramped compartment. As she saw Lindsay she gasped in surprise.

Lindsay stepped into the lift and said nonchalantly, 'Hello, Ruth, I didn't realise you still lived here.'

'Lindsay. What a surprise. I heard you'd left the country after . . . But . . . what on earth were you doing on the landing there? You hadn't come to see . . . I mean, you did know about . . .?'

Same old Ruth, thought Lindsay. Congenitally incapable of finishing her sentences. 'I got back a couple of weeks ago,' Lindsay said. 'I only heard about Alison last night. I guess I just wanted to make a sort of pilgrimage. For old times' sake, you know?'

Ruth Menzies gulped and nodded vigorously. 'I know what you mean. Antonis and I were thinking of selling up and moving out, you know? I couldn't face all the memories, it was all too . . . But anyway, we decided to stay a bit longer and see how . . .' The lift slid to a smooth halt and the doors opened.

'Nice to see you, Ruth,' said Lindsay pleasantly. 'Maybe we could get together some time and talk about old times?' The lift stopped at the ground floor and Lindsay stepped out.

Ruth's answer was cut short as the lift doors closed and carried her down to the basement. Lindsay walked back to her car, musing on the coincidence that had thrust her back into contact with Ruth. The mousey-haired art gallery owner had been Alison Maxwell's closest friend for years. About the only friend who hadn't been one of her lovers, Lindsay wouldn't mind betting. They'd been friends since schooldays, she seemed to remember, the classic pairing of the siren who needs the mouse to show her off to full advantage. Alison had been more than a little put out when insignificant little Ruthie had returned from a buying trip to Athens with a husband in tow. And not just any husband, but a handsome, dashing Greek three years her junior, who was determined to put Ruth's money to good use while he wrote the Great European Novel. Lindsay wondered idly if he'd managed to put pen to paper yet.

On her way back to Sophie's flat, Lindsay made a detour to Wunda Wines, a discount warehouse in Partick, where she bought a couple of bottles of crisp white Tokai di Aquilea to go with dinner. Even that little taste of the Veneto was better than nothing, she reflected as she drove back. She parked behind a Mercedes coupé and hurried towards the tenement entrance. She had only taken a few steps when she was brought up short by the sound of a familiar voice calling her name. A moment later, Cordelia was by her side.

Lindsay struggled to find something to say that wouldn't betray the confusion of emotions that were churning inside her. It didn't matter how many times she told herself it was over, her heart hadn't got the message yet. 'I like the new car,' she said sarcastically. 'Very tasty. Must be more money in the book business than I thought. Or was it another windfall from a rich relative?' she added, feeling ashamed as soon as the words were out of her mouth. She'd never been able to forgive Cordelia for the ostentatious luxury of her London home, bought with the money her grandmother had left her.

Cordelia failed to respond to Lindsay's barb. 'I had to get rid of the BMW. Some joyriders smashed into it outside the house one night, and the steering was never the same afterwards. When I sold the film rights for *Ikhaya Lamaqhawe*, I treated myself to the Merc,' she replied. 'But I didn't drive over here to discuss cars. Claire told me where you were staying. I need to talk to you.'

Lindsay felt anger rising up inside her. Hadn't Cordelia made her position clear enough the night before? 'What is there to say?' she demanded abruptly. She wanted this conversation over with. The longer it went on, the more upset she was going to become. 'You've obviously made your choices,' she snapped.

'At the time, it was the choice between loneliness and having someone to share things with. I missed you so much, Lindsay. And the months kept going by . . . well, I decided I couldn't go on hurting forever. Then I met Claire.' In spite of the conciliatory tone of her words, Cordelia's face was set in a stubborn expression of self-righteousness.

'Fine,' said Lindsay, cutting Cordelia off. 'I'll see you around.' She moved forward, but Cordelia was in front of her, barring her path.

'Wait,' she said urgently. 'Claire says you've agreed to try to clear Jackie. I wanted to offer my help.'

'That's very noble of you.' Lindsay snorted derisively, refusing to let herself be moved. 'Aren't you worried about the competition if Jackie gets out?'

Cordelia flinched, but didn't rise. 'We used to work well together on this kind of thing. I know you like bouncing your ideas off someone. Look, Lindsay, we might not be lovers any more, but I know the way your mind works. Let me help.'

In spite of herself, Lindsay was touched by Cordelia's

offer. 'Okay, let me think about it. I'm not making any promises, but I'll think about it.'

Cordelia smiled and Lindsay felt as if she would burst into tears. 'Thanks,' Cordelia said. 'You can get me at Claire's if you want to talk.' Then, with the impeccable sense of timing that always left people wanting more, she walked briskly back to her new Mercedes without a backward glance.

Close to tears, Lindsay stumbled blindly into the close and ran up the stairs to the first-floor flat. She walked into the hall, but before she could reach her room, Helen's voice rang out. 'Lindsay? Is that you? Thank God you're back. Rosalind's flat's been burgled!'

5

Less than an hour after she had left Caird House, Lindsay was heading back there, this time with Helen. 'I told Rosalind I'd find you and bring you round as soon as you got back,' Helen announced for the third time. 'I knew you'd be going back to Sophie's flat, so I thought I'd wait for you there. I still have a key, so I can feed her bloody tropical fish when she's away.' Why me, thought Lindsay wildly. Answering her unspoken question, Helen continued. 'With you being there this afternoon, Rosalind thought you might have noticed somebody hanging around. And besides,' she added mysteriously, 'There are things involved that I don't think Rosalind will be too happy to tell the police about.'

'What do you mean?' Lindsay asked.

'Oh, I'll leave Rosalind to tell you all about it. It'll be better coming from her. How did you get on with Claire? Tell all!'

Lindsay gave Helen a brief rundown on her day, punctuated at regular intervals with Helen's sharp exclamations. When she reached the meeting with Cordelia, Helen exploded in righteous anger as incandescent as her flaming red hair. 'The nerve of the woman!' she declared. 'I hope you sent her away with her guts in a paper bag!'

Lindsay drew up in Caird House car park, saying, 'What's the point, Helen? She's got every right to her own life. I was the one who did the walking.' She got out and slammed the car door, adding as they walked over to the flats, 'I don't think I was doing her much good by the end. As soon as I left, her writer's block disappeared, and she wrote the best book of her career, by all accounts. I guess she's better off without me.'

Before Helen could reply, Lindsay used Rosalind's spare keys to let them into the block and headed straight for the lifts. 'It's the eighth floor, isn't it?' she asked, her finger hovering over the button.

'That's right,' Helen replied, finally realising that Lindsay didn't want to discuss Cordelia further.

When they rang Rosalind's bell, the door was opened almost immediately by a uniformed police constable. 'We're friends of Ms Campbell,' Helen announced, sweeping past him in the narrow hall. 'She's expecting us.' Flashing an apologetic smile at the constable, Lindsay followed Helen through to the living room.

Rosalind was sitting in an armchair, looking dazed in the midst of the chaos that surrounded her. Her violet eyes were red-rimmed, as if she'd been rubbing them, her white hair in a disarray that was all the more shocking because of the contrast with her usual neatly groomed appearance. Papers were thrown everywhere, furniture had been overturned, carpets pulled up, and pictures hurled from the walls into corners where they lay surrounded by shards of broken glass. The drawers of the desk had been pulled out and emptied on the floor, and a bottle of ink had broken, leaving a permanent-blue puddle on a scattered pile of envelopes. Lindsay, who had only been in the flat a couple of times before, remembered how neat and orderly it had always been and felt a dim version of the shock that clearly possessed Rosalind.

Helen rushed impulsively across the room to hug Rosalind. 'I'll make a cup of tea,' Lindsay said, feeling useless. She went through to the kitchen where the burglars had also been active. All the storage jars had been emptied on the floor, and the contents of the cupboards were strewn everywhere. It didn't have the air of random vandalism, however. Odd, thought Lindsay. Almost as if they knew they were looking for something specific. Lindsay raked through the wreckage till she found a mound of teabags and put the kettle on. She stuck her head into the hall and asked the policeman if he wanted a cup of tea.

'Thanks very much,' he said gratefully, following her back into the kitchen.

'How many are there of you?' Lindsay asked.

'Just me,' he replied. 'I was told to hang on here till the CID could send somebody round. They've made some mess, eh?' he added almost admiringly as he looked around.

'You're not kidding,' Lindsay said absently as she brewed up. 'I've never understood why they feel the need to do it.'

'Anger and frustration, so they say. If they don't find any money or decent jewellery that they can sell easy, they take it out on the householder. I always tell the wife, leave £20 in a drawer in the living room. That way, if we do get some animal breaking in, they might not make a mess of the place.'

Crime prevention from the horse's mouth, Lindsay thought wryly. She handed a mug of tea to the constable and returned to the living room where Helen was sitting with her arms round Rosalind, who looked smaller and more vulnerable than Lindsay could have imagined possible. She handed them both a cup of hot tea, then settled down to wait for Rosalind to tell her what had happened.

Rosalind took a gulp of tea then gave Lindsay a weak smile. 'If I hadn't gone white at twenty, this lot would have done the trick. I'm sorry to drag you into this,' she said, clutching her mug as if it were a lifebelt in a stormy sea. 'But I needed your advice.'

'What happened?' Lindsay asked.

'I came back from the office in Edinburgh at lunchtime because I had a report to finish for my Minister by tomorrow morning,' Rosalind said. 'You can never get any serious work done in that office. The Minister's in and out all afternoon, wanting his hand held about something or other, so I thought I'd just pack up the draft and bring it back here.

'When I went to print out the finished report, I realised I was nearly out of computer paper. So I drove down to Byres Road and bought a box, then came straight back. I was only gone for about twenty minutes. As soon as I got out of the

49

lift, I knew something was wrong. The front door was open, you see. I dithered for a minute or two, wondering whether there was still someone inside, but then I decided, to hell with it, and went in. The place was empty, but it was like this. The policeman said he reckoned they must have been keeping an eye out for me, and just did a runner when they saw my car come back.'

'That's funny,' Lindsay mused.

'What's funny about that?' Helen objected. 'It's exactly what I'd do if I was a burglar.'

'Well, how would they know it was Rosalind's car, unless they were specifically targeting her? In a block this big, you'd have to be dead unlucky if the one car that came in while you were turning a flat over actually belonged to that flat's owner. It looks to me as if they came here with a particular goal in mind and they knew exactly who to keep watch for. This was no random opportunist burglary,' Lindsay said.

Rosalind paled. 'You mean, they were actually spying on me? Surely not! I don't have anything valuable.'

'Did they steal those papers you brought home?'

Miserably, Rosalind nodded. 'They walked off with the lot. And the disc from the computer with the finished report. They took all my other discs as well. Luckily, I've got back-ups of most of them safely stowed in Helen's flat.'

'Do you think the intent was to steal the draft?' Lindsay asked.

'How could it be? Nobody knew what I was bringing home. Not even my secretary knew exactly what it was about. God knows what I'm going to tell the Minister. I'm not supposed to let things like that out of my sight. He'll go absolutely apeshit.'

'Why?' Helen cut in, unable to restrain her natural exuberant curiosity. 'What were they about, for God's sake?'

'I can't say,' Rosalind said. 'Official Secrets Act.'

'I know all about that,' said Lindsay grimly. 'But look, you can trust us, Rosalind. We're not about to tell anyone. And the police are going to have to know, aren't they?'

Rosalind looked worried. 'Yes, they are.' She thought for

a moment, then made her decision. 'It mustn't go any further, and I really mean that, both of you.'

'You have my word,' said Lindsay.

'I won't tell a soul,' Helen said. 'Though God knows it'll kill me, keeping my mouth shut.' She pulled a face.

Rosalind gave a faint smile. 'I know you can keep quiet when you have to, Helen. The report was about the privatisation of prisons. They've been muttering about it for a while, but just like the poll tax, they've decided to try it out in Scotland first. You know the Tory theory – dump it on the Scots, that way if it doesn't work, we've not lost anything because the bloody Scots always vote Labour anyway.'

'Jesus,' Helen breathed softly. 'That's dynamite, Ros. What exactly are they planning?'

'I really don't want to go into details,' Rosalind said. 'But they're planning all sorts of shit like armed guards and high security isolation units for violent offenders. It'll mean the end of any kind of rehabilitation programmes for long-stay prisoners, among other things.'

Lindsay sighed. 'I can see why you're so worried. And if there were rumours around that you were working on it, there would be plenty of people who'd be happy to get their hands on the proposals. Any security firm who were thinking of bidding for the contract, for starters.'

'But I've already told you, no one could have known that this would be the one afternoon when the papers would be here,' Rosalind protested. She looked around the room distractedly, as if the chaos would provide her with some clue.

'Yes, that is a problem,' Lindsay admitted. 'But I don't quite understand why you wanted my advice. I mean, the CID and the Special Branch will be running around like blue-arsed flies till they get their hands on your precious briefcase.'

'That wasn't what I wanted to talk to you about. I know that you can't help me with the official stuff. I'm just going to have to pray that the police find my papers quickly. Then the relief might just stop the Minister from killing me. What I'm worried about is more personal.'

Lindsay lit a cigarette and waited. After a few moments, Rosalind disengaged herself from Helen's hug, took a deep breath and said, 'Did you ever meet my brother Harry?'

'The MP? No, I've actually met him, though I knew he was your brother, of course.'

'Lucky you,' Helen muttered. 'Harry's about as much use as a chocolate chip-pan.'

'All right, Helen. I know you can't stand Harry. But he's not as bad as you make out. Harry's the Labour member for Kinradie, in the Mearns. It's a long way from being a safe seat – it's mainly a farming constituency, and it was one of the few remaining Tory seats till 1983 when Harry won it the first time. So he has to maintain a respectable stance as far as the electorate is concerned. And his constituency party has a nasty right-wing rump that doesn't like a lot of his ideas, so they're always looking for an excuse to deselect him. He's done all the right things – bought a smallholding, married a nice girl who runs the farm while he's away. The only thing he's not managed to achieve in terms of respectability is to have kids.

'There's a good reason for that – Harry's actually gay. His wife knew what she was getting into when she married him, and they're good friends. I think Angela channels all her sexual energies into growing the perfect loganberry. But Harry's always been sexually active even though he's deep in the closet. He was a teacher before he got into politics, so he's always had the habit of being really careful about it.' Rosalind stopped abruptly, clearly not certain how to continue.

Helen jumped into the breach. 'What Rosalind isn't telling you is that Harry has a penchant for young boys. Don't get me wrong, he's not some kind of paedophile. He just prefers them in their teens. And, as we all know, that's still illegal in this benighted country. So Harry is no stranger to the meat racks round Blythswood Square. He likes the illicit thrill of the rent boys.'

'God, Helen,' Rosalind protested, 'you make him sound like some kind of sleazeball pervert. He's not like that. He's had a steadyish relationship on and off for years with Tom McNally.'

'One of his former pupils,' Helen interjected.

'Yes, one of his former pupils. But Harry never laid a finger on him while he was still at school. It was only after he'd gone to university that they started sleeping together,' Rosalind said defensively.

'I still don't see what this has got to do with me. Or the burglary,' Lindsay said, trying to break up the conversation between the other two women before it became a row.

'Sorry, I'm not explaining things very clearly,' Rosalind apologised. 'It must be the shock of all this. Harry spends quite a lot of time in Glasgow, seeing Tom and . . . other boys. When he's here, he uses my flat. I'm quite often away because of work.'

'And because of Bill,' Helen muttered. She got to her feet and began to wander round the room, unable to keep still. It was a constant source of amazement to Lindsay that in spite of Helen's phenomenal level of nervous energy, she still fought a constant battle with her weight.

'Yes, and because of Bill. That's the bloke I've been seeing recently. He lives in Edinburgh,' Rosalind explained. 'So Harry makes a lot of use of my spare room. Even when I'm here, it's not really a problem. We've always got along fine. But the spare room's been turned over as well. He has a desk in there with a locked drawer. The drawer has been forced and everything in it has been taken.'

'What exactly was in it? Do you know?' Lindsay asked.

'I'm not exactly sure,' Rosalind said. 'I've tried to get hold of him at the House of Commons, but he's not in his office. I'm waiting for him to call me back. But I know he has a Polaroid camera in there and I suspect he takes pictures of the boys he brings back here. They'd be dynamite in the wrong hands. A blackmailer or a journalist could really have a field day with them. But what really worries me is the HIV test results.'

'My God, he's not got AIDS, has he?' Helen asked. 'Poor bastard. Even creepy Harry Campbell doesn't deserve that!'

Rosalind ran a hand through her tousled white hair and shook her head. 'I don't know. I've been nagging him about having the test for ages. He's been with so many rent boys over the last few years, I've been scared stiff he'd be HIV positive. I thought he should find out, if only so he wouldn't infect anyone else. He's always resisted me, but a couple of months ago, he finally gave in and went for counselling and had the test. I know he went back for an appointment last week and he told me they'd given him the all-clear. But if there's anything in writing – appointment cards or a letter saying he's not HIV positive, then the only place I can imagine it would be would be that drawer. He thought he was safe here.' Rosalind's eyes quivered with tears. She was suffering a delayed reaction to the shock of the burglary, Lindsay realised.

'How can I help?' she asked gently.

Rosalind pulled herself together with difficulty. 'I wanted to ask whether you thought I should tell the police,' she said. 'And I wondered if you'd seen anybody hanging around when you were here.'

'I didn't notice anything,' Lindsay said. 'But when did it actually happen?'

'About four o'clock.'

Lindsay shook her head. 'It must have been just after I left,' she said. 'But as far as the police are concerned, I would be inclined to say nothing about photographs or blood tests. The police are a leaky sieve. Too many coppers are too pally with journalists for something like that to stay under wraps. Unless Harry is prepared to let the cat out of the bag, you'd better keep that stuff to yourself. They'll be pulling out all the stops to get your stuff back, and if they catch the guys who did it, they'll get their hands on the other stuff too. Then you'll get it all back with no one any the wiser. Hopefully.' She could already picture the headlines. The combination of AIDS, porno pictures and an MP would have the press pack on the doorstep faster than a major earthquake. To the tabloids, an all-clear result would be just as damning as a positive one. The fact of Harry having taken the test would be an admission of guilt in itself.

Rosalind nodded, but looked far from optimistic. 'You're right. But I needed someone else's viewpoint before I could bring myself to make the decision. Harry would never survive a scandal.'

Before she could say more, the door opened and two men walked into the room. The taller of the two, a balding man in his thirties whose shoulders looked one size too big for his sports jacket, said, 'Which one of you ladies is Rosalind Campbell?'

Rosalind got to her feet and said, 'I am. And you are?'

'Inspector Ainslie. Special Branch. I'll have to ask you two ladies to leave while we talk to Miss Campbell. I'm afraid we'll have to get the place fingerprinted too. If you ladies would be good enough to leave your names and addresses with the constable, then we can get your prints later if we need them for elimination,' he said authoritatively.

Lindsay and Helen picked up their coats and prepared to leave. 'I'll drop you back at Sophie's, Lindsay. Give me a ring when the boys in blue are finished, Ros. I'll come round and help you clear up,' said Helen on the way out.

They travelled down in the lift in silence. As they emerged into the car park again, Lindsay turned to look back at the block of flats, twinkling with lights in the early evening darkness. 'Not exactly a safe place to live, is it?' she said softly. 'First Alison, now this.'

6

Lindsay put her foot down hard on the accelerator as the motorway approach road suddenly turned into the fast lane. No matter how often she drove along Glasgow's urban motorway, she could never accustom herself to its vagaries. It had to be the only motorway in the world where you entered and left in the fast lane! Her nationalistic friends were convinced it was all part of an evil English plot to reduce the Labour-voting Scottish population in hideous road accidents, but Lindsay preferred to believe in the Department of Transport's incompetence rather than conspiracy theory.

She flicked the switch that put her engine into overdrive and turned the heater up full. Thundering down the motorway betrayed every draught in the elderly car's hood. At least it wasn't too far from Glasgow to the women's prison near Stirling where Jackie was being held. Claire had pulled strings to arrange an early visit for Lindsay, who had been instructed to say she was working for Jim Carstairs, Jackie's lawyer.

Just after ten, Lindsay pulled off the motorway and drove down the quiet country roads that brought her to the prison gates. A fifteen-foot-high fence of spiked metal stakes was topped with barbed wire, stretching as far as the eye could see in both distances. The gate was equally forbidding. Lindsay parked her car in the visitors' car park opposite the gates and crossed over. She rang a bell by the gate, and a woman in prison officer's uniform emerged from a small gatehouse. She opened a panel in the gate. 'Can I help you?' she asked pleasantly.

'Good morning,' said Lindsay. 'I've come to see Jackie Mitchell. Mr Carstairs arranged the appointment.'

'You're the woman from her lawyer's, are you? We were expecting you. Have you any identification?'

Lindsay produced her driving licence and a covering letter from Jim Carstairs which she'd collected *en route*. The officer examined them, then opened a small door set into the gate and indicated that Lindsay should enter. 'Just walk up the path to the first building and in the doors marked reception. Someone there will sort you out.'

Thanking her, Lindsay set off up the tarmac path. Her destination was a modern, three-storey block, like all the other buildings. Apart from the bars on the windows, it could have been a block of students' residences. The path was flanked by neat lawns. There was no one else in sight as Lindsay reached a pair of sturdy wooden doors with a black and white plaque that stated simply 'Visitors' Reception'. Lindsay tried the right-hand door, which opened on to a small room divided in two by a wide counter. On her side, there were several institutional plastic chairs. Behind the counter were two prison officers, whose conversation stopped abruptly as Lindsay entered.

Her bag was efficiently searched, then she was led through another door, down a cream-painted corridor lined with amateurish watercolours of the Stirlingshire hills, and finally through another door into a tiny interview room. The room had one large, barred window overlooking the lawns and a distant stand of mixed conifers. Its only furnishings were a small deal table and two plastic chairs. The vinyl floor was pocked with cigarette burns, doubtless as a result of the inadequate little tinfoil ashtray on the table. 'Sit there,' the officer said, pointing to the chair nearest the door. 'You must not touch the prisoner,' the officer said. 'If you want to offer her a cigarette, you should place the packet and the lighter on the table and let her pick it up. Is that clear?'

Lindsay nodded and immediately lit up, leaving the packet on the table beside her lighter. She had smoked less than half the cigarette before the door opened and another officer brought Jackie in. If she hadn't been expecting her, Lindsay would never have recognised the woman she used to know. When Lindsay had first met Jackie, she had been cheerful and vivacious. Her shapely figure, bordering on the voluptuous, had always been immaculately turned out in the height of fashion. Her copper hair had been cut and styled regularly. She could never have been described as beautiful, but her milk-white skin and her pale green eyes, which had always reminded Lindsay disconcertingly of gooseberries, had been carefully made up to show her to her best advantage.

The woman who was moving across the room towards Lindsay looked like a grotesque caricature of that Jackie Mitchell. She had put on weight, and her pasty face looked bloated and puffy. Her hair had lost its shine and was tied back untidily with an elastic band. The prison issue denim overalls made her figure look lumpy, with hips out of proportion to the rest of her. Her eyes looked dull and there were dark bruises underneath them. She barely seemed to notice Lindsay's presence as she slumped into the chair and reached for the cigarettes.

'Hello, Jackie,' Lindsay said quietly.

'Thanks for coming,' Jackie said, not sounding particularly grateful. 'Claire said she'd try to find you. I wish she'd been able to get you sooner.'

'I'm sorry too,' Lindsay said. 'But at least I'm here now. I don't know what exactly I can achieve, but I'll do everything I can to get you out of here.' There was an awkward pause.

'You do know I didn't do it, don't you?' Jackie suddenly demanded fiercely, challenging Lindsay with a defiant glare.

'If you'd been going to kill Alison, I don't think that's the way you'd have chosen,' said Lindsay.

Jackie gave a harsh bark of laughter. 'Damn right. If I'd killed Alison, I'd have made bloody sure I didn't get caught. She wasn't worth serving a life sentence for. But I don't have to tell you that. You know better than anyone what she was like, don't you?'

'I have very vivid memories of what Alison was like, yes.'

58

'I know, I know. She told me she'd had you on her hook. Told me that's why you had to do a runner to London. Told me you were scared of what she could do to you. I thought to myself then that if she could put the frighteners on someone as tough as you, I didn't have a cat's chance.' Lindsay listened, appalled, to Jackie's words.

'But that's not true,' she protested. 'I went to London because of Cordelia, not Alison. I'd finished with her long before I even met Cordelia. She was just trying to scare you, Jackie. I called her bluff, you see. I was the one that got away, and she didn't like that.'

Jackie's face crumpled and Lindsay thought she was on the point of tears. Instead, she crushed out her cigarette and lit another immediately. Lindsay noticed her nails were bitten to the quick. 'The bitch,' Jackie said bitterly, sucking the smoke deep into her lungs. 'My God, she deserved to die.'

'Want to tell me about it?'

'I still don't understand how it happened. I hadn't even thought about being unfaithful to Claire until I did so. I suppose we were in a bit of a rut, but it was a rut I liked. It was comfortable, it was home. Then Alison started planting her poison. It was all very subtle, just the odd sentence here and there, all calculated to make me start wondering if we were as solid as I thought.' Jackie rubbed her eyes. 'God, I was gullible.'

Lindsay nodded. 'She was good at that. I've seen her do it to other people.'

'But I fell for it. And then I fell for Alison. We'd gone out for a meal one night after I'd been working at the *Clarion*. We got royally pissed, or at least I thought we did. Looking back on it, I think I got royally pissed and Alison stayed sober. We went back to her place, lights down low, Mary Coughlan on the stereo, another little drink. Next thing I know, we're undressing each other and it's hands everywhere. And that was that. I was hooked.' Jackie stared bleakly at the wall, trapped by the memory.

'She was like a drug,' Lindsay said, caught in the memory

of her own affair. 'I couldn't get enough of her. It was as if the act fuelled the appetite.'

'That's it, that's exactly it. Sex with Alison was like living your fantasies. In a funny kind of way, I was almost glad when Claire found out. I thought that her knowing would break the spell, that I'd be able to escape Alison. But it didn't work, did it? Even though she's dead, I'm still her prisoner.'

'What actually happened that last afternoon?'

Jackie sighed. 'I told Claire I was going to end it, and I went round there all fired up with determination. Alison opened the door to me stark naked, and it took all my strength not to dive straight into bed with her then and there. But I made myself go through with it. I told her what I had decided, that I wanted Claire, not her.

'First, she tried to be seductive and talk me out of it. But I managed to stay firm. Then she lost her cool. Or at least, she seemed to. She burst into loud sobs and told me how much I meant to her and how she couldn't let me go. I was shaken to the core. I had to keep reminding myself that it was Claire I loved. It wasn't easy to hang on to that, faced with Alison in floods of tears.

'Then, when she saw that wasn't going to work, she started to threaten me. She told me she'd tell Claire all sorts of lies – that we'd had a threesome with a man, that I'd gone out with her to a club and we'd picked up two men and had sex with them, that we'd been using cocaine to improve our sex life. Oh God, you wouldn't believe the filth she was coming out with! And she said she'd spread all this poison round the city, make sure that no one gave me any work.' Jackie's voice cracked, and she lit another cigarette.

Lindsay nodded sympathetically. 'I know exactly what you mean. She tried the same routine on me. But I just laughed at her. I didn't have a lover to lose at the time, and I knew she couldn't destroy me professionally without damaging herself. The gamble paid off for me. But if she'd tried that on when I'd actually been with someone I loved, I doubt if I'd have been able to be clear-headed about it. You mustn't put yourself down for falling for it.'

Jackie shook her head. 'I can't help it. I mean, if I'd just stopped to think about it for a minute, I would have realised that there was no reason on earth why Claire or anyone else should fall for her lies. But I didn't stop to think. I should have been stronger, Lindsay. Then I'd have been out of there an hour or more before she was killed. I'd have had an alibi. Instead, I caved in and went to bed with her. You know what disgusts me most about myself? I actually enjoyed it. After all she'd said and done, I still loved every minute of it. Isn't that sickening?'

Lindsay could think of nothing to say that would ease Jackie's self-disgust. 'It's human,' was all she managed. 'What happened then?'

'Alison started shooing me out. She said her mother was coming to see her and she didn't want me wandering round with a just-fucked look on my face. So I got up and dressed in a hurry. I suppose that's how I came to leave my scarf behind. Then I got out of there. I stood on the landing waiting for the lift, feeling like a complete shit. I didn't want to go home. I couldn't face telling Claire I'd been so weak. So I left the landing and started walking down the stairs, just to give myself a kind of breathing space. But my legs felt shaky, so I sat down and had a cigarette. Then I carried on downstairs, got into my car and drove home. Mrs Maxwell says she saw me, but I didn't notice her. I was in too much of a state, I guess. The rest you know.'

Lindsay had listened to Jackie's account with a growing sense of helplessness. There wasn't even a loose strand anywhere she could start picking at to unravel this mess. 'Didn't you see anybody else at all?' she asked.

Jackie shook her head. 'Not a soul. But to be honest, if a rugby scrum dressed in tutus had been dancing the can-can on the landing, I doubt if I'd have noticed,' she added with a touch of fire. 'I was out of it, Lindsay, completely out of it.'

'Do you know who else Alison was sleeping with while she was seeing you?'

'I've no idea. Christ, Lindsay, you know how clever she was at keeping her secrets. She could have been screwing half of Glasgow and I'd never have known,' Jackie said with a swift flash of her old liveliness.

Lindsay sighed and helped herself to a cigarette. It wasn't just Jackie's body that had been coarsened by prison life. Lindsay remembered her as a precise user of language, unusual in the rough and tumble world of newspapers in that she seldom swore. Now she'd fit in comfortably on any ship's bridge, never mind a newsdesk. Lindsay gave a mental shrug and carried on with her fruitless questions. 'Was there any evidence at all that didn't fit the picture?'

'Not really. But Jim will show you all there is to see. It's hopeless, isn't it? I don't know why I was pinning my hopes on you. There's nothing anyone can do, is there?' Jackie said despondently, the animation that had briefly illuminated her face departing as swiftly as it had come.

'It's not hopeless,' Lindsay lied. 'I've hardly started. I've got one or two ideas of my own to pursue. I know most of the lads on the *Clarion*. There must have been some gossip kicking around at the time. And looking at the evidence might give me a few ideas. It's amazing what a fresh eye can come up with. Don't give up, Jackie. Alison Maxwell screwed up too many lives when she was alive. I'm damned if I'm going to stand by and do nothing while she screws up yours from beyond the grave.'

'Big words, Gordon,' Lindsay muttered to herself as she drove away from the prison, leaving Jackie behind her. 'And how the hell are you going to deliver this time?' In spite of her sympathy for Jackie, Lindsay had been only too glad to get away from the depressing encounter, especially after it became clear to her that Jackie knew nothing of Claire's affair with Cordelia. That would be a pleasant surprise for her to come out to, Lindsay thought angrily. No home, no job, no lover.

Lindsay thrust the thought of Claire and Cordelia away and reviewed what Jackie had told her as she drove back to Glasgow. No leads there, she mused. But she still had one or two cards up her sleeve. And maybe Jim Carstairs could give her some pointers that would be worth chasing up.

Less than an hour after she had left the prison, Lindsay was ensconced in the lawyer's secretary's office, ploughing through a thick file of all the case papers relating to Alison's murder. The police statements were interesting, as much for what they did not contain. They had been led straight to Jackie because of a name tape stitched into her scarf. In Jackie's statement, she'd revealed that it was a scarf she'd had since schooldays, hence the presence of the faded tape. Once they had Jackie in custody, she'd been picked out of an identification parade with no hesitation by Alison's mother, who had passed out cold as soon as she saw the woman she believed to be her daughter's killer.

Because they were certain they had the murderer, and because they were convinced it was an open-and-shut case, the police had not pursued any other lines of enquiry with much vigour. Judging by the statements from Alison's friends and colleagues, the questioning had been superficial in the extreme. By the time the papers had been passed on to the Procurator Fiscal for his decision as to whether there was enough for a successful prosecution, the case against Jackie looked overwhelming. And there were no other obvious suspects.

There was only one tiny piece of evidence which did not actually confirm Jackie's guilt. On the bedside table there had been a high-ball glass containing the remains of a whisky and water. There was a smudged lip-print on the glass, and faint traces of fingerprints. Only one was clear enough for the forensic scientists to lift a usable print. But it did not match Jackie's prints in any respect. Nor did it belong to Alison. They had half of a thumbprint from the glass, and the owner of that print was still unknown. Three hours later, that was still the only discrepancy that Lindsay could find in the case against Jackie. With a deep sigh, she closed the file and asked to see Jim Carstairs.

Lindsay was shown into a comfortable office, whose size was disguised by the piles of books, files and loose papers stacked everywhere. 'Come in, come in,' Carstairs greeted her. He was a tall, thin man in his early thirties, with narrow shoulders and bony wrists that stuck out of his fashionable double-breasted suit. 'Sit down, sit down,' he added. 'Sorry about the mess. The joiners have been promising to put my shelves up for months now, but they never appear. Now, how did you get on with the case papers?'

'They were heavy going,' Lindsay admitted. 'And I have to say there's not much there to lend support to the theory of Jackie's innocence. Apart from one thing.'

Carstairs nodded encouragingly. He reminded Lindsay of her Latin teacher, another ugly, skinny man who'd been nicknamed Plug because of his lack of physical charms. But he'd been a kind teacher, who had always managed to draw out even those most lacking in confidence. Feeling reassured, Lindsay went on. 'The glass,' she said. 'It doesn't fit.'

'Well spotted,' Carstairs said with an air of genuine delight at her perspicacity.

'And the police don't seem to have bent over backwards to try to find out who the mysterious thumbprint belongs to,' she went on.

'Good. Of course, I needn't tell you that pursuing that course of inquiry was virtually impossible for us. After all, I have no authority to go round fingerprinting people. With the whole population of Glasgow to go at, and no real suspects other than Jackie, we couldn't begin to unearth the owner of the print. If there had been someone else who had been an obvious suspect, we could have got their prints by some subterfuge, I suppose. But neither Claire nor I had the foggiest idea where to begin,' he apologised. 'However, from what I'm told, which squares with what I understand about fingerprinting techniques, it's likely that the print had been made that day. They certainly weren't the sort of residual prints that might have been left after the glass had been washed,' he continued enthusiastically.

'Who did the police fingerprint?' Lindsay asked, mildly irritated by Carstairs' failure to pursue the one lead that he and Claire had to the real culprit. God preserve me from falling into the hands of lawyers, she thought to herself.

'No one, really. They had no evidence apart from the glass that anyone else had been there. No one else had been seen or heard. Mrs Makaronas from the flat upstairs heard Jackie and Alison quarrelling, but that was all she admitted to having heard.'

'Would that be Ruth Menzies? The gallery owner?' Lindsay interrupted.

'That's right. A friend of the dead woman. Retains her maiden name professionally. Not a very helpful witness from our point of view. Now, as I was saying, the only direct evidence was the glass, and they didn't fingerprint all her friends and associates. In fact, they didn't even look too hard for her friends and etceteras, as you'll probably have picked up from the case file.'

Lindsay shook her head doubtfully. 'It's not much to go at. But at least it's a start. I was beginning to wonder if we were all wrong, and that maybe Jackie had actually done it, in spite of everything my instincts tell me about her and about this crime.'

Carstairs nodded. 'I know what you mean. I think we've all felt that momentary doubt. Including Jackie. I think there have been moments when she's wondered if she suffered some kind of brainstorm. The only one who's never doubted her innocence is Claire. She really has kept the faith.'

Pity she couldn't have managed faithful as well, thought Lindsay sourly. But she kept her thoughts to herself and got to her feet. 'Right,' she said. 'I'm off in pursuit of the missing thumb. I can't promise that I'll be able to get to the bottom of this, you do realise that? The trail I'm trying to pick up is very stale. Getting people to remember what happened four months ago is a tall order. Especially if one of them has something to hide.'

'I appreciate that,' Carstairs said, showing her to the door. 'But we owe it to Jackie to try, don't we?'

'I'll be in touch if I need anything,' she said on her way out.

Lindsay kept her word to the lawyer sooner than she expected. For when she returned to Sophie's flat, she found two men waiting for her.

'Miss Gordon?' Inspector Ainslie of the Special Branch asked as he and his colleague fell into step beside her. 'We'd like you to accompany us to the station. We've got one or two questions for you about Miss Campbell's burglary.'

7

'How many times do I have to tell you? I don't know anything about it!' Lindsay protested. She was sick of repeating herself. Ainslie ignored her denial and continued to put the same question, like a record with the needle stuck in the groove.

'What have you done with the draft report?' he asked her yet again.

Lindsay was bemused. When the two policemen had stopped her in the street, she had demanded to know what they wanted and why they thought she could help them. Ainslie had refused to answer any of her questions and had brought her to Maryhill Police Station, where she had been hustled into a small interview room, furnished with a table and two chairs. The room was hot and stuffy, and her head had begun to throb. It was all frighteningly reminiscent of another interview room she'd been interrogated in once before. The memory made Lindsay's palms sweat and the blood pound in her ears.

Neither police officer had attempted to explain what was going on. Ainslie had simply repeated his question over and over again. She had asked to call her lawyer, but her request had been ignored as completely as if she had never spoken. An hour had passed in this inconclusive but, for Lindsay, deeply unsettling pattern. Then, without warning, Ainslie got abruptly to his feet and walked out, slamming the door behind him. His junior sidekick followed him moments later, after fixing Lindsay with a long, hard stare.

She got to her feet and stretched her legs. It never crossed her mind to try leaving. She felt sure there would be someone outside the door. Lindsay rotated her shoulders and shook her wrists vigorously to loosen up her muscles. For some reason, they had decided she knew more about Ros's burglary than an innocent bystander should do. But she was determined to give nothing away. Something told her she was in for a long session.

A few minutes later, the door opened and a stranger walked into the room. His face looked as though he'd spent too much of his youth in a boxing ring. 'Miss Gordon?' he enquired mildly.

'That's right. Who are you?'

'Chief Inspector Fraser. Mr Ainslie tells me you're not being very co-operative,' he replied, lowering his bulky frame on to a plastic chair that didn't look equal to the task.

'Mr Ainslie might have earned my co-operation if he'd given me a clue as to why you've brought me here,' Lindsay said.

Fraser pulled a copy of the Scottish *Daily Clarion* from the inside pocket of his rumpled grey suit. 'Come on, Miss Gordon,' he said with an air of weariness. 'Don't tell me you haven't worked it out. We're not all daft in the force, you know. Your reputation has gone before you. So when we get a burglary involving politically sensitive information, followed by a press leak, and you're on the spot, you can't really be surprised if our fingers get round to pointing at you.'

'I'm sorry, I don't know what you're talking about. I don't know anything about a press leak. I haven't even seen today's papers. I left the house early this morning and I've been running around all day. I've not had a chance even to look at the front pages,' Lindsay explained.

Fraser shook his head sorrowfully. 'I'd hoped you could do a wee bit better than that. You must think I came up the Clyde on a biscuit. After my twenty-two years on the force d'you really expect me to believe that?'

'Whether you believe it or not, it's the truth,' Lindsay said stubbornly. 'Look, Chief Inspector. I'll happily answer any questions you want to put to me if you'll only do me the courtesy of either telling me what this is all about or letting me speak to my lawyer. I have rights, and I intend to exercise them.'

The Special Branch officer tossed the paper down on the table. The headlines screamed off the page at her. TOP TORY TO CASH IN ON PRISON PLAN,' the main banner said. Underneath, a smaller headline read, 'Jail sell-off means fat profits for Jedburgh'. Lindsay's heart sank. Whoever had stolen Rosalind's report hadn't hung around. The by-line on the story read 'By Bill Grace, *Clarion* Chief Reporter'. She knew Bill, and knew he was one of the best journalists in Scotland. He'd obviously used his extensive and varied contacts to turn a run-of-the-mill leak story into a major political scandal.

Appalled, she read on.

A top-secret plan to privatise Scotland's prisons will make the minister responsible a rich man.

Mark Jedburgh, the Scottish Office minister in charge of prisons, has an extensive shareholding in a security firm that has been gearing up to meet the challenge of running a top-security prison on the taxpayers' behalf.

According to a secret government report, revealed exclusively to the Scottish *Daily Clarion*, plans are well advanced to sell off Scotland's jails to the highest bidder.

The plans include armed guards, strict punishment regimes, increased security, drastic cuts in social and educational opportunities for prisoners and an end to all rehabilitation programmes for long-term violent offenders.

Vigilando Security Group are hotly tipped to win the first contract to run a private prison.

One of VSG's major shareholders is Mark Jedburgh, Tory MP for Central Borders. He owns 15 per cent of VSG. His wife Christina owns another 7 per cent.

Former prisoner Davey Anderson, who served three life sentences for murder and now works for a charity which helps to resettle ex-prisoners, said last night, 'This is diabolical. Jedburgh should resign at once. This plan is a recipe for riot.' (Continued p.3)

Lindsay looked up from the paper, hoping that her feelings of shock were reflected on her face. 'I knew nothing about this,' she protested. 'Ask Bill Grace. He'll tell you he didn't get it from me.'

'We've already spoken to Mr Grace,' Fraser replied. 'I bet you can guess exactly what he told us.'

'He refused to reveal his sources, I suppose. But surely if you asked him to confirm that it wasn't me, he'd tell you that, at least?' Even as she asked the question, Lindsay knew it was a vain hope. In Bill's shoes, she'd have admitted nothing.

'We did ask him, believe me, Miss Gordon. He simply said that he was not prepared to answer any questions at all relating to the source of his information. He made the perfectly reasonable point that if he started co-operating with us to the extent of eliminating people, we could go right through the names of every working journalist, civil servant and politician in Scotland till we got to a name he wasn't prepared to eliminate. So I'm afraid you're still very much in the frame.'

Lindsay sighed. 'Look, Chief Inspector. A year ago, I had a very bad time with the forces of law and order. So bad that I ended up leaving the country till the fuss died down. I'm sure your extensive enquiries will have already told you that. I've only just come home. Believe me, I'm looking for a quiet life these days. Do you really think I'd want to put myself in the same position all over again just to drop some junior Tory minister in it?'

Fraser pulled out a packet of cigarettes and offered one to Lindsay, who accepted gratefully, having smoked the last of hers twenty minutes before. He lit up, puffed for a few moments, then said, 'I'm not a psychologist. I don't pretend to understand what goes on in the minds of people like you. I'm a policeman, and what I'm trained to do is investigate crime. That means acquiring as many facts as possible and then making logical deductions. Now, the facts I have before me are these. A story based on a report stolen in a burglary yesterday has surfaced in a newspaper. A journalist who has a track record of writing this sort of anti-establishment story, who used to work for the very paper which carried the story, was on the spot. Not only in the building itself, but carrying a set of keys to the very flat that was burgled. Do you not think that I'd be failing in my duty to the taxpayers who pay my wages if I didn't pull that journalist in for questioning?'

Lindsay cursed silently. She'd been praying that Rosalind hadn't told the police that she had the spare keys to the flat. She'd have to try something else if she was ever going to get out of there. 'Come on, get serious,' she mocked. 'Rosalind Campbell's a friend of mine. Do you really think I'd stage a break-in and reduce her flat to a shambles just so's I could get a story? If that's how you think friends behave, you must have a bizarre personal life.'

Fraser shrugged, his beefy shoulders straining his suit seams. 'I've only got your say-so for this bosom friendship. You might have been stringing this woman along all the time. And besides, if you hadn't made a shambles of the place, we'd have been all the more certain it was you, wouldn't we? On the other hand, maybe you and Miss Campbell were in it together.'

Lindsay shook her head incredulously. 'I just don't believe you guys. Byzantine doesn't begin to describe your thought processes. For God's sake, why would Rosalind conspire with me to wreck her own flat?'

'We know one or two things about Miss Campbell too,' Fraser said flatly. 'We know, for example, that she's an active member of the Labour Party. Maybe she wanted this story to get out. I mean, what could be more damaging to the Tories?'

Lindsay stubbed out her cigarette angrily. 'If Rosalind had wanted the story to get out, don't you think she could have used her Labour Party contacts to leak it that way? She's not stupid, she could have covered her tracks easily enough.'

'Maybe she wanted her flat redecorated on the insurance.

Like I said, I'm not a psychologist. And all my years in the force have taught me that nine times out of ten, the obvious answer is the right one. You were on the spot. You had keys to the flat. And you've got the contacts to place that story,' Fraser summed up, ticking off the points on his short, thick fingers. 'Either you start to co-operate, or I'm going to charge you.'

'Fine. At least that way I'll get to see my lawyer.'

He smiled in a way that sent a chill down her spine. 'Eventually. I wasn't planning on charging you for a wee while yet. I'd like you to have every chance of showing your willingness to help us out.'

Fraser had backed her into a corner. She'd have to co-operate if she was to have any chance of getting home tonight. 'Okay,' she said. 'Thank you for finally telling me what all of this is about. I suppose I'd better keep my end of the bargain. I'll answer your questions now.'

Fraser nodded. 'Very wise. Let's start from the beginning. When did you get the keys of the flat?'

'Rosalind gave them to me the night before the break-in.'

'Why?'

'Didn't she explain that to you?'

'It's you I'm asking. Why did she give you the keys?'

'I wanted to take a look at the block,' Lindsay said, aware of how feeble her story sounded.

'Thinking of buying a flat, are you?'

'No. A friend of mine was murdered there last year. I've been asked to make some enquiries relating to her death,' Lindsay said defensively.

'So you think the police didn't manage to get the right person for Alison Maxwell's murder?' Fraser demanded.

He'd done his homework, Lindsay thought. 'Something like that,' she said.

'And you decided to come along on your white charger to show the woodentops how it should really be done, eh? I thought you said you were looking for the quiet life these days?'

Lindsay shrugged. 'I'm just doing a favour for a friend, that's all.'

71

'And I suppose that while you were there, you thought you'd just pop in to Miss Campbell's flat for a cup of tea, since you had the keys burning a hole in your pocket. Seeing that report on her computer screen must have been a hell of a temptation. I can't say I blame you. Any journalist worth their salt would have been hard pressed to ignore it.'

'I didn't go near Ros's flat. I was never on the eighth floor. I went straight to the sixth floor, had a look round then I left,' Lindsay stated.

'Surely you don't expect me to believe that?' Fraser asked incredulously. 'Missing out on the chance of a nice little earner like that? Come on, admit it, Miss Gordon, it happened just like I said. I've heard all the excuses. Now, how about coming up with the truth? It would save us all a lot of time in the long run.'

Lindsay shook her head vigorously. 'You're way off beam. Look, even supposing I had let myself into Rosalind's flat and seen the report, I wouldn't have needed to stage a burglary. I know about computers, for God's sake. All I would have had to do would have been to make a copy of the file on to another disc and walked out of there with it in my pocket. No one would have been any the wiser. When the story broke, no one would have been able to trace it back to me or to Rosalind. Like I said, Rosalind is a friend of mine. I wouldn't have wrecked her flat just to cover my back, not when I could have protected both of us by quietly copying the disc.'

For the first time, Lindsay thought she saw a flicker of doubt in Fraser's blue eyes. 'I don't know,' he finally said. 'Maybe all that sophisticated logic didn't occur to you on the spur of the moment. Maybe you just saw the chance and acted on it.'

'Look, apart from anything else, I wasn't even in the building long enough to make such a thorough job of it,' she protested.

'Protesting a wee bit too much, aren't we?' Fraser asked sarcastically. 'Just run through your movements yesterday afternoon for me. Let me work it out for myself.'

'I was with a lawyer called Claire Ogilvie until about

quarter past three. Then I drove straight to Caird House. I walked up from the garage to the sixth floor, stood on the landing for about three or four minutes, then travelled down in the lift with Ruth Menzies from Flat 7B. Then I drove to Wunda Wines on Dumbarton Road, bought two bottles of Italian wine and drove back to my friend's flat. Where your boys picked me up today. I arrived there about four. A woman called Cordelia Brown, who's staying with Miss Ogilvie, was waiting for me in the street. I spoke to her for a few minutes, then went upstairs. My friend Helen Christie told me about the burglary, and we went round to Rosalind's flat. Inspector Ainslie saw me there later.'

'I'll want a statement to that effect,' Fraser said, getting to his feet. 'Do you want to call your lawyer before you commit yourself to paper?'

Lindsay nodded, and at last she was escorted to a phone. She caught Jim Carstairs just as he was leaving his office, and he promised to come right away. To her surprise, Lindsay found her hand was shaking with relief as she replaced the receiver. Being in the hands of the police again had clearly frightened her more than she was prepared to admit to herself.

An hour and a half later, she stood with the lawyer in the police station car park, having written out a full statement of her movements the previous day.

'I don't think they're going to give up on you that easily,' Carstairs said.

'No,' Lindsay sighed. 'It looks like I've got a burglary to solve now as well as a murder.'

8

Lindsay drove past the floodlit car park of the *Daily Clarion* and parked on the street just past the modern skyscraper that housed the plant and offices of Scotland's top tabloid newspaper. She got out of the car, shivering as the damp evening chill made her fasten her sheepskin jacket, and walked towards the security office by the back door, the entrance used by the paper's many staff. It felt strange to be taking the familiar route back into a building that had once been as much home to her as her own flat. What felt even more strange was her certainty that inside she'd find the answers that would lead her to Alison Maxwell's killer.

Disneyland, she thought with a smile as she crossed the forecourt. That's what the printers had christened the building when it opened, moving the *Clarion* titles into the vanguard of the new technology. They'd been the first national daily paper to use computerised typesetting and full colour printing, and the initial hiccups in the system had led to the nickname, as frustrated workers had spent their shifts muttering. 'This disnae work, that disnae work. This is Disnaeland.'

Lindsay pushed open the door of the security office and walked into the stuffy room with its familiar odour of stale smoke, sweat and faint but unmistakable traces of printer's ink. The big balding man sitting at the desk that looked out over the forecourt got to his feet and exclaimed, 'It's wee Lindsay! How're ye doing, hen? We havenae seen you here for a few years!' He leaned forward to shake her hand and the buttons of his shirt gaped over his enormous beer gut, revealing a grubby white vest.

'I'm fine, Willie, just fine,' Lindsay replied, dredging his name up from her memory. 'I've been working abroad, but I'm back in Glasgow for a while. I just thought I'd pop in and see the boys. Do I need to sign the visitors' book before I go up?'

Willie roared with laughter. 'You?' he finally wheezed. 'Don't be daft. I know fine who you are. You're no' some IRA terrorist, are you? Away you go and see your pals.'

In the lift, instead of pressing the button for the third floor and the newsroom, Lindsay pressed the second-floor button. After she'd left the police station, she'd decided there was no time to waste in her pursuit of Alison Maxwell's murderer and Rosalind's burglar. The key to both of those lay, she believed, inside the *Clarion* building. And it was better to make a start at night when there were fewer people around. Besides, she had always got on well with the night duty librarian. She no longer had any right to use the *Clarion* library, but she couldn't see Martin refusing her.

Lindsay walked down the corridor, past the canteen where the tempting aroma of home-made soup nearly made her take a detour. Again, memory assailed her. Just after she'd first got it together with Cordelia she'd still been working in Glasgow, and when Cordelia came up from London they'd often spent Lindsay's meal breaks in a quite corner of the canteen, grabbing every chance to be together. Ironic, really, thought Lindsay. It was a murder that had brought them together and now another murder had driven them apart.

She carried on into the library. As always, the sight filled her with awe. On one side of the room, banks of ceiling-high metal cases housed quantities of newspaper cuttings, filed and cross-referenced, stored in huge mechanically driven carousels that were supposed automatically to produce the relevant cardboard folder. But this was Disnaeland, and at least one machine was usually out of order at any given time. On the other side of the room was the morgue – ordinary filing cabinets, crammed full of cuttings no longer current because they referred to events of more than fifteen years ago, or their subjects were dead. Above the filing cabinets there were rows of reference books. In a small annexe, there was a photocopier, a collection of back numbers of the daily and Sunday papers, and several tables where reporters could work away from the hurly-burly of the newsroom.

At a table among the filing cabinets, Martin Cameron the night librarian was sitting in front of a pile of the day's papers, carefully clipping items that were destined for the library's extensive files. He was so engrossed he didn't hear Lindsay enter, and looked up in surprise when she rang the bell for attention. As he recognised her, his pale face lit up in a welcoming grin and he struggled to his feet. 'Lindsay Gordon!' he exclaimed. 'What a nice surprise. Come on through.'

She lifted the flap in the counter and threaded her way through the filing cabinets to his side. She'd known Martin for years, and he'd always been her favourite among the bunch of oddballs who seemed to find their way behind the counter of newspaper libraries. They all had their foibles. Martin's had been importuning night-shift journalists into chess games which he won with depressing regularity. 'Hi, Martin,' Lindsay said. 'Good to see you. How are you?'

He shrugged. 'I can't complain, well I could, but you don't want to hear my problems. What brings you back to this den of vice?'

'I need some help, and I thought you might be able to oblige,' Lindsay said, perching on the edge of his desk.

'For you, Lindsay, anything!' Martin laughed. 'I'd guessed it wasn't just my company you were after.'

'Don't be daft,' Lindsay said. 'Seeing you is a bonus.'

Martin smiled. 'You always were a smooth operator. So what can I do for you?'

'I'd like you to have a look at the files relating to Jackie Mitchell's trial. And Alison Maxwell's by-line files,' Lindsay said.

Martin's eyebrows rose. But years of servicing the seemingly bizarre demands of journalists had rendered him immune to any serious curiosity. 'Nasty business, that was,' he said. 'You always did ask for funny things. Everything from famous murder cases of the fifties to the life and career of Tallulah Bankhead, as I recall,' he said over his shoulder as he walked towards the cuttings store. He pressed a button, and the hydraulics shuddered into noisy life. A few moments later, he returned with a bulging folder. 'That's the stuff about the murder and the trial. You can get started on that while I find Alison's stuff in the morgue.'

Martin began searching through one of the filing cabinet drawers while Lindsay took out her notebook and started reading the files of cuttings from the *Clarion* and other papers relating to Alison's murder and to Jackie's trial. It was full of sickening detail, and Lindsay noticed with distaste how the tabloids had gone to town on Jackie and Alison's sex lives. It was the kind of thing that was routine procedure in cases like this. She'd done it herself on occasion. But it left a nasty taste in the mouth when the stories referred to people she knew. She was glad she'd taken the decision not to earn her living like that any more. She'd grown tired of having to justify to herself the things she did in the name of journalism.

Lindsay worked through the file, noting down various details that were new to her. But she found little to suggest any new avenues to explore.

'There's Alison's files. Do you want a coffee?' Martin asked as he deposited two thick A4 manila envelopes in front of Lindsay.

'I could murder a mug of canteen soup,' she replied, glad of the chance to be left alone with Alison's cuttings. She knew exactly what she was looking for, and judging by what she'd read and been told, no one else had found it. Although Lindsay had discovered its existence years before, she believed it would still be there.

Martin left the library, and Lindsay immediately opened the two envelopes. She hastily flicked through the first bundle, which consisted entirely of yellowing clippings from the second half of Alison's career at the *Clarion*. Impatiently, Lindsay pushed them aside and started to search the other bundle. These clippings were older, the paper more brittle, and there were a few photographs and photostat sheets of typewritten copy among them. But there was still no sign of what Lindsay was looking for. She went through the pile again, this time opening out the larger cuttings that had been folded up to fit the envelope.

She struck gold on her third attempt. As she unfolded a cutting about Scottish rock bands, a slim white envelope fell out. Across the front was typed 'Confidential background', and the flap was tucked in at the back. Thank God Alison hadn't changed her habits! Without opening it, Lindsay stuffed the envelope in her pocket. When Martin returned with her soup, she was seemingly engrossed in a feature about comedian Billy Connolly.

'Mmm,' said Lindsay, drinking a mouthful of the rich chicken broth. 'That was just what I needed. I didn't realise how hungry I was till I walked past the canteen.'

'Found what you were looking for?' Martin asked as he settled down with his pile of papers again.

'Yes, thanks. You're a star, Martin. Who's on duty upstairs tonight?' Lindsay asked as she packed the cuttings back into their envelopes.

Martin told her, and at the name of Blair Craigie, Lindsay's ears pricked up. Blair had been her shift partner for the six months before she'd moved to London, and the close working relationship that had developed between them had spilled over into their private lives. They had often spent their days off walking in the mountains round Loch Lomond and the Trossachs. 'Great,' she said. Borrowing Martin's phone, she rang the newsdesk upstairs and spoke to Blair. He was due for a meal break in half an hour, and they arranged to meet in a pub some distance away from the office to avoid being sucked into a convivial journalistic gathering that would prevent them talking properly to each other.

Lindsay headed back to her car, waving a farewell to Willie as she passed the security office. She drove up the Clydeside Expressway and turned off at Partick. She cruised up Byres Road and parked outside Tennants Bar. She pushed open the door and stopped in astonishment. They'd renovated Tennants! She could remember when the spit-and-sawdust pub had been the most basic of hostelries. They hadn't even had a ladies' toilet. When women were caught short, they had to go into the pub next door. It created a problem near closing time, for the neighbouring pub shut half an hour before Tennants. But now, the bar was carpeted, the furnishings were new and she could see a sign saying 'Ladies' Toilet'. Lindsay walked up to the bar and bought a pint of lager.

She didn't have long to wait. Before she was half way down her glass, Blair arrived. He waved and headed straight for the bar, arriving minutes later at her table clutching two pints. He put the glasses down and swept her into his arms in a bear hug. 'When did you get back?' he demanded.

Breathlessly, Lindsay said, 'A few days ago. How's tricks?'

'You see it all,' he said expansively, running a hand over his sandy curls.

'That bad, eh? So, what's been happening?' Lindsay settled back in her seat to catch up on the newspaper gossip that she'd missed in her absence. Why is it, she wondered with amusement, that whenever two or more journalists get together, there isn't a reputation left intact by the end of the encounter?

'I think that's about it,' Blair said as he wound up. 'Oh no, wait a minute. Did you hear about Alistair McGrath's company medical?'

Lindsay shook her head. 'Tell me,' she said.

'Well, the doctor examined him, and he was asking him all the questions about medical history, smoking and all that. So he says, "And what do you drink?" Quick as a flash mad McGrath says, "What have you got?" ' Blair convulsed with laughter as he reached the story's punchline.

When Lindsay stopped laughing, she said, 'Time to be serious. I need your help, Blair.'

His eyebrows rose and he stroked his moustache. 'I hear that people who help you these days have a way of getting into bother,' he said carefully. 'Mind you, we've pulled each other out of the shit enough times. What's the problem?'

'Bill Grace's story this morning. About Jedburgh and the prisons. I need to know where he got it from.'

Blair whistled softly. 'Christ, Lindsay, that's a tall order. You'll have to form an orderly queue behind the Special Branch.'

'That's exactly why I need to know. The Branch picked me up this afternoon because they've got a bee in their bonnet that I was the person who leaked the documents to Bill.'

'But what's it got to do with you?'

'The story was based on a leaked Scottish Office draft report that was stolen yesterday afternoon. Unluckily for me, I happened to be in the building where the burglary took place. And with my track record . . .' Lindsay tailed off.

'I see. Christ, you've only been back five minutes and already you're causing mayhem. So you want to know who gave Bill his info so you can get yourself out of the firing line.'

'Not exactly,' she replied. 'Whoever did that burglary also walked away with some other bits and pieces that he'd no right to. The woman who was burgled happens to be a friend, and I promised I'd try to get them back for her. Look, you know me. I'm not going to grass Bill's source to the police. I believe in protecting sources as much as anybody. It's purely so that I can get this other stuff back.'

Blair looked doubtful. 'I don't know, Lindsay. It all sounds a bit iffy to me. Why don't you ask Bill yourself?'

Lindsay sighed. 'I don't think he'd tell me. We always got along all right, but we were never what you'd call buddies. He always treated me like a silly wee lassie who didn't really understand what being a hotshot reporter was all about. Anyway, I didn't want you to ask him straight out and drop yourself in it. Just a few discreet inquiries, that's all.'

Blair shrugged. 'Okay. But no promises. Where can I reach you?'

Lindsay gave him Sophie's number. 'Another thing . . .' she said.

'Oh God. What now?' Blair groaned. 'Don't tell me, let me guess. You want me to rob a bank riding blindfold on a unicycle?'

'The unicycle comes later. Jackie Mitchell has asked for my help. She claims she's innocent.'

'And you fell for that? Christ, Lindsay, I didn't think you were that naive. Haven't you read the court reports?'

Lindsay smiled wryly. 'Yes, Blair, I've read the court reports. And I admit that on the face of it, it looks like she did it. But I don't see how making a few inquiries can do any harm. And I promised I'd do what I could. I just wanted to ask you what the gossip was about Alison round the time of her death.'

Blair stroked his moustache and stared into his beer. 'Tell you the truth, everybody was so busy going "Fancy that!" over the shock horror revelations about Jackie that nobody else's name was mentioned. Whoever else Alison was seeing, nobody from the *Clarion* was putting their hand up. Mind you, after she got Jimmy Mills frozen out of the sports desk, everybody steered pretty clear of her.'

'I didn't hear about that. What happened with Jimmy Mills?'

'It happened about a year after you went off to London. Alison's version was that Jimmy gave her a lift home after a party, came up for coffee and raped her. She said she wasn't going to make a complaint to the police because she didn't want him to lose his wife and kids. Jimmy's version was that he'd been having an affair with her, but she'd cooled off and spread that tale to get him off her back. Jimmy had been doing regular shifts on the racing desk, but every time he was in the office when she was there, she would burst into tears and head for the loo. Eventually, the sports department decided they could do without the aggro and gave Jimmy the bullet. He was well pissed off about it.'

'I can see why the lads were steering clear,' Lindsay mused. 'Look, Blair, if you remember anything else that might be useful, give me a bell.'

'Okay. And I'll see what I can dig up about the Jedburgh affair.' He got to his feet. 'I'd better be getting back. Some of us have got jobs to go to,' he teased.

Lindsay finished her drink and got to her feet. She'd been glad to see Blair, but she was equally glad to see him go. The envelope was burning a hole in her pocket, and she was desperate to explore its secrets. The key to Alison's death was in her hands now, she felt certain.

9

Thank God for infatuation, Lindsay thought, as she sprawled across the bed in Sophie's spare room. If it hadn't been for her initial obsession with Alison, she'd never have known about the existence of the envelope and its contents. She sprawled across the bed in Sophie's spare room and sipped a glass of whisky and water. Sophie had instantly understood when Lindsay told her she didn't feel like discussing her Special Branch ordeal. She'd simply poured her a large drink and left her to herself.

Lindsay studied the envelope, tantalising herself before she opened it. It looked just like the one she'd discovered years before when, on fire with lust for Alison, she'd spent half of one night shift avidly reading every word her new lover had ever had published in the Scottish *Daily Clarion*. The contents of the envelope had shocked Lindsay, then amused her. But it was from the moment she understood the implications of what Alison had written that Lindsay dated her ultimate disillusionment.

At the time, it had seemed a strange place to leave a document of this sort. Lindsay had eventually come to the conclusion that Alison had hidden it there to avoid accidental discovery by anyone who regularly visited her flat. Anyone routinely looking something up in her by-line file would almost certainly have ignored it as journalists trawling through the files would only be looking for a specific story. It was only Lindsay's obsession with Alison that had driven her to open the envelope.

She supposed she should have left it where it was. Tampering with the evidence, Ainslie would doubtless call it. But if Alison had stuck to her old habits, the contents would be in her handwriting. There could be no dispute about their author. Lindsay pulled on a pair of thin leather driving gloves and opened the envelope. Carefully, to avoid destroying any existing prints, she removed its contents with a pair of eyebrow tweezers, then unfolded the thin sheets of airmail paper.

With a sigh of satisfaction, Lindsay surveyed Alison's secret dossier. There were about ten sheets of paper, all except the final page completely covered in the tiny neat handwriting that Lindsay recognised immediately. She turned straight to the last page. The final entry, dated the day before her death, began 'Ocz kjgdodxvg kjovoj: rdoc rcvo d xvi kmjqz do rjio ws gjib ijr!' and continued for another couple of lines. Lindsay crossed her fingers and prayed that Alison was still using the same simple alphabetic cypher that she'd used when they'd been lovers.

Lindsay turned back to the first page, which dated from six years previously. She'd be in this dossier somewhere, she knew. When she'd first found the document, she'd hastily photocopied it and taken it home to study at her leisure. The code Alison used hadn't taken much working out. It had been obvious to Lindsay that Alison's secret file was some kind of record of her sexual adventuring. It had seemed a strangely childish game to Lindsay. It was almost as if by committing it to paper in this way, Alison was proving something to herself about her desirability. Although Lindsay hadn't fully understood the reasons for it at the time, she now saw it as an expression of a deep-rooted personal insecurity, an emotional stunting that had left Alison trapped in adolescence.

But merely cracking the code hadn't been the answer. Translating the jumble of letters into proper English words had simply provided Lindsay with another problem. For Alison was too shrewd to leave an incriminating record of proper names. Instead, she referred to her lovers by nicknames, or where they were part of an established couple, in relation to their partners. It was often snide, seldom flattering to her conquests. Often, there were references to people before they actually became her lovers, showing each step in her campaign to include them among the notches on her bedhead. Each nickname was preceded by a date, and sometimes by a time and place. It was often followed by a comment on their performance or personality, and each neat entry ended with the ultimate childishness in Lindsay's eyes – a mark out of ten. Even the fact that Alison had given her 8.8 didn't vindicate the system for Lindsay.

She rubbed her tired eyes and put the papers to one side. She was too weary tonight for the close work involved in translating the dossier. Tomorrow, she'd get up bright and early and go down to the local print shop to make photostats of the sheets. That would save the originals from more handling than was strictly necessary. Then she could work her way through the list, and see where that took her.

Lindsay rolled off the bed and undressed, leaving her clothes in a pile on the floor, too tired even to throw them on a chair. She swallowed the remains of her drink in one and crawled between the sheets. She turned out the light and started to review her day. But she was asleep before she even got as far as the prison gates.

'I spent today decoding the entries. Here's a copy of the original, and here's a copy of my version of it. I've used highlighter pens to mark the ones that I think might have some relevance to my inquiries. As you'll see, about seventy per cent of her lovers were men, the rest women. Interestingly enough, although she often had several male lovers on the go concurrently, she usually stuck to one woman at a time.' Lindsay handed the sheets of paper to Claire.

She had arranged a meeting with her employer to discuss her progress so far, and to see if Claire could shed some light on the problem entries she'd uncovered. Lindsay had not bargained for Cordelia's presence at the meeting, and she felt distinctly uncomfortable at the sight of her former lover leaning over Claire's shoulder examining her work. They looked right together, she thought bitterly, in their designer jogging suits and trainers. Cordelia really had come home at last.

'What a weirdo!' Cordelia exclaimed as she read the entries. 'But how can we be sure that this is accurate? How do you know she didn't just make it all up?'

Lindsay blushed. 'The implication has to be that she told it like it was. If you'll take a look at the third page, there are several entries relating to me. Splash, she calls me. As far as I can recollect, her comments are accurate, if somewhat bitchy.'

'Why Splash?' asked Claire, flicking through to the relevant section. As she reached it her eyebrows rose. She shoved her glasses up her nose and looked up questioningly.

'I suppose because Lindsay was being a little megastar and always getting the front page at the time. You know, Claire, the front page is the splash. That's right, isn't it?' Cordelia said, the smile on her wide mouth failing to reach her grey eyes. Lindsay said nothing, while Cordelia read the sentences Claire pointed out to her with her pen. Cordelia giggled. 'Only 8.8, Lindsay? I thought you reckoned you were at least eleven out of ten!'

'Like wine, I've improved with age,' Lindsay retorted caustically, feeling herself blush in spite of herself. 'I'd like to get down to the business in hand . . . If you'll turn to the second-last page, you'll see the first entry which I interpret as relating to Jackie.'

' "The legal eagle's eager beaver: easier than I thought to get her to break the rules! 7.2." Is that the one you mean?' Claire asked bleakly. Her small, neat features looked pinched and she seemed to hunch into herself.

Lindsay nodded. She was beginning to feel sympathy for Claire. She knew how much she'd have hated it if their positions had been reversed and she'd been hearing this about Cordelia. She wished there was a less embarrassing way of dealing with Alison's diary, but forced herself to press on. 'If you look further down, you'll see another half-dozen entries over the next couple of months. The last one, made a couple of days before her death, says, "Spent all afternoon doing very traditional things with champagne.

She's less fun than I expected. Still a bit of mileage, though. 6.8." That must have been the afternoon before you overheard the phone call. It certainly undercuts the prosecution's argument that Alison was desperate to hang on to Jackie.' Catching Claire's look of distaste, she added, 'I'm sorry if this is very painful. But I think it might hold the key.'

Claire nodded sadly. 'I understand that.' She took a deep breath and visibly pulled herself together, flicking her hair away from her face. 'I just find the whole thing deeply sick. Most people grow out of that sort of silly childishness by their early teens. Alison Maxwell must have been really screwed up. But I still can't forgive the way she screwed up other people to make herself feel better. Now, Lindsay, what do you make of these other entries? And why have you picked them out in particular?'

'I've disregarded the bulk of the entries because they relate to affairs that ended at Alison's instigation when she had grown tired of the individual. Once she had decided it was the end of the line, that was it, you see. No recriminations, no exposure, just goodnight Vienna. And I've set aside for now any of the ones where she was clearly not happy with the outcome but where she seems to have taken no action. I've marked ones where she appears to have done something to cause damage to the person who upset her. Those people might reasonably be deemed to have some kind of grudge. I've also left ones that were still current at the time of her death.'

Claire nodded, completely restored to her brisk, cool legal persona. 'Fine. Can we go through these now?' Cordelia, obviously feeling left out of the conversation, got to her feet and refilled everyone's glasses with chilled Chardonnay.

'Thanks,' Lindsay acknowledged curtly. 'Starting in reverse order. The very last entry is one I am completely confounded by. "The political hot potato. With what I can prove, it won't be long now. Let's hope for some originality between the sheets!" I haven't the faintest idea who that refers to. But then, it's three years since I spent any time with Alison. It's unlikely that I would know.'

'It looks as if it's someone she hadn't actually slept with yet, since there's no rating,' Cordelia chipped in.

'You could be right,' Lindsay agreed reluctantly. 'What I propose, Claire, is that if you don't understand any of these references either, I'll discuss them with Jackie to see if she's got any ideas.'

Claire nodded. 'I can't imagine that many of them would mean much to me, but I'll certainly try to help. But what about your former colleagues at the *Clarion*? Surely they might have a better idea?'

'I'd already thought of that,' Lindsay said. 'It's a distinct possibility, which I've got covered. I don't want to raise your hopes, though. Anyone who was having an affair with Alison at the time of her death has had plenty of time to cover their tracks, don't forget. Now, if we could get started? "Ali and his technicolour dream ceiling. He's starting to feel too secure. Time his cage was rattled a little. 6.3." I rather think that might refer to Alistair Anderson.'

'The painter?' Claire asked, surprise showing in her blue eyes.

'That's right. He was an old buddy of Alison. She used to use him as a public escort when she needed a man on her arm. He painted the mural on her bedroom wall, and he did one on Ruth and Antonis' ceiling. Their sexual relationship was still current.'

Claire shook her head, bemused. 'I know Alistair. He wouldn't hurt a fly. Unless . . .'

'Unless what?' Cordelia demanded, settling herself down on the sofa next to Claire and reaching out for her hand.

'Unless someone was trying to stop him painting, I suppose.'

'If you know him, why don't you see what you can do by way of checking him out?' Lindsay said. 'I only ever met him once at a party, so I've no excuse for talking to him, really.'

'How on earth do I do that?' Claire asked. 'I thought that's what I was paying you for.'

'It would be easy,' Cordelia interjected, seeing Lindsay's angry flush and knowing how near an explosion was. 'Don't forget, Claire, I know Lindsay's methods,' she added lightly.

'We could invite him round for dinner, work the conversation round to Alison's death and ask him if he remembers what he was doing at the time, all very casually, a bit like the "what were you doing when Kennedy was shot" conversation.'

Claire shrugged doubtfully. 'I suppose so. Well, Lindsay, what other little jobs do you have for me?'

'There's one I've marked on the last page. "Davina's Duck. Wonder when he's going to settle his account? I told him I'd make him pay for flaunting her under my nose, and I meant it. 7.1." Mean anything to you?'

Claire nodded slowly. 'Davina and Donald Mottram, I suspect. Donald's an accountant with Porterhouse's. Davina was very into the arts. I've seen them at a few openings and parties where Alison was too. But they split up a few weeks ago. Davina ran off with Bill Herd the ethnologist to some South Pacific island. I wonder if that had anything to do with Alison's death?'

'One way to find out,' Lindsay said. 'I know Donald Mottram slightly. Rosalind went out with his brother once. I can check that one out. Next is "Macho the Knife. Brought his work into the bedroom. All that was missing were the stirrups to stir me up." He didn't score too well, either. A mere 5. And she makes a snide remark later about his wife having to nurse his ego, which might mean he's married to a nurse. He sounds like a gynaecologist to me. And one of their encounters took place at GWI, which I take to be the Western Infirmary. I'll ask Sophie if she can think of anyone there who might fit the bill. But I've saved the best – or the worst, depending on your point of view – till last. Look at the one I've highlighted in blue.'

' "Greek God. She'll never sell a work of art that wonderful. 8.4," ' Cordelia read out.

'That's the one. It can only refer to Antonis Makaronas,' Lindsay said.

'Who is . . .?' Claire asked.

'Ruth Menzies' husband. Ruth was Alison's best friend. Ruth runs an art gallery off Byres Road. They live in the flat above Alison's. And as you'll no doubt remember, at

Jackie's trial, Ruth gave evidence that she was in the flat that afternoon. I don't know if Antonis was at home, or how long Ruth claims she was there for. Ruth met Antonis a couple of years ago when she was on a business trip in Greece. He was a self-styled writer playing bouzouki in a taverna to make ends meet. It was love at first sight, at least on Ruth's side. They were married days later and Ruth came home with a suntan and a husband. She supports them both while he supposedly is writing the Great European Novel. Except that it now looks like he was running his fingers over Alison rather than a word processor keyboard. It's got to be one hell of a motive for both of them. If I was a gambling woman, I'd be giving very short odds on one of that pair as my chief suspect.'

Claire smiled grimly. 'You've certainly come up with some interesting leads. Well done.'

'Thanks,' Lindsay said drily. 'There's also someone who used to work at the *Clarion* with an axe to grind against Alison. A guy called Jimmy Mills. Alison made some extremely unpleasant allegations about him, and he lost all his shifts on the sports desk as a result. I'll be checking that out too.'

Before Lindsay could say more, the phone rang and Claire jumped to her feet. 'Excuse me,' she said, hurrying out of the room. 'I'm expecting a call from a client. I won't be long.'

Left alone with Cordelia, Lindsay felt wrong-footed. She stood up and picked up her jacket. 'I'd better be going anyway,' she said awkwardly. 'I'll just wait and see if Claire's got anything else to say, then I'll be on my way.'

'Don't rush off,' Cordelia said, getting to her feet. 'Look, Lindsay, I know this is all a bit difficult, but I want us to stay friends. I'd hoped that if I could help you by working with you on this business that maybe we could build some bridges.'

'I think we've burned all our bridges, don't you?' Lindsay said bitterly, walking over to study one of the quilted wall-hangings. 'Besides, you seem to get along much better without me. Judging by what the critics have to say about the new book, I'd say that my departure was the best thing that ever happened to you, professionally speaking.'

'Have you read it yet?' Cordelia asked, moving towards her.

Lindsay deliberately walked away from her, putting a sofa between the two of them. Her face felt as if the muscles had seized and it seemed to take an extraordinary effort to speak. 'No,' she said. 'I guess I got used to getting complimentary copies of Cordelia Brown books. I haven't got back into the habit of actually buying them.'

Cordelia flushed and then frowned. Somehow, she kept her voice even and friendly. 'I haven't got any spare copies here, but I'll let you have one when I get back to London,' she said.

'Don't bother. I'm sure I can afford a copy, on what Claire's paying me,' Lindsay retorted sharply, not trusting herself to be anything other than combative. 'You really don't owe me anything, Cordelia.'

'That's not true, you know that.' Whatever Cordelia might have been going to say was lost as Claire walked back into the room.

The awkward silence that greeted her brought an angry frown to her face. Her eyes glittered behind her glasses, and she moved swiftly to Cordelia's side. 'Are you off, then?' she demanded.

Lindsay nodded. 'I've got work to do. I'll speak to you as soon as I've got anything to report. Let me know how you get on with Alistair,' she said abruptly. 'I'll see myself out.'

Lindsay rushed out of the flat and ran down the stairs. Catching her breath in the street outside, she was overwhelmed by the desire to kick and punch and gouge someone, anyone, but preferably Claire bloody Ogilvie. Shaking with emotion, she slumped in her car seat. When was she going to stop loving Cordelia?

10

Lindsay's fury had subsided by the time she returned to Sophie's. The sudden recollection of a thought that had drifted across her mind as she'd been dropping off to sleep drove thoughts of Cordelia far away. Fraser had been too quick off the mark with Alison Maxwell's name. He was Special Branch, not CID. He would normally have had no involvement in a routine homicide like Alison's. Yet as soon as she'd mentioned murder in connection with Caird House, he'd known instantly whose murder she was talking about.

Could there be any link between Ros's burglary and Alison's death? It seemed too much of a coincidence that the break-in had happened on the very day that Lindsay had started her enquiries, and at a time when she was actually in the building. But the idea of Ros and Alison as lovers was ridiculous, even to Lindsay's suspicious mind. Although her two closest friends, Helen and Sophie, were gay, Ros herself had never been interested in women except as friends. Lindsay had sat through too many slightly drunken conversations with the three women to believe that even Alison Maxwell's charisma could have disrupted Ros's lifelong exuberant heterosexuality. Besides, there was nothing in Alison's notes that sounded even remotely like Ros.

If there was a link, it had to be Harry. The idea of some sexual connection between them seemed unlikely. Perhaps they shared a lover? Could Harry Campbell be the 'political hot potato' of Alison's dossier? As Lindsay threw herself down on the couch, the headline of an article about vaccines in a medical journal lying on the side table caught her eye. 'I wonder,' she muttered aloud.

Harry had visited the AIDS clinic for his test. But if anyone was a candidate for the terrifying virus, it had to be Alison, given the extent of her promiscuity. Could Alison have seen him there? Could she even have been blackmailing him? Lindsay wouldn't put it past her.

It was about time she started asking some questions. Lindsay leaned over and picked up the phone. She dialled a number and drummed her fingers impatiently on the arm. 'Come on Ros,' she muttered to herself. 'Answer the goddamn phone.' On the seventh ring, Rosalind answered. 'Hi, Ros, it's Lindsay.'

'Have you got some news for me?' Rosalind demanded eagerly.

'Not yet, but I'm working on it. Hopefully tomorrow.'

'Oh.'

Lindsay didn't need to see Rosalind to sense her disappointment. 'Don't worry, it's all under control,' she lied uncomfortably. 'How were things at work?'

'Don't ask. I feel like a haddock. By half past nine this morning, I was gutted, filleted and battered. On a popularity rating of one to ten with my minister, I come around minus ninety-nine.'

'Poor you,' Lindsay sympathised. 'Have you spoken to Harry yet? Do you know exactly what was taken?'

'I finally got hold of him about midnight last night. He's in a hell of a state. You can imagine – he's phoning me every hour to see if there's any news. He's convinced his perfect little world is going to come crashing round his ears any minute now. He's going to try to get up here tomorrow, and he'll want to have a chat with you. As to what's missing – I was more or less right. There were photographs of various rent boys. And I don't mean happy family snaps. There were a couple of letters from Tom. And Harry's appointment card for the AIDS clinic and the counselling service. Luckily for him the tests were negative. But in the wrong hands, the combination of the pictures, the letters and the very fact that he's had the test makes for a very unpleasant conclusion.' There was a note of desperation in Rosalind's voice that Lindsay found hard to reconcile with her normal cool control.

In response, she tried to fill her own voice with confidence and certainty. 'Well, I'll do everything I can. I should be able to find out where the *Clarion*'s story came from. Once I've got that sussed, then we can't be too far away from our burglar.'

'I appreciate all you're doing, Lindsay. Just make it as quick as you can, eh?'

'Will do. Listen, Ros, I need some more help on the Maxwell investigation . . .' Lindsay let her unspoken request hang in the air.

Rosalind sighed. 'Sure. What can I do for you?'

'It's all a bit delicate. I'm trying to track down the people Alison was sleeping with around the time of her death. I've got good reason to believe that one of them was Donald Mottram. Didn't you go out with his brother a few years ago?'

'That's right. Duncan and I were together for about six months . . . God, it must be four years ago now. But we've stayed vaguely in touch.'

'How well do you know Donald?' Lindsay asked, lighting a cigarette. Old habits die hard, she thought ruefully to herself. She could survive for days at a time in her outdoor routine in Italy without recourse to a cigarette. But put a phone in her hand, and it was second nature to have a cigarette in the other. Lindsay shook herself mentally and listened to Rosalind's response.

'Not too well, I'm afraid. I know him to say hello to in the street.'

'But not well enough to set up a meeting with him?'

'Afraid not. But why don't you just make an appointment to see him professionally?' Rosalind suggested. 'It wouldn't be unreasonable for you to need to see a tax specialist. You've been working abroad, you've no idea what your tax position is on your foreign earnings. You can tell him I recommended you – he sorted out a problem with the Inland Revenue for me a couple of years ago.'

'That's a good idea. But how do I get him talking about Alison?'

'You're the journalist. I thought your forte was getting people to talk about things they didn't want to discuss?' Rosalind teased.

'Miracles take longer,' Lindsay muttered. 'By the way,' she added, trying to sound nonchalant. 'Did Harry know Alison at all?'

'Harry?' Ros's astonishment was obvious even in one word. 'I don't think so, Lindsay. He certainly never mentioned her to me. I suppose they might have had a nodding acquaintance from the lift or something, but I don't think he knew her at all.'

'I just wondered if her murder had unsettled him at all,' Lindsay said lamely.

Ros laughed. 'It did. He got very jittery about us all being murdered in our beds. I think he's been rather more discriminating about who he brought home since then. Why d'you ask?'

'It's probably nothing. It just seemed odd to me that the burglary happened just after I started looking into Alison's death. Must just be a coincidence.'

'It struck me last night, actually. But I can't for the life of me see what the connection could be.'

'You're probably right. If anything occurs to you, let me know. And thanks for the suggestion about Donald. I'll get back to you.' Lindsay rang off and pondered. She made a mental list of things to do in the morning. First, make an appointment with Donald Mottram. Second, get hold of Jimmy Mills and pump him about Alison. She vaguely remembered him from her days at the *Clarion*, but she'd have to work up an excuse for seeing him. Third, arrange a meeting with Ruth and Antonis. And she'd have to pump Sophie about Alison's gynaecologist. It was all becoming very complicated.

Lindsay rolled off the couch and poured herself a whisky, wandering through to the kitchen to top it up with water.

She felt restless and uneasy. Until she had more information, she was deadlocked. She glanced at the kitchen clock. Ten past eight. Too late to go to the theatre or the cinema. Idly, she wondered where her friends were. Helen was probably out socialising or talent-spotting at some avant-garde play in a church hall with an audience comprising three old biddies and the cast's lovers. Sophie would be at the hospital, dealing somehow with a level of human misery Lindsay could only guess at. How she coped with the tragedy of the AIDS babies without cracking up Lindsay couldn't fathom.

'A good read, that's what I need to take my mind off all the hassle,' Lindsay told herself, striding through to Sophie's study. The small, high room was lined with built-in bookshelves filled with medical textbooks and modern novels. It also contained a desk, a computer, a filing cabinet and a single divan bed. Lindsay started looking for something appealing that she hadn't read. Her absence from Britain for so long meant there was a considerable backlog of new novels for her to work her way through, and Sophie was always well-supplied with the latest fiction. As she scanned the shelves, one book seemed to leap out to catch her eye. In bold black capitals on a gold spine, Lindsay read IKHAYA LAMAQHAWE: CORDELIA BROWN. As if she were mesmerised, Lindsay lifted her hand slowly and took the book from the shelf. Lindsay stared bleakly at the dustcover with its embossed three-quarter profile of a black woman, head back, fear straining her skin taut over her jaw and neck.

Lindsay subsided on to the divan and forced herself to open the book. Carefully, as if she were handling a delicate mediaeval manuscript, Lindsay turned the pages. She read the dedication with a wry smile. 'To all those who have the courage to fight for truth and against oppression wherever it is found, no matter what the personal cost.' Perhaps she hadn't been so far from Cordelia's thoughts after all.

Taking a deep breath, Lindsay began to read the novel. She knew ten pages into it that it was good, no doubt about that. The writing was taut. Not a word was wasted. And the atmosphere was extraordinary. Lindsay could almost smell the world that her former lover had created so painstakingly.

96

She shook her head in amazement. Cordelia had somehow managed to get under the skin of South Africa from thousands of miles away.

And the style was a logical development from everything Cordelia had done before. It was so stripped down, so lacking in decoration. Yet it somehow managed to be rich at the same time, the sort of writing that forced you to read slowly because you wanted it to last. Lindsay felt a new respect. She'd always been impressed by Cordelia's careful plotting and her scrupulous use of language. But with this book, she had achieved her real potential.

The book dropped into her lap. She felt hurt that she'd been cut out of the process of creating this book, and of the joy Cordelia must have felt in it. Lindsay knew her reactions were childish and maudlin, but that didn't make them any less real. She was so lost in her thoughts that she didn't hear the front door opening. Sophie called out, 'Anybody home?' and, seeing the light in the study, she walked in. At once, she registered the fallen book and Lindsay's misery. Dropping her briefcase, Sophie sat down by Lindsay's side and pulled her into her arms. 'It hurts, doesn't it?' she murmured.

The sympathy destroyed the last remnants of Lindsay's self-control, and the tears in her eyes overflowed down her cheeks. She shook with sobs as Sophie calmly stroked her back, saying nothing, letting her cry herself out. Eventually, Lindsay pulled brusquely away, rubbing at her eyes with her fists. 'I'm sorry,' she gulped. 'It all got too much.'

'Want to talk about it?' Sophie asked.

'What's to say? Reading this, I'm not surprised I've lost her. Do you know, I didn't have the faintest idea she was working on this? She must have been researching it before I had to do a runner. But I was so wrapped up with what I was doing I never even noticed,' Lindsay said unsteadily.

'No point in blaming yourself,' Sophie said. 'You had your own problems at the time. You were under a lot of pressure too.'

'That's no excuse,' Lindsay muttered. She was wallowing in self-pity, and no amount of good sense was going to interfere with her self-indulgence.

'Stop beating yourself up, Lindsay. These things happen,' Sophie sighed. Then she adroitly shifted the subject, knowing it was the best way to dig Lindsay out of her gloom. 'Look at me and Helen. Towards the end, we were living separate lives. Half the time, I didn't know what was happening in her world, and she was so revolted by mine that she acted like she didn't even know what I did for a living.'

'But you two always seemed so supportive of each other,' Lindsay said, diverted from her own misery by this revelation, just as Sophie had planned.

Sophie shrugged. 'If it's supportive to say, whatever you do is all right by me, and then make no effort to find out what the other is doing, then we had a supportive relationship.' Sophie got to her feet and for the first time Lindsay noticed the deep lines of exhaustion round her eyes. 'Anyway, enough of my troubles. Have you eaten?' Lindsay shook her head. 'Well, I don't know about you, but I'm starving. Come and tell me about your day while I throw some dinner together.'

'I'll give you a hand.' Lindsay followed Sophie and found her pulling the crisper out of the fridge. Sophie picked up a sharp kitchen knife and started chopping vegetables into a big wooden salad bowl. Lindsay picked up a carrot and chewed it idly, feeling vaguely guilty about imposing her problems on Sophie when it was obvious she had more than enough stress in her own life. 'What kind of day have you had?' she asked.

'Pretty shitty. Delivered a baby this morning, mother's an IV heroin user, virus positive, starting to develop AIDS-related symptoms,' Sophie said dispassionately. 'We won't know if the baby's carrying the virus till the last traces of his mother's blood have left his system and we can test him, but he's not looking too good. Imagine your first experience outside the womb being heroin withdrawal,' Sophie sighed as she savagely attacked a lollo rosso lettuce.

'I don't know how you do it,' Lindsay said.

Sophie stopped chopping.

'Matter of principle,' she said. 'After all, according to you journalists, AIDS is the disease that proves God's a lesbian.

Least I can do is help the poor unfortunates who are stricken by it.'

Lindsay looked puzzled. 'I'm not with you.'

'Well, the moral majority as represented by our beloved tabloid columnists spent a lot of time telling us that AIDS was a gay plague sent by God to punish the sodomites. So if AIDS is God's punishment, it must follow that the people God identifies with and loves best must be the people least at risk. And since non-drug-using lesbians are statistically the lowest risk group . . .'

In spite of herself, Lindsay laughed. 'That's sick,' she said.

'Gallows humour. One of the lesser known medical specialities. If I didn't laugh, I'd crack up completely. Now, tell me about your day. How are your inquiries going?'

Lindsay brought Sophie up to date, finally adding, 'Do you know a gynaecologist at the Western who fits the description Macho the Knife? Possibly married to a nurse?'

Sophie barely paused for thought before replying. 'Yes, as it happens. Why?'

'He could be on my list of suspects for Alison's murder,' Lindsay replied, picking up a chunk of mozzarella cheese and dicing it into tiny cubes.

Sophie stopped cutting carrots into neat batons with surgical precision and stared at Lindsay. 'Ian McIntosh? You've got to be joking! He's all mouth and trousers. You're not seriously trying to tell me he was bonking Alison Maxwell?'

'Why not?'

'Well . . . It's just that he's one of those guys who's always cracking *double entendres* and pretending he's a superstud. In my limited experience, those types seldom actually do what they're always mouthing about. He's not been married that long. Can't be more than eighteen months or so,' she added thoughtfully.

'And is his wife a nurse?' Lindsay probed insistently, her earlier misery forgotten in the joys of the chase.

Sophie nodded. 'Yes. A theatre sister, I think. But how on earth would he have met Alison? I can't imagine their social circles overlapping,' she mused as she threw the carrots into the big wooden salad bowl and started to cut up some cauliflower florets.

'Maybe she was his patient,' Lindsay said.

'Dear God. I suppose you could be right. Do you want me to see if I can take a look at the records?'

'Would you? That would be terrific,' Lindsay enthused, glad to feel she was getting somewhere at last.

'No problem. I like to feel useful.' Sophie threw the last of the ingredients in the bowl and took a bottle of home-made dressing from the fridge. She sprinkled it over the salad and began to toss it vigorously. 'Besides, I don't like doctors who abuse their position.'

'Good. Then can you arrange for me to meet this guy McIntosh?'

Sophie laughed. 'My God, I'd forgotten what a pushy little shit you can be when you've got a bee in your bonnet. I'll see what I can do.'

After they had eaten, Lindsay curled up on the couch and continued to read Cordelia's new novel. Sophie settled down beside her with the British Journal of Obstetrics, a comforting arm round Lindsay's shoulders. Just after eleven, Sophie finished reading her periodical and yawned expansively. 'I'm ready for bed,' she said. 'How are you feeling now?'

Lindsay shrugged. 'Pretty raw, to tell you the truth. Losing Cordelia's taking a bit more getting used to than I expected.'

'Come to bed with me, then,' Sophie said. Seeing the look of surprise on Lindsay's face, she laughed softly. 'Sorry, not the most romantic proposition you've ever had, is it? It's just that . . . well, you look fairly cuddle-starved to me. We both need a bit of loving and comfort, I'd say. And we've been friends for long enough to trust each other. No strings, Lindsay, just a bit of shelter in the storm.'

Lindsay felt the prickle of tears in her eyes as she hugged Sophie. 'Thanks,' she whispered. 'If you hand out prescriptions like this to all your patients, no wonder you're such a success!'

Sophie grinned and kissed Lindsay's forehead. 'If you saw

my patients, you wouldn't even think of making a scurrilous suggestion like that!'

Afterwards, they lay sprawled chaotically together in Sophie's king-sized bed, the room illuminated with the eerie glow of the ten-foot long fish tank that occupied most of one wall. 'Mmm. It's been a long time,' Lindsay murmured.

'For me too. You're the first since Helen,' Sophie confessed with a distant smile. Her eyes had lost the weary look they'd held earlier.

'You surprise me,' Lindsay said. 'A woman of your charms. I didn't think you'd be on the loose for long, to be honest.'

'After Helen, it would take someone rather special to interest me,' Sophie said with a trace of bitterness unnoticed by Lindsay in her post-orgasmic haze.

'I'll take that as a compliment,' Lindsay purred as she leaned over and picked up her cigarettes from the bedside table.

'You should. I've always had a soft spot for you, you know?' Sophie said, stretching luxuriously.

'I'd no idea. Personally, I'd always thought Helen was far luckier than she deserved to be. So how come we never did anything about it till now?' Lindsay asked as she lit up and inhaled deeply.

Sophie propped herself up on one elbow and stroked Lindsay's side. 'Well, I was with Helen, then when I wasn't with Helen any more, you were with Cordelia. Speaking of whom, how are you finding working for Claire?'

'Uncomfortable,' Lindsay said, luxuriating in her new lover's touch. 'It's not easy maintaining a coolly professional relationship with her when Cordelia's around all the time. Though I suspect that after tonight all that might have changed.'

Sophie stopped in mid-stroke. 'I wonder . . .' she murmured.

'What?'

'I wonder if it's deliberate, Cordelia always being around?' Sophie said thoughtfully.

'I don't understand,' Lindsay said. 'Why should it be deliberate?'

'Say for the sake of argument that Claire's heart isn't really in it. She doesn't really want you to discover Alison's murderer.'

'You mean she doesn't believe in Jackie's innocence at all?'

'No, no,' Sophie said impatiently, sitting up and hugging her knees. 'Jackie's innocence isn't the issue. I mean, she's obviously fond of Jackie and would be happy for her if she were released. But say Claire didn't want you to uncover the truth. What better way of distracting you than by ramming Cordelia down your throat at every opportunity?'

'But why on earth would she want to do that? I mean, why bother asking me to investigate in the first place if she then goes out of her way to distract me?' Lindsay demanded, completely confused.

'It would make perfect sense if Claire Ogilvie killed Alison Maxwell.'

11

Lindsay woke from a confused dream of being lost in an African township, searching vainly for Cordelia, to Sophie gently shaking her awake.

'I made you a coffee. I've got to run, but you said you had a lot to do today, so I thought I'd better wake you. You were sleeping like the dead,' Sophie greeted her.

Memory of the night before flooded back to Lindsay, and a satisfied grin spread across her face. 'You did right,' she said. 'So the bumper sticker is really true?'

'What bumper sticker?'

' "Gynaecologists do it with their fingers," ' Lindsay teased.

'We do other things with our fingers too,' Sophie exclaimed, grabbing Lindsay and tickling her ribs.

'Whoa!' Lindsay yelled. 'Mind the coffee!'

Sophie hugged her. 'I'll see you later,' she said, kissing her smiling mouth.

'I can't wait!'

The stinging needles of the shower chased the last trace of sleep from Lindsay's brain. She wasn't ready yet to examine the new basis of her relationship with Sophie. Her body felt relaxed and comfortable after their love-making, but her head was still spinning with the implications of Sophie's bombshell. Why hadn't *she* thought of Claire? If Jackie hadn't been the obvious choice, Claire could well have been the next person the police would have looked at.

As she towelled herself dry, Lindsay examined the idea step by step. Claire had carefully presented an image of herself as cool and rational, the woman who had been hurt but who had forgiven. But what if the reality had been different? What if she had known Jackie well enough to realise that she would never be able to rid herself of her obsession while Alison was still alive? She could easily have gone to the block of flats and waited in the rubbish chute cupboard till she saw Jackie leaving, then slipped in to Alison's flat and killed her. But if so, why was she going through the charade of asking Lindsay to help clear Jackie's name?

Sophie's answer to that was the double bluff. What would someone in Claire's position be expected to do? Answer: she'd be expected to do exactly what she had done. Anything else would have looked suspicious. Added to that was Claire's insistence when she'd first briefed Lindsay that she didn't have to uncover the true identity of the murderer, merely cast enough doubt on Jackie's conviction.

And the fact remained that she hadn't actually tracked Lindsay down. What if her involvement with Cordelia had started as a convenient distraction for the one woman who could reasonably be expected to know where to look for Lindsay? Once Claire and Cordelia were lovers, there would be a certain reluctance on Cordelia's part to searching too diligently for Lindsay, after all.

Sophie had also come up with another interesting angle. 'Claire may not have intended to frame Jackie, just to kill Alison,' she'd mused. 'After all, she couldn't have known Jackie was going to sit around on the stairs like a lemon. And Claire could have had no way of knowing that the body would be discovered so soon. The arrival of Alison's mother plus Jackie's bizarre behaviour might have screwed up Claire's plans completely.'

'But if she hadn't meant to frame Jackie, why use her scarf?' Lindsay had objected. Thinking it over now, she felt deeply confused. Maybe she was letting herself place more weight on Sophie's suggestion because she instinctively disliked Claire for coming between her and Cordelia. Well, there was one simple way to see if there was anything in the idea. She'd have to check Claire's ablibi for the time of the murder. Oh boy, that was going to be a fun question to ask her employer!

Lindsay shivered as she wrapped herself in a bath towel. She'd still not acclimatised to the cold Scottish winter after so long in the warmth of the Adriatic. The thought of the freezing February air outside made her feel like diving back under the duvet and staying there till spring. Instead, she huddled over the gas fire in the living room with the phone and a mug of coffee. This question mark over Claire was going to have to be sorted out, and soon. She fished Claire's card out of her bag and dialled her office.

When she was put through, she said, 'Lindsay Gordon here. Can we meet for a talk later today?'

'Have you some progress to report?' Claire asked neutrally. There was no eagerness in her voice, thought Lindsay.

'Sort of,' Lindsay stalled. 'What time would suit you?'

'I'll be leaving my office around three. I'm taking some paperwork home. Come round any time before six.'

'That'll be fine. See you then.'

Next, Lindsay rang directory enquiries for the number of Porterhouses' office. After dialling, she was quickly connected to Donald Mottram's secretary. She explained her need for an urgent appointment to discuss her tax problems.

'Could you be at the office in half an hour, Miss Gordon?' the secretary enquired. 'One of Mr Mottram's clients has just rung to cancel his appointment, so he'll be free then. Otherwise, it would be next Thursday before I could fit you in. He has a very full diary just now.'

Lindsay couldn't believe her luck. What a good game this was! She could get her year's accounts done at Claire's expense. 'I'll be there,' she promised. 'Where exactly are you?'

After the call, Lindsay checked out her clothes. If Donald Mottram was the ladies' man she took him for, she might just get under his guard with the fluttery female act. Desperately, she searched through her bags. There was nothing there that would remotely fit the bill. Cursing under her breath, she ran through to Sophie's room and opened the wardrobe. They were near enough the same size, though Sophie was taller, and Sophie had always had impeccable taste in clothes. Unlike me, thought Lindsay, choosing a smart red woollen dress with matching shoes. She pulled open the top drawer of the dressing table and hastily applied some eyeshadow and mascara. Thank God she still had the healthy remains of her Italian tan! She surveyed herself in the mirror, far from happy with the overall effect. 'Relax, you're looking good,' she muttered, trying to convince herself.

Precisely half an hour later, Lindsay was shown into Donald Mottram's businesslike office. The walls were covered with grey hessian shot with apricot and cream, their sole decoration a moody photograph of a blood-red sun setting over the Glasgow skyline. The yuppies really are here to stay, she thought moodily. As she entered, Donald Mottram rose from a grey leather swivel chair and extended his hand across a wide grey desk. He was quite short, but stocky, with shoulders and chest that looked bulky inside his smart business suit. His short black hair clung to his head in tight black curls shot with grey. His strong-featured face reminded Lindsay of a prize bull. 'Miss Gordon,' he said. 'I'm delighted to meet you. Do have a seat.'

Lindsay settled into a deep grey leather armchair, took a deep breath and told a white lie. 'I think we've met before, actually,' she said. 'At one of Ruth Menzies' private views? Alison Maxwell introduced me to you and your wife.'

The muscles of his jaw tightened momentarily, but he managed to smile and said, 'I'm sorry, I don't remember. One meets so many people at these dos. Now, what can I do for you?'

Lindsay launched into an account of her chaotic finances while Mottram made careful notes on a foolscap pad. At the end of her recital, he put his pen down and smiled. 'Well, Miss Gordon, I don't foresee too many problems with this. If you can let me have the necessary paperwork by the end of the week, I'll get your accounts formally prepared.'

'Thank you so much,' Lindsay said, carefully crossing her legs and swinging her foot in its red stiletto, wishing she had Sophie's long legs. 'I don't know what I'd have done without you. It's been preying on my mind. Then I remembered Alison saying you were the best tax accountant in Glasgow, and if I ever needed help I should come to you.'

Mottram gave a smug smile. 'We aim to please,' he said.

'Such a blow, Alison's death. I couldn't believe it when I heard it. We were so close,' Lindsay said, trying to look woebegone and unthreatening while feeling like a grade one fool.

'Yes, it was a terrible shock,' he replied shortly.

'I didn't even hear in time to get to the funeral,' she added. 'Were you there?'

Mottram shook his head. 'No. Like you, we were out of the country at the time. My wife and I were on holiday in Madeira. We got back the day after the funeral.'

Lindsay didn't know whether to be glad or sorry at his response. It looked as if he was out of the running. One suspect fewer. But she wouldn't have minded so much if Donald Mottram had been the killer. She didn't like this smooth accountant whose eyes were fixed greedily on the line of her calf. Hastily, Lindsay uncrossed her legs and got to her feet. 'Well, Mr Mottram, I won't take up any more of your valuable time, and I'll get that paperwork to you as soon as possible.'

He moved quickly round his desk to escort her to the door, his hand proprietorially on the small of her back. 'If you're going to be in Glasgow for a while, perhaps we could meet for a drink to discuss your future business plans,' he said.

'That would be nice,' she said sweetly. 'I'd like to meet your wife again.'

Mottram frowned. 'I'm afraid that won't be possible. My wife and I are separated, and she's living in Samoa.'

'Oh, I'm so sorry, I didn't realise,' Lindsay stammered, putting her hand to her mouth to hide her grin.

'I'm not. Sorry, that is,' Mottram said with a predatory smile. 'We'd been on the rocks for a long time. The holiday in Madeira was something of a last ditch attempt to get back together again. But it didn't work out. So I'm footloose and fancy free.'

'I'll give you a ring about that drink,' Lindsay lied as she made her thankful escape.

Back at the flat, she cleaned the make-up from her face and climbed back into her own clothes, glad to shed the false skin she'd assumed for the interview. It looked as if Donald Mottram was off her list of suspects, but she wanted to make absolutely sure. She called his office and asked to speak to his secretary again, slipping back into the persona of the dizzy woman. 'I'm so sorry to bother you again,' she said. 'Mr Mottram was telling me about the wonderful holiday he had in Madeira last year, and I foolishly forgot to write down the name of the hotel he was staying at. It sounded so lovely, I wanted to make a note of it. I don't suppose you know what it was?'

'If you'll just hold the line, I'll look it up for you,' the secretary replied. Moments later, she was back. 'The Hotel Miramar,' she said.

'Thank you so much,' Lindsay gushed. 'I don't suppose you know if they're open all year round, do you? Only, I was thinking we might go next winter.'

'I've no idea, I'm afraid. But Mr Mottram was there for the first fortnight in October, so they're definitely open then.'

'Thank you. Oh, I'm so pleased you were able to help me. So nerve-racking, isn't it, going on holiday when you don't know what the place is like? Thanks again.' Gratefully, Lindsay put the phone down.

Five minutes later, she was talking to the manager of the Hotel Miramar. 'We met a couple while we were on the island last year, and we wanted to get in touch with them, but foolishly, I've lost their address. I wondered if you could help me?'

'Certainly, madam,' the crisp English voice replied. 'Can you tell me their names and when they were staying?'

Within two minutes, she had eliminated Donald Mottram from her enquiries, making a mental note to ask Claire for expenses to cover the damage she was doing to Sophie's phone bill.

Lindsay glanced at her watch. It was still only half past eleven. Maybe she should ring Ruth and set up a meeting with her and Antonis? She'd already cleared with Sophie the possibility of inviting them round to the flat for dinner. She was almost looking forward to putting her chief suspects under the microscope.

Before she could do anything more, the phone rang. 'Hello?' she said.

'Can I speak to Lindsay, please?'

'It's me, Blair,' Lindsay said, recognising his voice instantly.

'Hi. Listen, I think I've got something for you. I was on the night shift again last night, so I took the opportunity to go through the credits book,' he said, referring to the ledger that sat on the newsdesk, where the names of freelances and tipsters to whom the paper owed money for stories or information were entered. 'Our blue-eyed chief reporter wasn't giving anything away about his sources, so I thought the book might hold a clue.'

'But surely they wouldn't be daft enough to credit anyone for the story? They must have known the police or the Special Branch would be all over them after a leak like that,' Lindsay protested.

'You're right. But the guy would have to be paid somehow, wouldn't he? So I looked very carefully through the credits for the last few days, and I think I might have cracked it.'

Lindsay felt the adrenalin coursing through her. Good old Blair! He was like a terrier with a rat when he got his teeth into something. 'Go on,' she said eagerly, grabbing a pen and notepad.

'On the day the story came in, there's a payment of £150 to one particular freelance. On the following day, a payment of £200 to the same guy. And yesterday, another payment of £150. Making a total of £500 so far. All the payments were marked down as being for stories that all made page leads. And the payments are about the going rate for strong exclusive page leads. But all the stories appeared in the paper with staff by-lines. Now, I don't have to tell you that it's not unusual for us to put a staff by-line on a story when all the staff reporter has done is rejig the intro or add a couple of paragraphs. So I thought I'd do a little check to see whether that was what had happened in this case.' Blaire paused for dramatic effect.

'And?' Lindsay asked impatiently.

'It would have been easy in the old days when we had everything on paper. But nowadays, the computerised newsdesk is cleared out of stories on a daily basis. So I couldn't access the material directly. However, over the last few months I've been doing a lot of night shifts and I've got pally with the night systems editor. So, in exchange for a half-bottle of Grouse, which you owe me, by the way, I got him to give me a complete trail on the copy for those stories.'

'Wonderful, Blair, you're a star. So what did you learn?' Lindsay demanded.

'None of the stories in question came from the freelance who has been paid for them. One came from a reader's phone call. One seems to have been brought in by the reporter herself. And the third one came as a tip from a different freelance altogether. Which means that our freelance friend has been paid a total of £500 for stories he had nothing to do with.'

'Which means that he's done something that requires payment which they don't want to put through the books,' Lindsay breathed. 'I think you've got him, Blair.'

'I think so too. Want to know who it is?' he teased.

'Of course I do!' Lindsay yelled.

'Barry Ostler.'

Blair's words immediately conjured up an image in Lindsay's mind. Barry Ostler. Early fifties, small, running to fat, silvery white hair cut like Elvis. The sort of chauvinist pig who, in spite of all the evidence to the contrary, lived inside the illusion that he was irresistible to women. She'd had to work with him a couple of times and had hated every patronising minute of it. 'That sleazeball?' she said. 'Is he still making a living?'

'He doesn't do much for us these days. But he seems to do all right. He's still driving around in that big American gas-guzzler.'

'Does he still live in Pollokshields?'

'Far as I know. His number in the contacts book is still the same.'

'Blair, I owe you one.'

'You owe me several after this,' he told her. 'But I'll settle for dinner at the Koh-i-Noor.'

'You're on. Can I add to my debt? Just a simple query this time.'

Blair groaned. 'Nothing's ever simple with you. Go ahead, what is it this time? Lord Lucan's phone number, maybe?'

'Where can I find Jimmy Mills these days?'

'I don't even want to know why you're asking me this, Lindsay. Jimmy's got a job in Motherwell. He's the sports editor of the local paper. He drinks in the pub opposite the office. You'll usually find him there between half one and three. That do you?'

'Perfect. Thanks again. I'll give you a ring in a couple of days to fix up that meal. Okay?'

'Okay. And Lindsay . . .?'

'Yes?'

'Be careful out there. Don't take chances with Barry Ostler. He's a nasty piece of work. He's obviously taken a lot of care to cover his tracks on this one. He's going to be very twitchy about you turning up and pointing the finger.'

'Yeah, I know. Don't worry, Blair. I'll cover my back. And yours. Thanks again.'

Lindsay put down the phone with a sigh of satisfaction. Things were starting to move at last.

12

The Printer's Devil was an old-fashioned working-man's pub. There were no modern frills – just a scattering of wobbly tables and chairs, a couple of fruit machines and a long wooden bar in front of shelves of spirits and glasses. When Lindsay walked in just before two, it was moderately busy. Half the clientele were dressed in grubby overalls stained with the printer's ink that betrayed their occupation. Lindsay walked straight up to the bar, looking neither right nor left, aware of the eyes appraising the stranger. She ordered a pint of lager, then slowly looked round the scruffy tavern. She was relying on the journalistic tradition of never showing surprise when a face from the past walked into a press pub. Unless the journalist in question operated in an area of direct competition, it was also regarded as bad form to pry too closely into what they were doing there. And if, when questioned, they hedged, it was an unwritten rule that you didn't carry on probing. She didn't think Jimmy would be too surprised to see her here. Any journalist doing a job in Motherwell would naturally gravitate to the Printer's Devil.

She soon spotted her target, sitting at a table with three other men, engrossed in a game of dominoes. Jimmy Mills hadn't changed much in the three years since she'd seen him last. With his build, he could have been one of the jockeys whose racing cards he'd sub-edited for years. As she watched him, he glanced up, feeling her eyes on him. His face registered uncertainty then surprise. He sketched a quick greeting with a handful of dominoes.

Lindsay walked across the room towards him. But before she reached the table, the hand came to an end and Jimmy hastily got to his feet and met her half-way. 'Lindsay Gordon, isn't it?' he asked with the lop-sided smile she remembered. Thanks God for the instant camaraderie of journalists the world over. Once met, a contact for life, even if they can't stand the sight of each other! 'What brings you to these parts?' Jimmy added. 'Hot on the trail of some world exclusive?'

'Something like that,' she said. 'Let me get you a drink.'

'Thanks. I'll have a wee goldie,' he replied, walking back to the bar with her.

'A whisky, please,' Linday said to the barmaid, before turning back to Jimmy. Close up, she noticed his straight dark hair was still free from grey hairs, though there were a few more lines round his quick brown eyes. 'I didn't know you lived out this way,' she said.

'I don't. I'm still living in Partick. I'm working across the road now. Sports editor, for my sins,' he replied with a rueful grimace.

'Oh, I hadn't heard. I knew you'd left the *Clarion*, but I didn't realise you were in Motherwell,' Lindsay lied, hoping she sounded convincing. The last thing she wanted was for him to suspect their encounter wasn't entirely fortuitous.

'It's not the kind of thing you shout about, is it? What about you? Still working for the *Clarion*?'

Lindsay shook her head ruefully. 'No. They kind of fell out with me. And you know what they're like. Long memories. They don't give you a second chance.'

'Don't I know it,' Jimmy said bitterly.

'I heard you had a bit of bother too. Alison Maxwell, wasn't it?'

'Aye, Alison bloody Maxwell. Funny, isn't it? You'd read her work and think, what a bloody good journalist. And then you'd get to know her and find out she was the biggest bitch in town,' he said with a bitter bark of laughter.

'Yeah,' Lindsay agreed. 'Mind you, if they kicked out all the journalists whose private lives don't match up to their talent, there would be a lot of empty newsrooms.'

'I know, but Alison Maxwell was in a class of her own. If anyone deserved what they got, she did.' Jimmy added some water to his whisky and took a sip. 'I was surprised at Jackie Mitchell, though. Never thought she had it in her.'

'If you push people hard enough, they'll do anything to get out.' Lindsay said. 'And when it came to pushing, Alison was the expert. As I found out the hard way.'

'You?' Jimmy exclaimed, his face a caricature of astonishment.

'Me,' Lindsay said. She expected that, like most people on the *Clarion*, Jimmy had always known she was gay, but he had seemed genuinely surprised about Alison. 'I was young and daft, Jimmy,' she explained. 'And she really knew how to put on the ritz. I was completely dazzled by her. But when I finally saw what she was really like, I had a hell of a job to get her claws out of me.'

'I wish I'd known that,' he replied. 'I could have done with a few tips. That bitch wrecked my career. Damn near wrecked my marriage too. I put out the flags when I heard that she was dead, I can tell you.' He pulled a pipe out of his pocket and started poking viciously at it with a tool he took from another pocket. Lindsay couldn't remember him having this particular mannerism, and wondered if he were using it to cover his nervousness at the way the conversation was going.

'It's kind of like Kennedy, isn't it? I bet anyone who had had a run-in with Alison could tell you exactly what they were doing when they heard the news of her death,' she probed.

'You're not wrong,' Jimmy said, pushing tobacco into his pipe as if he were trying to suffocate it. 'I was at home in my bed with the 'flu. I heard it on the local news at half-past ten. I tell you, it was the best cure I ever had. I felt like a new man, you know? While she was alive, there was always the threat hanging over me that she'd contact my wife and tell her the same poisonous lies she put round the office. Can you believe it? Me, a rapist? For God's sake, she was bigger than me!'

'I suppose a lot of people breathed a sigh of relief when

114

Jackie was arrested, though,' Lindsay said, refusing to be sidetracked by Jimmy's indignation.

'How do you mean?' Jimmy asked, draining the last of his whisky. 'Another pint?'

Lindsay nodded. 'Well, if the police hadn't got hold of Jackie so quickly, they'd have been picking over Alison's past in all its gory details. Every poor sod like us who'd had anything to do with her would have been put under the microscope. There would have been a few ruined marriages after that.'

'You're not kidding. I never thought of it like that. I suppose the police did me a favour, really.' He used several matches in a bid to light his pipe, realised he'd packed it too tightly and started prodding the tobacco with a spent match in an attempt to loosen it.

'Especially since being in your bed with the 'flu isn't much of an alibi,' Lindsay added jocularly. 'Mind you, I suppose your wife was your alibi.'

'Well, she wouldn't have been as it happens. She'd taken the kids round to her mother's so they wouldn't catch it too. So she'd have been round there, giving them their tea. She probably wouldn't have been home till about eight o'clock. No, my alibi was the 'flu. It was that epidemic that went round. You must have written the 'Killer 'Flu Bug' stories. I could hardly walk to the toilet, never mind strangle anybody.' Jimmy had finally got his pipe going, and he visibly relaxed as his head was engulfed in a cloud of blue, aromatic smoke.

Lindsay chuckled. 'I can beat that, Jimmy. I was in Italy at the time.'

'On holiday, were you?'

'No, I was working over there.'

He grinned. 'All right for some. Christ, you wouldn't catch me coming back here if I could get a job over there. A bottle of wine and a place in the sunshine, eh? What more could anybody ask for?'

Lindsay was content to let the conversation slip into more general channels now she had the information she wanted. When she finished her drink, she glanced at her watch and said, 'I'd better be off. I've got to meet a punter in ten minutes. It was nice bumping into you, Jimmy. All the best with the new job.'

'Thanks, Lindsay. If you see any of the boys from the *Clarion*, tell them I was asking for them.'

Lindsay drove back down the motorway, thinking over what Jimmy had told her. It would have been easy enough to exaggerate his illness for the benefit of his wife and the doctor. But how would he have known he would find Alison alone, unless they were still on good enough terms for him to have made an arrangement to see her? And why kill her then? The crisis was over and he was clearly getting his life back together again, even if the *Motherwell Tribune* sports desk wasn't as well paid or prestigious as the *Daily Clarion*. Still, he'd said himself that while she was alive he'd had to live with the constant edge of fear that one day she might extract a crueller revenge. And all that displacement activity with his pipe could have disguised a multitude of emotions. No, she couldn't write Jimmy off just yet.

She glanced at the dashboard clock. Just after three. She should drop in at Claire's on the way back. Lindsay would have dearly loved to put off so potentially awkward an encounter, but she knew it would have to be faced sooner or later. Better sooner.

Lindsay rang the entryphone buzzer for Claire's flat. There was no reply. After a couple of minutes, she rang again. She was on the point of giving up and going back to Sophie's when the loudspeaker crackled incomprehensibly. 'It's Lindsay,' she shouted into it. The door release buzzer sounded, and Lindsay hurriedly pushed the door open. On the third floor landing, the door stood ajar. Cautiously, Lindsay pushed it open and walked in. 'Hello?' she called out.

'In here,' came a voice from the bathroom. But it wasn't the voice Lindsay expected to hear. It was, unmistakably, the voice of the woman who had been her lover for more than three years.

'It's Lindsay,' she said.

116

'I know who it is,' Cordelia replied, emerging from the bathroom wearing nothing but a towel that ended too many inches above her knees for Lindsay's peace of mind. Her black hair was damp and tousled, her shoulders glistening with drops of water. 'I was in the bath,' she said unnecessarily.

Lindsay stared at her with a mixture of astonishment and desire. Then anger and self-disgust quickly took their place. How dare Cordelia wind her up like this with Claire only feet away!

As if reading her thoughts, Cordelia let a slight smile appear on her lips. 'Claire's not here,' she said. 'She had to go over to Edinburgh at short notice. Something about getting an injunction in the High Court on behalf of one of her clients. She tried to phone you and let you know, but there was no reply. She said, if you came, to apologise on her behalf.'

'I see,' Lindsay croaked through dry lips. Embarrassed, she cleared her throat and said, 'I've been out working on the case. Interviewing suspects. You know the drill.'

'I know the drill,' Cordelia murmured, moving closer to Lindsay. 'Who better? Now you're here anyway, why don't you come through and have a coffee?' She put her hand out to touch Lindsay's arm.

Lindsay flinched from her former lover's touch as if it had been a blow. 'Thanks all the same, but I'd better get on,' she replied. 'After all, Claire is paying me. We don't want to waste her precious time, do we?'

'Oh Lindsay, stop being so prickly. Relax.' She ran a hand through Lindsay's hair, sending an involuntary shudder through her body. 'Come and tell me how you've been getting on. I can pass it on to Claire, and that'll save you having to come back later.'

Cordelia smiled wickedly and walked confidently through to the kitchen. As if pulled by an invisible string, Lindsay followed, hating herself for her susceptibility. She stood in the doorway while Cordelia poured out two mugs of coffee from a jug and put them in the microwave. Cordelia leaned back against the kitchen unit, looking relaxed and, to

Lindsay, unbelievably sexy. Although it was only hours since she had been lying in Sophie's arms, it might have been a lifetime ago for all the effect it had on Lindsay's reactions. 'Have you made much progress?' Cordelia asked.

Lindsay shrugged. 'Some. But if you don't mind, I'd rather wait till Claire's here. There are one or two things I want to ask her about, so I might as well save it till then. If she's got any queries, we can sort them out on the spot.' Realising that she sounded churlish, Lindsay softened her tone and struggled for something to say that was emotionally neutral but offered some kind of olive branch. 'Do you know if she's done anything about Alistair Anderson yet?' she managed.

Cordelia showed no reaction to Lindsay's words except a slight raise of her eyebrows. She took the coffees out of the microwave and said, 'Here you are,' holding one out to Lindsay, who came warily across the room to take it. 'She's organised a small drinks party for this evening. Alistair's one of the guests. So we might have something for you tomorrow.' She moved closer to Lindsay, penning her into a corner of the kitchen, and put down her coffee. 'Why are you so nervous of me?' Cordelia asked innocently. 'You're acting like I'm the big bad wolf.'

'Is it any wonder I feel a bit nervous?' Lindsay demanded. 'Here I am, trapped in the kitchen with a half-naked woman. I mean, Claire could walk in at any minute. And the last woman who found herself in a compromising position with one of Claire's lovers ended up dead,' she added, falling into the old habit of telling Cordelia exactly what she was thinking.

Cordelia laughed delightedly. 'You're surely not suggesting that Claire killed Alison? Oh Lindsay, you really are something else again! But set your mind at rest. Claire won't be back for a couple of hours at least. She's not going to catch you in a compromising position. Besides, she's an adult. She's not the sort of woman who indulges in temper tantrums.' Cordelia reached out and gently stroked the side of Lindsay's head.

Lindsay felt her defences dissolve under the familiar

touch. 'Meaning that I am?' she asked, desperately trying to fight her feelings and provoke a less intimate atmosphere. Being alone with Cordelia at such close quarters was uncomfortable, but she was determined that she wasn't going to let her former lover defeat her.

'You are a very passionate woman, Lindsay. And sometimes that passion shows itself in ways that are less comfortable than your stunning lovemaking,' Cordelia teased.

'Yes, well, that's something you won't have to deal with any longer,' Lindsay replied, feeling herself start to sweat.

'I never imagined I would, but I miss your temper, your passion, your arrogance. It's not too late, Lindsay. We could make up for lost time,' Cordelia murmured persuasively, letting the towel fall away from her slim body and moving into Lindsay's arms.

As she felt Cordelia's lips on hers, Lindsay suddenly came to her senses. She turned her face away, saying, 'Wait a minute.'

With a puzzled look on her face, Cordelia stopped. 'It's all right,' she soothed.

'No it isn't,' Lindsay protested, feeling confused. 'It's all wrong. What about Claire? You made your choice, Cordelia, and it wasn't me.'

'It wasn't so much a choice as a default. I was lonely, Lindsay. And I was confused. I still am, come to that. As soon as I saw you the other night in Soutar Johnnie's, I couldn't help thinking I'd made a stupid mistake. Maybe if I hadn't kept on running into you, maybe if we weren't living in the same city, I'd have been able to carry on with Claire without these doubts surfacing all the time. But every time I see you, I get all churned up again. I can't forget the way I feel about you. Oh Lindsay, let's give it another try.'

Cordelia's voice held a note of pleading Lindsay had never heard before. But something was wrong. Lindsay couldn't put her finger on it, but something didn't ring true in Cordelia's words. She'd only started seriously seducing rather than teasing after Lindsay had voiced her suspicion of Claire. Did Cordelia genuinely want her, or was she simply trying to protect Claire from Lindsay's inquiries? In bed, with her defences down, Lindsay knew she'd believe anything Cordelia wanted her to. She felt torn. In spite of the peace she'd found the night before with Sophie, her body told her to ignore her doubts and follow her instincts into bed with Cordelia, but inside her head, a voice screamed 'No!'

Lindsay pushed Cordelia away and moved back towards the door. 'No,' she said. 'No.'

'But why not?' Cordelia asked, her voice trembling. 'We still care about each other. I can see you still love me, for God's sake!'

'But it's not just between you and me any more, is it? This is so dishonest, Cordelia. If you'd really wanted me back, why didn't you just leave Claire and come back to me? I might have believed you then. But this? Trying to seduce me in Claire's kitchen? Were you planning on bonking me in Claire's bed?'

Cordelia flinched at Lindsay's words and took a tentative step towards her. But Lindsay shook her head angrily and Cordelia stopped in her tracks. 'I didn't mean it to be like this,' she protested. 'It's just the way it happened that's all.'

The feebleness of her response fuelled the rage that had begun to burn in Lindsay. 'Apart from anything else, I'm still working for Claire. How the hell can I carry on with that if I'm sleeping with you? I still don't hear you saying you're going to leave Claire and come back to me! After what we've had, do you really think I'm going to settle for being your bit on the side?' Lindsay demanded angrily.

'It doesn't have to be like that. You don't have to work for Claire. And I don't have to stay here, where Claire's still around to cause confusion. We can go back to London together. Start again. Give it another try.' Cordelia pleaded.

Lindsay's heart sank. Cordelia's words served only to confirm her suspicions that her motives were suspect. Was Cordelia protecting Claire after all? 'And just abandon Jackie?' she blurted out. 'No way. I made a commitment. I've started, so I'll finish, like the man says. Besides, it's not just Claire who's involved,' she blurted out.

Cordelia paled. 'What do you mean?'

Lindsay silently cursed herself. She hadn't meant to tell Cordelia about Sophie. 'Nothing,' she mumbled.

'It's that bloody Helen, isn't it?' Cordelia demanded. 'I always knew she fancied you. Couldn't wait to get her claws into you, could she?'

'It's not Helen. It's Sophie. And you've no room to talk about people who couldn't wait,' Lindsay shouted, almost glad of an excuse to pick a fight. Anything to escape a situation that she was finding increasingly intolerable. 'You knew I'd be back. You knew it wasn't *you* I was leaving. But you couldn't give me time, could you? I hadn't been gone six months when you were throwing yourself into Claire's arms. I never looked at another woman in all the time I was away. And when I did come back, it was straight to you. Or it would have been if you hadn't been too busy bedding your new girlfriend.'

Cordelia scowled. 'How the hell was I supposed to know when you were coming back? Or even if you were coming back?'

'How could I let you know? It's not as if I went away without a word. The whole point of me leaving the country was so the security forces would get off my back. I knew they'd be tapping your phone and checking your mail. The last thing I wanted was for you to have to suffer even more because of my pig-headed principles.' Lindsay stood staring defiantly at Cordelia's naked body. She wasn't going to give in, she wasn't, she kept telling herself. She shook her head. 'I think it's too late,' she sighed. 'I think it's too late for both of us. I'm sorry, Cordelia. But you turned your back on me when you started living with Claire. Now I'm turning my back on you. Sophie has made me feel good for the first time in months. And I don't believe any more that loving more than one person is a good thing multiplied. It's not. It's a good thing divided.'

'But we need each other,' Cordelia pleaded. 'Don't be so stubborn. You know we belong together. Sophie can't give you what I can. Sophie won't be any use to you trying to track down a killer. Sophie doesn't know the way your mind works. She won't put up with your crazy working routines, all those unexplained absences.' Her face was flushed and angry, her straight brows twisted in a frown.

'At least Sophie's loyal. Sophie never made a pass at me while she was still living with Helen, or while I was with you.'

Cordelia flushed a deeper scarlet. 'You'd better go,' she said softly.

'That's the first sensible thing you've said today,' Lindsay replied. 'I'm sorry it had to end like this, Cordelia.'

The cliché was still ringing in her ears as she stumbled blindly from the flat and ran through the streets to her car. It was fully five minutes before the shaking in her hands subsided enough for her to drive the car safely. Lindsay drove back to the flat like a maniac, desperate to shut the door on the world and lose herself in drink.

13

Once the emotional storm had abated, Lindsay found herself ravenous. Cursing Cordelia, she fixed herself a bacon sandwich. 'Damned if I'm going to let her interfere with this job,' she muttered as she slung her dirty plate into the sink. Fired with anger and energy, she grabbed the phone and rang Ruth Menzies at her gallery. 'It's Lindsay Gordon, Ruth,' she announced. 'I'd really like to get together with you and Antonis. Are you free tomorrow evening for dinner?'

Ruth was instantly flustered by the positive approach, which was what Lindsay had banked on. 'Well, I . . . em . . . there's nothing in the diary, and Antonis hasn't said anything about . . .'

'That's great. I'm really looking forward to seeing you both again. Half past seven suit you? I'll expect you then. 21 Halbeath Drive. First floor, right hand flat. The name on the bell is Hartley. Got that?'

'Yes, I think so,' Ruth stammered, repeating the address.

'See you then,' Lindsay said cheerfully. 'Bye.' She put the phone down with a grin. It had been a pushover. Ruth was far too polite and diffident to ask her what the hell she was playing at. They were hardly friends, after all. If it hadn't been for Alison, they'd have been little more than nodding acquaintances.

The adrenalin surge that had carried her through the phone call to Ruth soon abated, however, leaving her feeling worn out and confused. What exactly had Cordelia been playing at? Had it been because of genuine feelings for Lindsay? Or was it about protecting Claire, either by distracting Lindsay or by making sure that she was privy to Lindsay's every move? Whatever her motives, Cordelia had defeated herself by her appalling sense of timing. She knew only too well that the way to Lindsay's heart was via her body, and she'd gone straight for her weak point. She'd have stood a good chance of success if she'd made her move anywhere other than her lover's flat.

Lindsay shrugged and looked at her watch. Half past four. The next burning item on her agenda was to confront Barry Ostler. But she felt too drained even to plan their encounter, let alone carry it out. It would have to wait till morning. That left her with a couple of hours to kill before she could reasonably expect Sophie, so Lindsay decided to cook something for dinner. She was half-way through an inventory of the store cupboard when the phone rang.

'Hello?' she said wearily as she picked it up.

'Well, love certainly knocked the ginger out of you,' Sophie's familiar voice teased her. 'You sound like you've got the weight of the world on your shoulders.'

'Sorry. It's nothing to do with you, I promise. I've just had a particularly difficult afternoon.'

'Will it keep, or do you want to tell me all about it now?' Sophie asked kindly.

'It'll keep. What can I do for you? I mean, I take it you didn't just ring up to whisper sweet nothings down the phone?'

Sophie laughed. 'I think we're both a bit too long in the tooth for that. Though I must admit it's been kind of difficult to concentrate today. However, that isn't why I rang. As you correctly deduced, I do actually have something to say.'

'McIntosh?' Lindsay asked eagerly.

'I looked up the records. He did a routine D&C on Alison just over a year ago, in December 1988. She had a follow-up appointment three months later, at the beginning of March 1989, then nothing.'

'I see . . .' Lindsay mused.

'I thought you'd be interested. He's just written a fairly pedestrian paper on combating post-partum infection, which is actually very relevant to my work, so I rang him up and suggested we meet for a drink,' Sophie continued.

'Well done! When?'

'This evening. Half past six in The Cricketers. If I can make a suggestion?' Sophie asked tentatively.

'Please do. I need all the help I can get.'

'Why don't you arrive about five to seven? Then I can introduce you. You can give me some spurious phone message, from Helen or someone, asking me to call her between seven and half past. Then I can slope off to the phone and you can do your Perry Mason bit with him. How does that sound to you?'

'Sophie, you are a star. I couldn't have plotted it better myself. I owe you one.'

'I'll collect later,' Sophie replied, her voice heavy with innuendo.

'It'll be my pleasure.'

'Mine too, I hope. See you in The Cricketers.'

'Yes. And Sophie – thanks.' Lindsay switched the phone off and grinned, delighted that Sophie had so swiftly proved Cordelia wrong. So much for her insistence that Sophie would be of no use in a murder enquiry! She checked with her copy of Alison's list and found the dates referring to the man they believed to be Ian McIntosh. Interestingly, Alison had made a passing reference to him around the time of her operation. But they hadn't actually become lovers till a few weeks after her follow-up appointment. So technically, she had no longer been a patient when she had started sleeping with him. Lindsay wondered fleetingly how the General Medical Council would view that. When did a patient stop being a patient, as far as disciplinary matters are concerned? Could he have been struck off for his affair with Alison?

No point in cooking a meal now, Lindsay thought. She'd treat Sophie to a takeaway after they'd seen McIntosh. Then they could switch off the phones and forget about Alison Maxwell for a while. She'd tell Sophie about Cordelia's futile seduction attempt, and show her that last night had been more than a desperate search for comfort. Feeling pleased with herself, Lindsay ran a hot bath and soaked in it for an hour while she read a new crime novel she'd found on Sophie's shelves. As she skimmed forward to check the ending, it amused her that she had spotted the murderer eighty pages before the detective did. If only real life were so simple!

After her bath, she put on a clean pair of Levis and her Aran sweater, pulling a face at her limited wardrobe. When she'd come back from Italy, she'd gone back to Cordelia's to drop off her lightweight clothes and pick up some winter outfits. But she hadn't anticipated being away for more than a couple of weeks. She was going to have to go down to London with a van soon and clear her possessions out of Cordelia's house. And she'd have to find somewhere to live in Glasgow till her own flat became vacant in July. Whatever was on the cards for her and Sophie, she felt wary about moving in on a semi-permanent basis, even supposing Sophie wanted her to. After Cordelia, Lindsay needed a place to call her own, a place she couldn't lose on the whim of her lover.

At twenty to seven, she left the flat and drove to The Cricketers, the pub attached to the local cricket club. Instead of planning her encounter with Ian McIntosh, she was too busy with the rosy glow of memories. When she'd lived in Glasgow three years before, she and Sophie had often met here after work in the long, warm summer evenings, sitting out in the garden, drinking cool lagers, putting the world to rights. Cordelia Brown had only been a name on a book jacket to her then.

Impatiently, Lindsay shook off the past and took a deep breath. She walked into the bar and immediately saw Sophie sitting at a window table with a slim man in his thirties. Ian McIntosh had straight, light brown hair cut like Robert Redford's. As Lindsay approached, however, she noticed that the youthful image presented by his fashionable casual clothes was tarnished by the network of fine lines round his eyes and mouth.

As Lindsay reached the table, he leapt to his feet and

turned a poor imitation of Redford's engaging boyish grin on her. 'Hi,' he said effusively. 'Sophie mentioned you'd be joining us. You must be Lindsay. Nice to meet you. Any friend of Soph is a friend of mine. Let me get you a drink. Same again, Soph?'

'Thanks. I'll have a pint of lager,' Lindsay said as Sophie nodded. Lindsay's eyebrows rose as he headed for the bar. 'I thought you said you only knew him slightly.'

'I do. This is the longest I've ever spent in his company. I told you he was full of shit.'

Before they could say more, McIntosh returned with a round of drinks. 'Aren't I the lucky man, surrounded by two lovely ladies,' he said, preening himself.

There was nothing one could say to that and remain within the realms of social politeness, Lindsay thought. Ignoring him, she turned to Sophie and said, 'By the way, before I forget. Helen rang just as I was leaving the flat. She asked if you could ring her between seven and half past. She said it was urgent.'

Sophie nodded. 'Thanks.' She glanced at her watch. 'I'll give her a ring in a minute.'

'Don't let me interrupt your professional conclave,' Lindsay said. 'Just ignore me if you've still got business to discuss.'

'Ignore you? Impossible,' McIntosh said archly. He smoothed his light-brown hair in what was clearly a habitual gesture.

'It's all right, we've finished. Ian's given me a couple of ideas about procedures we can implement that should reduce our infection rate.'

'Think nothing of it, Soph,' he said magnanimously, turning his calculated smile on her. 'But let's not bore your friend talking shop. Soph tells me you're a journalist. What sort of stuff do you do?'

Lindsay shrugged. 'This and that. Anything that comes along, really. I'm a freelance, you see, so I have to pick up every little titbit I can. You live by your wits, and what you can winkle out of people.'

'Fascinating,' he said. 'It must be very interesting.'

'People always think so,' Lindsay replied ruefully. 'But it's not always glamorous or exciting. A lot of the time it's excruciatingly boring. You can spend a whole day waiting for the one phone call that you need before you can get an inch further on a story. Or you can sit and freeze in your car outside someone's house waiting for them to come home. And you have to be just as polite to the creeps as the nice guys. It's not a bit like *All the President's Men*.'

Sophie got to her feet. 'If you'll excuse me, I'll just make that phone call,' she said.

'Don't leave us alone too long,' McIntosh replied with an exaggerated wink. 'We might not be able to control our basic animal urges, you know!'

Lindsay watched Sophie cross the room, wondering how she put up with men like McIntosh with such equanimity. Collecting herself, she turned back to the gynaecologist and said casually, 'I used to work at the *Clarion* here in Glasgow. I believe we had a mutual . . . how shall I put it? Acquaintance?'

He looked slightly disconcerted and flashed the grin at her. Lindsay looked forward to wiping it off his self-satisfied face. 'Really?' he said casually. 'I don't think I know anyone who works there.'

'She doesn't work there any more. She's dead now. Alison Maxwell?'

McIntosh refused to meet Lindsay's eyes and nervously ran a hand over his light-brown hair. 'Maxwell . . . Maxwell? Oh yes, I remember now. She was a patient of mine for a short time about a year ago.'

'A bit more than a patient, I think.' Lindsay let her comment hang in the air.

'I think you've got hold of the wrong end of the stick, Lindsay,' he said sincerely. 'I can assure you that my relationship with her was purely professional.'

'Alison and I were very close, you know,' Lindsay said. 'She told me everything. I think I was a kind of insurance policy for her, you know? If anything were to happen. Which of course, it did.'

'I don't know what you're getting at, but I don't like your

tone one little bit,' he blustered, all traces of the irritating grin gone.

'You must have been very relieved when she was killed. Especially when the police arrested Jackie Mitchell so quickly that they didn't have to bother investigating Alison's other relationships,' Lindsay stated coldly, abandoning all efforts at finesse. They'd be wasted on McIntosh, she decided.

'That's an outrageous and scurrilous suggestion. I barely knew the woman,' he parried weakly, looking round desperately, clearly wishing Sophie would return and rescue him from Lindsay's attentions.

'Barely being the operative word,' Lindsay remarked drily.

'What the hell has all of this got to do with you?' he said angrily. 'You'd better be very careful what you say. There's such a thing as the law of slander.'

'I just wondered what you were doing on the afternoon Alison was killed,' Lindsay said coolly.

McIntosh jumped to his feet. 'I'm not sitting here listening to this one minute longer!' he exploded.

'I wouldn't do anything rash if I were you, Ian. You see, Alison kept a diary. Names, times, dates, places. It could be dynamite in the wrong hands. Like the General Medical Council. Or your wife, perhaps. Like I said, I was Alison's insurance policy. Now why don't you just sit down and discuss this reasonably?'

The strength seemed to disappear from McIntosh's legs and he crumpled back into his seat. 'You blackmailing bitch,' he spat. 'Two of a kind, you and Maxwell. Well, *she* got what *she* deserved.'

'What do you mean? Was Alison blackmailing you?' Lindsay blurted out. She was no stranger to Alison's emotional blackmail, but McIntosh's tone indicated more than that.

'I never said that,' he objected. 'You're the one doing the blackmailing.'

'I don't see you running to the police. Though I must say I'm seriously thinking about doing just that. You might as well tell me, doc. What were you doing on the afternoon she was killed?' Lindsay demanded.

'How the hell should I know?' he hissed through lips drawn tight over his even white teeth.

'I'd have thought that the evening you heard the news of her death would be printed indelibly on your mind. Come on, Ian, you can do better than that. Maybe the diary would help to jog your memory? After all, you can probably remember the occasion you had a bonk in the Western Infirmary?'

His eyes narrowed. 'I'll get you for this,' he said.

'I don't think so,' Lindsay said. 'I'm like Alison. I take out insurance for dangerous situations. What were you doing that afternoon?'

He scowled and said, 'Not that it's anything to do with you, but I was in theatre till about five o'clock. Then I went up to the University Library to do some reading. I got home about seven o'clock.'

'And can anybody verify that you were in the library?' Lindsay continued relentlessly. Now she had him on the run, she was determined to press home her advantage. If she didn't nail him now, she knew she wouldn't get another chance.

'What? Three, four months later? You must be joking!'

'Interesting, Ian. You have motive, and opportunity. And as a doctor, you'd know exactly how to strangle someone most efficiently.'

He looked angrily at Lindsay, speechless for once. His face was white with fear or rage. She couldn't decide which was the stronger emotion. Recovering himself, he spluttered. 'You're off your rocker. Look, even supposing I had a fling with Alison Maxwell, it was long after she stopped seeing me as a doctor. I had no reason to kill her. Besides, the police got the murderer. Another one of your journalist pals. Is that what all this is about? Frame me to let your pal go scot free? Well, it won't work. I never went near her flat that day, and you can't prove I did.' He spoke with the childish defiance of a small boy who's been caught stealing sweets from the local newsagent.

Before Lindsay could reply, Sophie walked back across the bar. As she came into McIntosh's sight, he pushed himself to his feet. 'You bitch!' he hissed. 'You fucking set me up. You haven't heard the last of this!'

Sophie stared open-mouthed at her colleague as he stumbled unsteadily away from the table and out of the bar. 'Jesus Christ,' she said. 'You really rattled his cage.'

Lindsay gazed out of the window at the disappearing form of Ian McIntosh. 'Tell me, Sophie. Did he look to you like a man with nothing to hide?'

14

Lindsay performed the dicing-with-death routine required of any driver attempting the first exit off the urban motorway south of the Kingston Bridge. 'Shit,' she yelled, as she dodged a Ford Cortina seemingly hell-bent on suicide. Quarter to nine on a Friday morning was not the best time to negotiate the complexities of the motorway bridge, she decided as she swung down the spiralling exit ramp and on to the street below. But by making an early start, she hoped to catch Barry Ostler on the hop.

Sophie had been touching in her concern, without making Lindsay feel at all claustrophobic in the way that Cordelia sometimes had. 'Be careful,' she had urged. 'He might not be as gutless as Ian McIntosh. I spend enough time in hospitals as it is without having to visit you.'

Lindsay had put a brave face on it, dismissing Sophie's fears. But she felt far from confident at the thought of confronting Ostler. But at least this time she was well-prepared, she thought as she drove through the south side streets lined with tenements. She had rung Helen the night before, driven by a vague recollection that she'd heard Ostler's name linked to the Labour Party. Helen had been extremely useful, dredging her memory for a few snippets of gossip. 'Barry Ostler's a real scally,' she'd said. 'He's one of the rent-a-thugs on the right wing of the party. He's been responsible for spreading several of the nastier rumours that have surfaced about the Left over the past few years. You remember when there was that big scandal a couple of years back about Gordon Graham's expenses – the word then was that it was Ostler who broke into Gordon's offices to steal his papers. There was never any proof, but no one was really in any doubt. A few press leaks have been traced back to him too. You know the kind of thing – stories that are essentially true but are twisted so that they sound like there's something really nasty in the woodwork behind them. Barry Ostler's idea of party democracy is that he and his pals make all the decisions and everybody else falls into line, or else.'

Interesting, Lindsay thought as she approached the area of Pollokshields where Ostler lived. She had no difficulty remembering his address, having dropped him off at home on both occasions they'd worked together. He preferred her to drive – that way he could drink all day without having to worry about being breathalysed.

She turned off the main road and threaded her way through the back streets till she found the slightly shabby 1960s block of flats where Ostler lived alone. His big silver Buick was parked outside, looking like a dinosaur among the Japanese runabouts scattered along the rest of the street. Lindsay found a nearby parking space and carefully set the car alarm. She pushed open the doors and walked up one flight of concrete stairs. The block had grown even more seedy since she'd last been here, with graffiti on the walls and the smell of stale urine in the air. Obviously Barry Ostler wasn't doing too well, or he'd have found himself somewhere more salubrious to live.

Lindsay rang the bell and waited. There was no reply, so she rang again, then banged on the door for good measure. She was soon rewarded by the door opening a crack. Barry Ostler's unshaven face appeared, his white quiff awry, eyes screwed up against the light. A blast of sour breath and stale tobacco smoke hit Lindsay as he growled, 'What the hell's going on?'

'Hello, Barry,' Lindsay said with a smile. 'You going to leave me standing on the landing like the rent man?'

'Lindsay Gordon? What the hell are you doing here?' he mumbled as he opened the door wider to reveal a beer-gut in an off-white singlet hanging over a pair of striped pyjama trousers.

'Did I get you out of your bed? I'm really sorry,' Lindsay lied. 'I just wanted a wee word with you about something. I could come back later if it's not a good time.'

'You might as well come in now you're here,' he said grudgingly, turning his back on her and padding down the hall in bare feet.

Lindsay followed him, closing the door behind her. The flat smelled of too many cigarettes and fry-ups. The frowsty hall led straight into an untidy living room, with several empty beer cans and the remains of a Chinese takeaway littering the floor round a single armchair that faced the television. Lindsay perched gingerly on the edge of a sofa whose Dralon cover felt slightly tacky to the touch.

'There's no milk so I cannae offer you a coffee,' he said brusquely as he lit a cigarette and shook with a spasm of coughing. 'So what the hell brings you out here at this time of the morning?' he finally gasped.

'I want the stuff that was nicked from Harry Campbell's desk,' Lindsay said bluntly.

Ostler ran his hand over his stubbly chin and gave the chesty wheeze that passed for laughter with him. His gut wobbled sickeningly in rhythm with the wheeze. Lindsay struggled to keep a sneer from her face as he recovered himself and said, 'Christ, I see your interviewing technique hasnae improved any. Lindsay, I don't have a fucking clue what you're on about.'

'Okay, Barry. I thought maybe we could do this the quick way, but you've obviously got some time to kill. Let me tell you a wee story. On Monday afternoon, there was a burglary in North Kelvinside. Some confidential Scottish Office papers were stolen from a senior civil servant. Also on the missing list are the contents of a desk belonging to Harry Campbell, MP for Kinradie. The next day, the Scottish *Daily Clarion* had a cracking splash based on those Scottish Office papers. Now, I'm no Sherlock Holmes, but it seems to me that whoever gave that nice wee exclusive to the *Clarion* has either got Harry Campbell's papers or else knows where they are. Does that seem about right to you so far?'

Ostler took a long drag on his cigarette. 'So far, so good, Enid Blyton. But what has all that got to do with me?'

'I've got proof that it was you who sold the story to the *Clarion*.'

He looked shrewdly at her. 'You're bullshitting me, wee lassie. How can you have something that doesn't exist?'

'Oh, it exists, all right. Because it was you who sold the story, Barry. So that means you've either got Harry Campbell's papers or you know who does. And Harry wants those papers back very badly. That's why I'm here.' Lindsay pulled opened her handbag and, under the guise of removing her own cigarettes, checked that her tiny voice-activated tape recorder was working.

'Even supposing it was me who gave the story to the *Clarion*, why the hell should I help you? I mean, if Harry Campbell wants those papers back so badly, they must be worth something. Maybe even another splash in the *Clarion*, eh?' Ostler said craftily, lighting another cigarette.

'They are worth something, Barry,' Lindsay replied. 'Shall I tell you exactly what they're worth?'

He nodded, appearing vastly amused. 'You tell me.'

'They're worth about six months. That's what you'll get if I tell the police it was you who leaked the story to the *Clarion*.'

'Now wait a minute,' he said apprehensively. 'Just wait a minute. What are you saying?'

'I've had the police on my back. For some reason, they seem to think it was me who leaked the story. After all, I've got more of a track record than you when it comes to breaking stories that embarrass the government. It would make my life a lot easier if I didn't have the Special Branch breathing down my neck. If I give them you on toast, and tell them where the evidence is that ties you to the burglary, everybody will be happy. Well, me and the police'll be happy, anyway.'

Ostler shook his head slowly. 'And I always thought you were such a nice wee lassie. Fancy you threatening to shop a fellow journalist just to get a wee bit of peace and quiet. And how much work do you think you'd get in this city if you did that?'

Lindsay shrugged. 'To tell you the truth, Barry, I've been thinking lately that maybe journalism isn't really my game. So being on the blacklist wouldn't exactly break my heart. But I'll do you a deal. You hand over the papers and I won't shop you.'

'Lindsay, I'd gladly give you Harry Campbell's *billets doux* if I had them. But what I haven't got, I can't part with,' Ostler countered, spreading his hands in an exaggerated Latin shrug.

'But you know where they are,' Lindsay said flatly.

'Now, how would I know that?'

'Because whoever gave you the prison privatisation story also has Harry Campbell's papers. And only someone who had seen those papers or had had them described to him would refer to them as *billets doux*. I never gave you any indication of what those papers were. You just gave yourself away, Barry,' Lindsay observed.

'Maybe, but a good journalist never reveals his sources.'

'Well, that lets you off the hook, Barry. Not even your best friend would describe you as a good journalist. Look, I've not got all day. I've told you the deal. You can come across now and I won't tell the police it was you. Or you can sit there on your big fat principles and wait for the Special Branch to come knocking. What's it to be?' Lindsay was almost beginning to relish her role as the tough nut.

Ostler sighed and lit another cigarette from the butt of the previous one. 'Okay. It was me leaked the story. But I've no idea who did the burglary. The papers were shoved through my letter box in a brown envelope on Monday night. I don't know where they came from.' Lindsay stared at him, for the moment mute with a mixture of outrage and admiration at his brazen effrontery. 'Sorry I can't be more help,' he added urbanely.

Lindsay smiled in spite of herself. 'That's life,' she remarked, getting to her feet. 'Well, I'd better be off now. I've got a policeman to see about this burglary. I'm sure they'll be delighted to hear who was really responsible.'

Alarmed, Ostler jumped to his feet. 'Now wait a minute! You said you'd do a deal.'

'That's right. The deal was that I got Harry Campbell's papers back. No papers, no deal. I mean, what's in it for me otherwise?'

'But I told you,' he said desperately. 'I don't know where the papers came from!'

'You must think my head's full of mince, not brains,' Lindsay said, moving towards the door.

'No! Wait a minute,' Ostler said, sagging back into his chair like a deflated balloon. 'I'll tell you. It came from a lad called Alex McNaught. He's a rent boy, hangs about on the meatracks down Blythswood Square. I met him on a story I was doing a few months back. I thought he was a pretty smart cookie, so I told him to stay in touch. He brought the papers to me late on Monday afternoon.'

'You're seriously expecting me to believe that a rent boy was smart enough to spot the implications of a bundle of Scottish Office papers? You sure you weren't there with him, turning the place over?' Lindsay asked sarcastically.

'Who are you accusing of burglary? What do you take me for?' Ostler demanded self-righteously.

'I'd rather not answer that, Barry, if you don't mind. So where do I find him?'

'I don't know,' Ostler whined. 'How the hell would I know?'

'You might know if you put him up to it,' Lindsay said shrewdly.

'Oh for fuck's sake, Lindsay, gie's a break! I told you, I don't know where he lives.' Lindsay noticed a sheen of sweat on his pasty features. A moment ago, she wouldn't have believed it was possible for him to look less appealing. Now she knew different.

'You've told me a lot of lies this morning and it's not even half past nine yet. Come on, Barry, I'm doing you a favour. Do me one,' Lindsay pressed.

'Some favour,' he muttered. 'Okay, you win. He lives in Springburn. He's got a bedsit there. I don't know the exact address.'

'You can do better than that, Barry. How about some directions?'

Ostler sighed deeply. 'You're a hard bitch, Lindsay Gordon. Anyone ever tell you that? Up Springburn Road, first left after a pub called The Spring Inn. Second right and it's the third or fourth house on the left. It's got a blue door. Satisfied?'

'That better be good info, Barry. Or I'm down the road to the police first thing tomorrow. Cheerio then. It's been nice seeing you again,' she threw over her shoulder as she made her way with relief out of the fetid atmosphere of Ostler's flat.

'Aye, and I hope your next shite's a hedgehog,' he called as she slammed the front door behind her.

Gleeful, she ran down the stairs. At last she had something positive to tell Rosalind! But what Ostler had told her hadn't eliminated the possibility that the murder and the burglary were linked. Perhaps Alex McNaught was the connecting link. After all, Ian McIntosh had hinted that Alison was into blackmail. What better source of compromising information than a rent boy?

Lindsay stopped at the first callbox she came to and rang Claire's office. She had a momentary pang of apprehension as she waited to be connected. Would Cordelia have said anything about her visit yesterday? 'Can I see you this morning?' she asked when she was finally put through to Claire.

'I can fit you in for ten minutes in half an hour. Otherwise it will be this evening,' Claire said briskly. 'I'm sorry about yesterday, by the way. Cordelia said you'd had a wasted journey.'

'No problem. See you in half an hour.' Lindsay hung up.

Thirty minutes later, she was walking into Claire's comfortable office high above the city skyline. The lawyer was seated behind a wide and uncluttered desk, looking utterly in command of her situation. A desk lamp was switched on, making her white-blonde hair gleam ethereally. She reminded Lindsay strangely of a modern version of Joan of Arc, with her small, chiselled features. She'd look stunning in a suit of shining armour astride a white horse, she thought in surprise. 'You seem to like having a view,' Lindsay remarked as she settled into a tweed-upholstered sofa.

'It prevents claustrophobia,' Claire remarked absently, signing a piece of paper on her desk. She put her pen down and gave Lindsay her full attention. Her face looked calm and untroubled. Whatever Cordelia had told her about Lindsay's visit, it obviously hadn't been the truth. 'Now, where are you up to?' she asked tartly.

Lindsay gave Claire a swift rundown on her progress so far, while Claire jotted notes on a legal pad. Lindsay concluded by saying, 'And tonight, Ruth and Antonis are coming to dinner. All I need is one shred of evidence, and this whole thing could be wrapped up by the end of the weekend. But how about you? How did you get on with Alistair?'

'It seems you'll have to remove him from your list of possible suspects,' Claire said, pushing her glasses up her nose in the familiar gesture. 'On the day Alison was killed, he was in Aberdeen. Between four and five o'clock, he was giving a lecture at the art college, and afterwards he was discussing the lecture with several of the students. He learned about Alison's murder later that evening when he saw the television news in his hotel room. I've already checked his story, and it seems he was telling the truth.'

'In a funny way, I'm glad about that. I've always liked his paintings. They're so full of life and colour,' Lindsay said.

'If that's all, Lindsay . . . I have another appointment in a minute,' Claire said, ostentatiously consulting her watch.

Lindsay swallowed hard. The moment had come, and her bottle had nearly gone. Giving a silent prayer, she said, 'One more thing. There's no pleasant and polite way to ask this, Claire, but I hope you won't take it the wrong way. Even though you're paying me to carry out this inquiry, I still have to be impartial. And if I was a police officer, I'd have to ask you this.' Claire looked puzzled, but Lindsay struggled on. 'What were you doing at the time of Alison's murder?'

Claire looked furious, two bright spots of colour rising on

her pale cheeks. Then quickly she saw the funny side and laughed, tossing her fine hair back. 'Well done, Lindsay. Hang on just a minute, would you?' She buzzed her intercom and said, 'Mrs Cox, would you bring me in my diary for last year, please?' Then she turned back to Lindsay and said, 'As far as I can remember, I was in a meeting all afternoon. I left the office about half past five and I was at home when Jackie arrived.' She broke off as her secretary walked in with a large leather-bound desk diary. Claire quickly flicked through the pages then pushed it across to Lindsay. 'There you are. 3.30. Meeting with Colin Amis, Duncan McIver, David Milne. I can give you their phone numbers if you want to check.'

Lindsay was forced to smile in spite of her suspicions. 'But you've no alibi for the crucial time, have you?'

Claire returned her smile. 'It doesn't appear so. But I'd have had to have been incredibly lucky not to have been spotted by someone if I'd been running to such a tight schedule. Besides, I had no motive for killing Alison. Jackie and I had settled our differences. As far as I was concerned, her visit to Alison's flat was for the sole purpose of ending their liaison. If I'd have been going to kill Alison, I'd have done it either before then or after. Not at that particular point. And why on earth would I hire you to investigate if I was the murderer?'

'It's a good double bluff,' Lindsay retorted.

This time, Claire's smile had a hint of steel in it. 'I'm sure if you really want Cordelia back, there are easier ways of going about it than trying to implicate me in a murder. Now, if there's nothing else?'

Claire's words were like a slap in the face. Cordelia had obviously given Claire a highly sanitised version of their encounter, revealing only Lindsay's suspicions. Claire had been playing with her all along. Furious, Lindsay got to her feet and marched to the door. 'I'll be in touch when I've got something to report,' she said angrily. 'And don't kid yourself that I'd cast suspicion on you for Cordelia's sake. As far as I'm concerned, you're more than welcome to her.' And as she strode through Claire's outer office, Lindsay realised with a feeling of shock that she had meant exactly what she said.

15

'Can you talk, Ros?' Lindsay asked cautiously when she was finally put through to Rosalind's office extension.

'Yes, I'm alone. Have you got any news?' she inquired eagerly.

'Progress at last. I think I know who our burglar is.'

'That's terrific news! How on earth did you find out?' Rosalind asked, her voice full of admiration.

'Trade secret,' Lindsay replied modestly. 'But I can tell you that the burglary appears to have been carried out by a rent boy called Alex McNaught. Does the name mean anything to you?'

'Can't say it does. But if he's one of Harry's little friends, there's no reason why it should. I never meet them. But if he knew his way around the building . . . Does this tie in with Alison's murder, like you thought it might?'

'I can't quite see how. Why do you ask?' Lindsay asked.

'It's just that . . . It might be nothing, but she did a five-part series on AIDS for the *Clarion* last year. About how it's spreading into the heterosexual community. Maybe she ran into him then?'

Lindsay's thoughts were racing. Rosalind's words seemed to confirm her hunch about a connection. Casting Harry as the 'political hot potato' suddenly seemed far more credible. On impulse, she stalled Rosalind with, 'Possibly. It'll have to be checked out, though.'

'I agree. Do you know where to find this McNaught?' Rosalind demanded.

'I think so. But before I go any further, I think I'd better speak to Harry. When is he coming up?' Lindsay asked.

'He'll be here late tonight. He was supposed to be spending the weekend in Kinradie, but after this business, he cancelled his Saturday morning surgery and he's not going up till Sunday. Do you want to come round later on?'

Lindsay thought rapidly. With Ruth and Antonis coming for dinner, she really didn't want to commit herself to anything more that evening. 'Not tonight, Ros,' she said. 'Sophie and I have got dinner guests. Business rather than pleasure, if you catch my drift.'

'No problem. Why don't you come round for breakfast in the morning and take it from there?'

'That would be perfect. What time?'

'Nine okay? Harry should have surfaced by then. He'll be your friend for life after this, Lindsay. And so will I, come to that.'

'Don't fall at my feet with gratitude till I've actually got Harry's papers back,' Lindsay warned. 'It might not be entirely straightforward, I shouldn't have to tell you that. Tell Harry it might cost him to get his stuff back.'

'He won't quibble, don't worry about that. He'll think it's cheap at the price to preserve his respectability,' Rosalind said bitterly. 'See you tomorrow morning.'

Lindsay put down the phone and started preparing for the evening's dinner party. Plenty of good food and good wine to relax them and put them at their ease, she had decided. She'd worked the menu out and stopped to do the shopping on the way back from her sticky encounter with Claire, and she surveyed her purchases with satisfaction. She wondered if she could claim her outlay back from Claire as a legitimate business expense. Maybe she should have broached the subject before she accused Claire of murder, Lindsay thought ironically.

First, she put some water on to boil, then quartered the two pheasants she had bought from the game butcher. There was a glut of pheasants this year, they'd never be cheaper, he had informed her as he'd talked her into buying the brace. She tipped the pheasants into the boiling water, then added carrots, onions, and spices. She left it to simmer while she chopped vegetables ready for the soup she was planning as a starter.

Once the pheasant was cooked, Lindsay stripped the flesh from the bones and set about assembling the complicated dish of bastilla: layers of filo pastry, pheasant, flaked almonds and egg custard. After half an hour's work, she looked with satisfaction at the finished pastry parcel, all ready to be popped in the oven to cook. The soup was also bubbling merrily. For dessert, she'd bought some Italian ice cream which she planned to serve with a sauce of puréed fruit from the rumtopf Sophie prepared every year with 160 proof Austrian rum. If they hadn't drunk enough wine to loosen their tongues, she'd get them pissed on the pudding.

By six, everything was ready, and Lindsay poured herself a glass of wine on her way to the bath. Sophie arrived from work just as Lindsay was towelling herself dry. She looked stunning in a scarlet and cream leisure suit. 'Doctors never looked like this when I was young,' Lindsay commented as Sophie pulled her into her arms and kissed her heartily.

'Probably just as well! How's my favourite detective today? Did Barry Ostler eat you alive?' she asked.

'He was just like the Red Queen,' Lindsay replied. 'Wanted me to believe six impossible things before breakfast.'

'But did you get Harry's papers back?'

'Not as such,' Lindsay admitted. 'But I've got a pretty shrewd idea where they are. I'm meeting Harry for breakfast tomorrow, and then we'll go and see if we can get them.'

'There's a treat for you,' Sophie teased. 'A breakfast meeting with one of our leading politicians. Rather you than me.'

'What's he like?' Lindsay asked, following her through to the bathroom where Sophie quickly stripped off and dived into the shower.

'He's a pain,' Sophie shouted. 'The sort who makes you feel distinctly iffy about gay solidarity. He's basically a chancer. He tells people what he thinks they want to hear.'

'Sounds like the perfect recipe for a politician,' Lindsay called back.

'Harry's problem is that Ros got all the brains in that family. Harry's not half as bright as he'd like people to think he is, which is why he's only ever going to be a back bencher. Speaking of recipes, what time are our guests due?'

Lindsay checked her watch. 'In an hour.'

'Oh good,' said Sophie, emerging dripping from the shower. 'Time for some fun, then.'

Antonis wiped his mouth delicately on his napkin and favoured Lindsay with his most ingratiating smile. Looking at him, she could see exactly why Ruth had fallen for him. He had pale olive skin that hadn't gone sallow even in the depths of the Scottish winter. Lindsay suspected him of patronising the sunbeds at the Western Baths. His deep-set brown eyes oozed a sincerity she found spurious. A full moustache drew attention away from his aquiline nose and failed to cover a cruel twist to his full mouth. 'May I compliment you on the exquisite dish, Lindsay? I have not tasted such fine pastry since I left Greece,' he said in his precise English with its faint trace of an accent.

'If I was you, Lindsay, I'd take that as a bit of a back-handed compliment. In my book, the Greeks don't go down among the great pastry cooks of the world,' Ruth said with a giggle in her voice that Lindsay suspected had a lot to do with the amount of Chardonnay she'd drunk. Her own muddy complexion was flushed and her eyes were glazed over.

Antonis frowned slightly. 'Do not mock at me, Ruthie,' he said softly but with a hint of menace.

Ruth flushed, but before anyone could say more, Lindsay stepped into the breach. 'I'm glad you enjoyed it. I must say I had a lot of fun cooking it. I missed cooking anything more elaborate than pasta when I was in Italy. There's a limit to what you can do with a couple of gas rings and a grill.'

'Are you now back for good?' Antonis asked politely.

'I don't really know,' Lindsay replied. 'I'm not exactly

144

flavour of the month as far as journalism is concerned, and I don't really know what else I'm capable of doing to earn a living.' She took a deep breath. The conversation so far had been superficial to the point of boredom. It was time she got to work. 'And the changes there have been while I was away certainly haven't been for the better. Imagine how I felt, coming home to find one of my mates behind bars for murdering one of my ex-lovers!'

'Did you really not know anything about . . . about Alison till you got back?' Ruth asked, pushing back the mousey wisps of hair that had escaped from her inefficiently constructed French pleat.

Lindsay shook her head. 'Not a thing. It completely shattered me when I found out what had happened.'

'It was a devastating experience for all of us,' Antonis said gravely, playing with the stem of his wine glass. Lindsay noticed with a shiver of distaste that even his fingers were covered with fine black hairs.

'Jackie especially, considering she didn't do it,' Sophie said dryly, getting up to fetch another bottle of wine.

Ruth nodded vigorously. 'I've never been able to believe she was guilty,' she said sagely.

'Why's that, Ruth?' Lindsay asked. 'After all, it was partly your evidence that convicted her.'

Ruth looked as if she might burst into tears. 'I know. I . . . I could hardly sleep for days afterwards. But I couldn't lie, could I? Not about what I heard. But it seemed so . . . so cold-blooded. To make love to her, then to do that.'

Antonis ran a hand through his luxuriant dark hair and said in the exaggeratedly polite tone of voice one uses to a small child who is letting the side down in public, 'But I have told you before, Ruthie, we do not know what took place between them. Alison could be very provoking. I have watched her deliberately goad people to anger.'

'I know, darling. But Jackie? I mean, we knew her. She was always so . . .' Ruth tailed off under his gaze.

'Alison must have said something to provoke her to fury,' Antonis stated with an air of finality. He drained his glass and refilled it from the fresh bottle.

'It must be a terrible memory for you to live with, Ruth,' Sophie said. 'To think that if you'd only done something when you heard them quarrelling, Alison might still be alive.'

Ruth's bottom lip trembled, but before she could speak, Antonis butted in authoritatively. 'Ruth has tortured herself enough with that thought. I have told her, there was nothing she could have done. Even if she had diverted Jackie that day, there would have been another time.'

'Que sera, sera, eh?' Lindsay said. Antonis' attempts to cut short any discussion of Alison's murder had made her even more determined to pursue it. 'But you'd already left by the time of the actual murder, hadn't you, Ruth?'

Ruth seized Lindsay's comment like a drowning woman a raft. 'That's right,' she replied. 'I had gone back to the gallery. I had some clients to phone, and the girl who runs the gallery for me had gone off early to the dentist. But it never occurred to me that it was anything other than a tiff. Then when I got back about seven, the whole block was in an uproar. There were policemen everywhere. I nearly collapsed when I heard the news.'

'Luckily, I came home soon after Ruth,' Antonis said. 'She was in a state of complete terror.'

Lindsay cleared the dishes and brought the ice cream to the table. 'That's funny,' she said. 'I thought someone had told me you were there too all afternoon.'

'You must have misunderstood,' he said, fixing her with a suspicious look. 'I was out all day. I went through to Edinburgh to have lunch with my literary agent, then I visited some friends at the university.'

'It must have been a terrible blow to you both,' Lindsay continued relentlessly. 'She was very close to the two of you.'

'I'm surprised you let Antonis near Alison, Ruth,' Sophie said lightly. 'After all, she had a nasty habit of poaching other people's property.'

Antonis smiled politely, revealing slightly crooked but brilliant teeth. 'Ah, but Ruth knows I am devoted to her only.' He was fiddling with his wine glass again, throwing

146

quizzical glances at Lindsay and Sophie as he listened to his wife.

'I think a lot of that has been exaggerated,' Ruth said primly. 'A lot of rumour and gossip. If half of it were true, well, there would have been a lot of people rejoicing at her death, wouldn't there? But everyone was really upset.'

'They'd be bloody silly if they did dance on her grave with a police investigation in full swing,' Sophie muttered.

'I think Ruth has a point,' Lindsay said, pouring oil on the deliberately troubled waters. Sophie was playing her pre-arranged part of grit in the oyster almost too well. 'But on the other hand, if Jackie hadn't been arrested, I think she and Claire would have been keeping very quiet about her connection with Alison.'

'But didn't people know about it already?' Ruth asked.

'If you hadn't lived in the same block as Alison, would you have known?' Ruth shook her head at Lindsay's question. 'And you were her closest friend. So it's fair to assume there must be other people out there with sufficient motives that no one knows about. Ice cream and fruit sauce, anyone?'

Lindsay dished up the dessert as the conversation continued. Antonis leaned back in his chair and said, 'Motives are all very well. But no one is interested in motives now. There is someone paying the price for the crime. That keeps the police happy.'

'But she's innocent!' Lindsay protested.

Antonis shrugged expressively. 'Excuse me, I do not mean to be rude. I know she is a friend of yours. But I did not know the lady in question very well. You say she is innocent. But a court has said otherwise.'

'And that's the end of the matter?' Sophie enquired casually, spooning the rich fruit sauce over her ice cream.

Again, he shrugged. 'It should be. You Scots are so proud of your judicial process.'

'So we just forget about it? Even if a mistake has been made? Even if the murderer is free now? Relaxing after a good dinner like us?' Lindsay asked, deliberately not looking at anyone.

Antonis' dark eyes narrowed. 'There is still the small matter of proof.'

'I think what Lindsay's getting at is that by examining the motives of other people it might be possible to come up with enough reasonable doubt to get Jackie out of prison,' Sophie said.

'There must be some clue somewhere as to who her other lovers were,' Lindsay said. 'Didn't she keep a diary or anything? Ruth, you were her best friend. You must have some ideas.'

Antonis froze with a spoonful of fruit half-way to his mouth, and cast a startled look at his wife. But Ruth only shook her head. 'You know how secretive she could be. And there wasn't any sign of a diary or anything among her papers.'

'Did you have to go through them, then?' Lindsay probed.

Ruth played nervously with her fork and spoon. 'No. But I helped her mother pack everything up after the police had finished with the flat. We didn't really look at anything . . . we just packed all her letters and cuttings and computer discs into boxes. Neither of us could bear to read anything that would remind us of her. We were still in shock, you see. Her mother took it all home to Dundee with her. I suppose one day she'll be able to bring herself to . . .' Ruth tailed off, looking as if she was about to burst into tears.

'So no one actually looked through it? Not even the police?' Lindsay asked.

'I don't know. I don't think so. It didn't look as if it had been disturbed,' Ruth said.

Antonis leaned forward and put his strong, hairy fore-arms on the table. 'Why should they have studied her documents?' he asked intensely. 'They already had their hands on Alison's killer.'

'True,' Lindsay sighed, pushing away her empty plate and lighting up a cigarette.

'Must we carry on talking about this?' Ruth suddenly said. 'I'm sorry but I just find it so . . .'

'It is distressing,' Antonis agreed with a heavy finality in his voice that even Lindsay couldn't argue with. 'And it is in the past now. I think we should leave the dead in peace. Tell me, Sophie, what progress are you making in the care of your AIDS patients?'

Sophie closed the door behind Ruth and Antonis with a huge sigh of relief. 'That,' she complained as she returned to the living room, 'was above and beyond the call of duty.' She collapsed on the sofa with a groan. 'They are dire!'

'I know,' Lindsay commiserated. 'I'm sorry. Let me get you another brandy.'

'Please,' Sophie begged. 'Promise me we don't have to have them round for dinner ever again.'

'I promise. I'll tell you something, though. That Antonis is a very cool customer. If I hadn't known he was one of Alison's lovers, I'd never have guessed from that performance,' Lindsay announced as she poured Sophie's drink.

'And he trotted out his alibi as if he'd been waiting for months to get the chance to parade it before someone. Makes you wonder, doesn't it?'

'It sure does. Maybe I should take a little look at Antonis' movements. Though I don't quite know how I'm going to manage it. You performed beautifully, by the way,' Lindsay congratulated her as she handed her a glass of brandy.

'Perhaps I've finally found my natural role in life. Ms Nasty to your Ms Nice. So, what do you think? Any closer to an answer?'

Lindsay shrugged. 'What is it the song says? "There are more questions than answers, And the more I find out, the less I know!" ' She paced the floor as she worked through the facts she had gathered. Past experience had taught her that the best way to order her thoughts was to bounce them off someone. And when it came to providing her with stimulating responses, Sophie had already proved herself that evening.

'Claire has no alibi, and she has motive,' Lindsay began, ticking people off on her fingers as she paced. She worked her way through Claire, Jimmy Mills, Ian McIntosh, Ruth and Antonis, and concluded, 'What we are distinctly lacking is any proof.'

'What about the thumbprint that you told me about? Couldn't we get prints from all those suspects and see if any of them match?' Sophie suggested.

Lindsay sighed. 'I guess it might have to come to that. But I can't see the police being very co-operative. And I really haven't the faintest idea if you can get freelance fingerprint experts to check out any prints we might obtain by subterfuge. I don't know, Sophie. I'm completely confused.' She threw herself down on the sofa beside Sophie.

Sophie tickled the back of her neck, sending shivers of pleasure down Lindsay's spine. 'The darkest hour is just before the dawn,' she consoled. 'Come on, let's go to bed. Maybe sleeping on it will help to clarify your thoughts.'

Lindsay grinned. 'Personally, I've always found that vigorous physical activity is a great mental catalyst.'

'So go out for a jog!'

16

It was loathe at first sight. Lindsay hadn't been in Harry Campbell's company for five minutes before she knew for certain they would never be friends. When she arrived at Rosalind's flat, he was sitting at the kitchen table, nervously drumming his fingers while Rosalind waited on him. As Lindsay entered, he half-rose from his chair and offered her his hand.

'Lindsay? I'm glad to meet you. Rosalind has told me so much about you. I understand we're deeply indebted to you for all your hard work in tracking down our burglar. Well, let me say now, we won't forget what we owe you. Coffee? Orange juice? Rosalind, see to our guest, will you?' he smarmed.

Lindsay shook the warm, soft palm he held out, and before Rosalind could do anything, she helped herself to orange juice and coffee. Being with her big brother might reduce Rosalind to the level of obedient schoolgirl, but Lindsay didn't want to be part of it. She sat down and appraised Harry Campbell. Leaving aside the possibility that he was Alison's 'political hot potato', if he was going to be by her side on the showdown with Alex McNaught, she wanted to know exactly what she was getting into.

He was in his late thirties, though he looked younger. His pepper and salt hair was neatly barbered, as was the still-dark moustache, which Lindsay guessed was there to hide the weakness of his thin mouth. His eyes were dark blue rather than violet like Ros, but they had the disconcerting habit of sliding away from direct contact. He was, she supposed, fairly handsome in an almost feminine way. But there was nothing arch or camp in his manner or his dress. He wore a crisp white shirt with a tweed tie, and tweed trousers. The matching suit jacket was slung over the back of the kitchen chair on which he sat. If he hadn't been a politician, he might have been deputy headmaster at a country primary school. He wasn't a natural number one, Lindsay decided almost immediately.

Before he could launch into his party political broadcast, Lindsay turned to Rosalind and commented on her success in restoring the flat to its previous state of neatness.

'Helen helped me,' Rosalind said. 'I don't know what I'd have done without her. Actually, once we'd cleared up the mess, it didn't take too long.'

Harry was clearly impatient of such domestic chit-chat. 'So,' he said portentously. 'You're the young woman who succeeds where our incompetent police force fails? Tell me, how did you discover the culprit's identity?'

'I'd rather not say,' Lindsay replied coldly. 'I promised I wouldn't reveal my source. But the information is sound.'

'Oh, I'm not doubting that for a moment,' Harry said hastily. 'I was just curious.'

'Lindsay has all sorts of contacts,' Rosalind said as she put a plate of scrambled eggs and bacon in front of Harry. The smell made Lindsay feel vaguely nauseous after her over-indulgence the night before. 'What would you like to eat, Lindsay? We've got eggs, bacon, mushrooms, sliced sausage, black pudding, potato scones . . .'

'Just toast, please. And some Marmite, if you've got it,' Lindsay replied. 'Harry, what can you tell me about Alex McNaught?'

Harry flashed an uncertain look at Rosalind, who said reassuringly, as if to a small child, 'It's all right, Harry. You can trust Lindsay.'

'I'm sorry,' he said, forcing a quick, artificial smile which revealed a row of perfect crowns. 'I'm not accustomed to being able to trust members of your profession.'

'Don't worry about it,' Lindsay said wearily. 'You're not alone. Now. About Alex McNaught?'

Harry sighed and picked at his breakfast. Finally, he said, 'I met Alex about six months ago. I picked him up in the city centre and brought him back here.'

'Wasn't that taking a bit of a chance?' Lindsay enquired, buttering a slice of toast and adding a thin coating of Marmite.

'As things turned out, it seems so. But I didn't think it was at the time. He didn't know who I was. I mean, he knew my name was Harry, but he didn't know I was an MP. I mean, I'm not exactly Neil Kinnock, am I? I'm hardly a household name in Kinradie, never mind Glasgow,' he said bitterly.

'So you brought him back here. And?'

'Well, we went to bed together. I took some Polaroid photographs of him.' Harry looked embarrassed. 'Look, this is all a bit awkward, you know.'

'Better me than the Special Branch,' Lindsay commented, despising him for his lack of bottle.

'I suppose so. Well, I paid him, and drove him back to where I'd picked him up. I saw him again a couple of times over the next six weeks or so. And that was that. He was really a rather boring boy. Not someone I'd want to spend a lot of time with.'

Lindsay found a moment to wonder just why she was putting herself out for this unpleasant politician. Then she caught sight of Rosalind's worried expression, and bit on the bullet. 'When you say you saw him, do you mean you brought him back here for sex?' she asked bluntly.

'That's right.'

'Fine,' she said. 'What I suggest we do is this. I think we should go round to his flat now, while there's still a chance that he'll be there. Initially, I want you to wait in the car while I see exactly what the score is. I suspect he'll want money in exchange for your things, since they could earn him a fair amount if he goes to the papers. Once I've persuaded him we can do a deal, I'll bring you in to negotiate the nuts and bolts. Then we'll take it from there. How much money have you got on you?'

153

Harry looked confused and pulled his wallet out of his jacket pocket. He took a quick look inside and said, 'About £50.'

Lindsay shook her head. 'That's not going to be nearly enough. Have you got any cash cards?'

Harry nodded reluctantly. 'I've got a couple of those gold cards that let you draw £500 at a time.'

'Let's hope that'll be enough,' Lindsay said.

Harry looked dismayed. 'You mean he might want more than £1,000?'

'Harry, if I had what he's got in his possession, and if you weren't Ros's brother, I could be ten grand richer by teatime. Get away with £1,000 and you'll be doing very well. Now, when you've finished tucking in, I think we should get round to Springburn.'

As she followed Ostler's directions, Lindsay broke the edgy silence in the car. 'By the way Harry, did you know Alison Maxwell?'

He frowned as if trying to recall where he'd heard the name. 'Maxwell? Oh yes, the woman who was murdered in Caird House. No, we'd never met.'

His response seemed so natural that Lindsay was tempted to believe him. Then she remembered the necessity for all politicians, especially the ones with skeletons in the closet, to learn how to lie expertly, and reserved judgment. If there was a connection between Harry and Alison, straight questioning wasn't going to bring it to light.

She pulled up outside a three-storey detached Victorian house slotted incongruously among blocks of council flats. Its grey stucco was peeling off, giving the building a scabby, down-at-heel look. The door, once painted royal blue, was now overlaid with a layer of city grime. Leaving Harry in the car, Lindsay walked up the path and studied the house. Most of the curtains were closed, but a few were drawn back to provide unappetising glimpses of typical bed-sit land. On the door jamb were a dozen bell pushes, only a few of which had names scrawled on their labels. Lindsay scrutinised them carefully, but the name McNaught was nowhere to be seen. Undeterred, she pressed the bell marked Flat 1. There was no response, so she worked her way methodically down the bells. Eventually, Flat 5 produced a response.

The door inched open to reveal a sleepy looking young woman in a grubby dressing gown. 'What is it?' she demanded grumpily.

'I'm sorry to disturb you,' Lindsay said. 'But I was looking for Alex McNaught and I didn't know which flat was his.'

'Flat 9,' the girl muttered crossly. 'I wish they'd all put their bloody names on the bells,' she added as she moved to close the door.

'I'll just come in, then,' Lindsay said, moving forward forcefully. 'It'll save Alex coming all the way down to open the door.'

'Please yourself,' the girl said with a shrug, moving back to allow Lindsay in. Before Lindsay could thank her, she retreated down the dim hallway and disappeared through a door at the far end.

Lindsay looked around her. The only light in the hall came from the dirty fan light above the door. Several doors opened off the hall, with cheap plastic numbers screwed to them. To her right was a rickety table with a scatter of mail in brown envelopes lying on it. She checked the letters, and soon spotted an unemployment benefit cheque addressed to McNaught. G-day, she thought happily. If he was expecting his Giro, he might well be in a reasonably good mood.

Ahead of her was a flight of stairs, surprisingly elegant in spite of its shabby carpet. Obviously a remnant of the house's former glory, Lindsay thought as she climbed. On the first landing, there were three numbered doors, from six to eight, and two other doors labelled 'toilet' and 'bathroom'. The whole place was seedy and smelled of unidentifiable cooking odours, strongly reminiscent of her student days. She took a deep breath and climbed the second flight, narrower than the first. Five doors opened off the landing, four of which were numbered. Lindsay stepped up to the door of Flat 9 and knocked loudly.

For a moment there was silence, then she heard soft

footsteps cross the room. 'Who is it?' a voice nervously demanded.

'A friend,' Lindsay said, feeling foolishly like a player in a bad TV show.

'What friend?' came the suspicious response.

'I've got a proposition for you, Alex. A nice little earner. Barry Ostler sent me,' Lindsay tried, feeling no less foolish. She heard the lock turn, then the door opened on a chain.

A thin, frightened face appeared in the crack. 'Who are you? What do you want with me?'

Obviously not the usual, Lindsay thought wryly. 'I need to talk to you, Alex. Can we do it privately, or do you want the whole house to know your business?' she said with a smile.

Alex looked her up and down, then, deciding she represented no threat, slipped the chain off the door and let it swing open. He stepped back and Lindsay entered his home. It was a large, square room, containing a three-quarter bed, a rather dilapidated wardrobe, a chest of drawers, a table with two kitchen chairs and two old-fashioned armchairs. In one corner was a sink and a Baby Belling cooker. A gas fire on full was blasting out dry heat. The room was surprisingly clean, and the walls had been painted magnolia in an attempt to brighten the place up. There was a poster-sized photographic reproduction of a naked body-builder opposite the bed.

Warily, they eyed each other. He was wrapped in a sheet which did nothing to hide the fact that he was slim to the point of emaciation. Probably using speed, thought Lindsay as she caught a whiff of his rancid breath. But she could see his appeal for the men who frequented the meatracks. He was waif-like, with tousled blonde hair and wide, hazel eyes. He had an air of corrupted innocence which Lindsay guessed would attract a man like Harry.

'What do you want, then?' he asked in a parody of aggression.

'My name's Lindsay Gordon,' she said. 'You've got something a friend of mine wants very badly.'

'I don't know what you mean,' he replied so quickly it had to be an automatic reflex.

'We're willing to pay you for it, Alex. Nobody's trying to rip you off. Whatever deal you had lined up with Barry Ostler, I'll make sure you don't lose out,' Lindsay said.

'I still don't know what you're on about,' he said stubbornly.

'I think you do, Alex. How much did he pay you for Rosalind Campbell's Scottish Office papers? Not much, I bet.'

He looked startled and flashed a glance at his rumpled bed. 'You've got the wrong guy,' he stammered.

Lindsay shook her head. 'No way. Look Alex, stop pussyfooting. There's no problem. All I want is to arrange the purchase of certain items in your possession. You're not going to get into trouble. Unless of course, we can't come to some sort of arrangement. Then you are going to be in so much trouble your head won't stop spinning for a week,' she added pleasantly.

Alex looked scared. He retreated to the table and picked up a packet of cigarettes. He lit up, never taking his eyes off Lindsay, who followed his example. She exhaled smoke slowly and perched on the arm of one of the chairs. 'It's very simple, Alex. You stole Harry Campbell's papers and photographs. He wants them back. He's sitting in my car downstairs, waiting to hear your terms. I promise you, whatever Barry Ostler said he'd give you, we'll match. But Harry's very upset. He doesn't want any publicity. So if we can't do a deal, he's going to shop you to the police for the burglary. Not to mention the fact that you're earning while signing on as unemployed. None of us wants to go down that road, do we? Now, can we talk properly?' Lindsay urged. She really didn't want to give him a bad time, but she suspected it wouldn't be necessary.

Alex nodded uncertainly. 'Just suppose you're right. How much is it worth?' he said, trying to sound defiant.

'How much did Barry pay you for the Scottish Office stuff?' Lindsay asked.

'None of your business,' he retorted.

Lindsay smiled. 'Alex, I used to be in the newspaper business myself. I know exactly how much Barry got for that

story. And I bet you didn't get more than £100 of his £500.'
The expression of surprise on his face told Lindsay all she needed to know. If she knew Barry, Alex would have been lucky to see £50. And now she'd sown a seed of doubt in his mind about Barry's trustworthiness.

'He said the other stuff would be worth a lot more,' Alex said.

'How much more? Come on, Alex, the sooner we get this settled, the sooner I can get back to my girlfriend. This is not my idea of a fun Saturday morning.'

He scowled. 'Barry said he'd pay me £500,' he said, obviously naming a figure off the top of his head. Lindsay almost felt sorry for him. Ostler was using him, and it was clearly a position Alex was so accustomed to it no longer surprised him.

'We're prepared to equal that, and add a little bit more on top for your trouble,' Lindsay said. 'How does £750 sound to you?'

'I suppose so,' he replied grudgingly. 'But I'm not handing anything over till I get the money.'

'That seems perfectly reasonable to me. What I suggest we do is this. I'll go down and tell Harry to go and fetch the cash. Then he can bring it back here, and the two of you can make your swap. That way, Harry can check he's getting everything back. Is that okay with you?'

'I don't want to see him,' Alex blurted out. 'Can't you handle it all?'

'Afraid not. You see, I don't know the details of every single item you removed from his desk, but Harry does. It's okay. He's not going to give you a bad time. I'll be back in a minute, okay?'

He nodded reluctantly. Lindsay left him and ran down the stairs. He was pathetic, she thought to herself as she walked down the path towards her car. She'd be happy to bet that he hadn't even had the nous to make copies of the stuff he'd stolen. But then, in his favour, she'd seen no sign that he planned to blackmail Harry, merely to cash in on his secret.

Harry was cowering in the seat of the car, a newspaper hiding his face. When Lindsay pulled the door open, he nearly jumped out of his skin. 'Well?' he demanded. 'Have you sorted him out?'

'£750. You go and get the money and come up to Flat 9. Alex will hand over the stuff so you can check it.' And that will be the end of this whole sordid business, she thought wearily to herself.

'£750? Couldn't you get him any cheaper than that? I'm not made of money, you know,' Harry protested.

'I told you before, if you get change out of a grand, it's cheap at the price. Just be grateful I'm not charging you for my time on top of what you're paying Alex,' Lindsay snapped, furious at his pettiness. She handed him the car keys. 'Be very careful with the car. I'll see you back here as soon as you can make it.'

'Aren't you coming with me?'

'For Christ's sake, Harry, surely you don't need a minder to go to a cash machine? I'm going back to make sure Alex doesn't do a runner,' Lindsay said over her shoulder as she marched exasperatedly back to the house. Suddenly Alex McNaught's company seemed more appealing than that of Harry Campbell MP.

By the time she returned, Alex had dressed in a tight white teeshirt and shrink-to-fit jeans that hugged his narrow hips and slim legs. He gave Lindsay a nervous grin and asked, 'Did he agree?'

'He did,' she replied.

'Christ, I bet that hurt,' Alex said, pulling a face. 'Getting that guy to part with money was like getting blood from a stone. Want a coffee?'

He'd obviously decided she was okay, Lindsay thought. She wondered if it was the line about getting back to Sophie that had swung it. 'I'd love one,' she said. 'Milk, no sugar.'

He turned off the kettle he'd already set to boil and made two mugs of instant. 'How come you got into this?' he asked, settling down in the chair nearest the fire.

'It's a long story,' Lindsay said. 'His sister's an old pal of mine. And you?'

He shrugged. 'He picked me up one night. He must have

liked what he got, because he came back for more. We must have been together half a dozen times or more over the next couple of months.' So Harry had been rather economical with the truth, Lindsay thought without surprise. 'Then he just stopped seeing me. You know how it is,' Alex continued. 'Then I saw his picture in the paper and realised he was this respectable MP.'

'You mean you hadn't realised before then who he was?' Lindsay demanded sceptically.

Alex scowled. He was used to people not believing him, but he'd never learned to like it. 'How could I? Christ, the only time I buy a paper is for the racing. Besides, he's not exactly a hot shot, is he? I mean, who the hell even knows where Kinradie is? It's not as if he was a Glasgow MP, or one of those guys that're always on the telly shouting off about the poll tax. He's a no mark. His picture was only in the paper because they were doing some big thing about marginal seats. Anyway, I figured there must be some money in it for me, so I asked Barry.'

'How do you know him,' Lindsay asked, curious to see if his version would tally with Ostler's.

'He did a story a while back, looking for rent boys who'd been with a judge. I couldn't help him, but I kept his number. You never know, do you? Anyway, he said if I could get any proof, it would be worth a few bob.'

'So you broke into Ros's flat? Nice one, Alex,' Lindsay said cynically.

'I didn't know it was her flat, did I? I thought it was his own place. When I saw the woman's stuff in the bathroom, I just thought he was probably married. A lot of them are. I never met her. I only saw a photo of her once in the kitchen. I never thought I was robbing her. I just waited till I saw her going out, then I nipped in. I lifted everything I could see that looked official, like Barry told me to. I thought all the papers and stuff I took were his. How was I to know she worked for the Scottish Office?'

'So how come you didn't hand Harry's personal stuff over to Barry with all the official papers?' Lindsay enquired.

Alex looked slyly at Lindsay, clearly pleased with his own

cleverness. 'I figured that if I gave him everything at once he might not pay me what he owed me. And I didn't know if we'd get away with it. If the police had traced the story back to Barry and lifted him, I'd have had to do a runner. This way, I held on to something that was worth a bob or two.'

'Quite a profitable wee break-in,' Lindsay said wryly.

'Technically, it wasn't a break-in. I just made it look like one. I had keys,' he said importantly.

'Handy that Harry gave you the keys to the flat,' Lindsay remarked, trying to hide her surprise.

Alex gave her a sideways glance. 'He didn't actually give them to me,' he muttered.

Lindsay grinned. Another thing Harry had been less than frank about. There had been no mention of missing keys. 'You mean you helped yourself?'

'Something like that,' he admitted. 'In my line of business, you never know what might come in handy. You can sometimes sell things, if you catch my drift.'

Lindsay nodded. 'Yes, I can see that having the keys to such a nice block of flats could be very profitable. So how come you never sold them?'

'After that woman was murdered there, the place was jumping with police. It wouldn't have been too clever to mess about there, would it? And then I kind of forgot about it again till I saw Harry's picture.'

'You knew about the murder?' Lindsay asked, delighted that he'd brought it up himself. 'Did you know the woman that was killed?'

'No.' Alex looked chagrined at the admission.

'Did Harry ever mention her to you? That she was someone he knew?'

'Harry? No, he never talked about anything like that. Besides, that was the last time I saw him.'

'You mean, you were with Harry on the day of the murder? You were actually in the building?' Lindsay fought to keep her excitement under control.

'I was more than there. I saw the murderer,' he said self-importantly.

'You what?' Lindsay exploded.

Alex smiled, pleased with himself. 'I saw the murderer.'

17

Lindsay could only stare at Alex. But as she evaluated what he'd said, a faint scepticism crept in. 'How did you manage that, then?' she demanded.

He gave her the smile and the wide-eyed stare. 'I'd been with Harry. I left the flat about six o'clock. I remember the time, because Harry'd just put the radio on for the news. Bor–ring! Anyway, I waited for ages for the lift, then I decided to go down the stairs because I was in a hurry. I had an appointment, see? I was just pushing the door open on to the sixth-floor landing when this woman came tearing out of a flat and ran down the stairs ahead of me. I don't think she noticed me, but I saw her all right. You got any fags?'

Lindsay automatically handed over her packet. 'So . . . why didn't you go to the police when you heard about the murder?'

'Are you kidding?' Alex expostulated. 'For a kick off, I'm under age. I'm only seventeen. Soon as they started asking me what I was doing there, I'd be right in the shit. Besides, in my game, you have to be discreet. The word goes round that you blab to the police about where you've been and who with, you might as well be dead. Anyway, think about it. Who's going to take the word of a rent boy?'

What he said made sense, Lindsay thought. Her head was buzzing with the possibility that this was the break she needed. But she had to check that it wasn't Jackie he'd seen leaving the flat. She chose her words carefully. 'I suppose you followed the case in the papers?'

'Of course I did.'

'So you must have realised that your evidence would have helped the police nail Jackie Mitchell. They'd have been so glad to get someone backing up their version that they wouldn't have probed too closely into what you were doing there.'

Alex looked at her as if she were extraordinarily stupid. 'Don't you understand? The woman I saw wasn't the one they did for it.'

Lindsay's heart lurched. This really was what she'd been waiting for. 'What did she look like, then, this other woman?'

'What's it to you?' Alex asked, suddenly suspicious again.

'Just nosy,' Lindsay lied.

'Well, she was wearing one of them ski caps so I couldn't see her hair. The weather was hellish that day, I remember I got soaking waiting for the bus. But I'd know her again anywhere, sure I would,' he said.

'Well, was she tall or short? Thin or fat?' Lindsay pushed.

'I don't know. I'm not very good at describing people. She was just ordinary, I suppose. But what's the big deal anyway? Oh, wait a minute. You weren't thinking Harry had anything to do with it?' Laughter bubbled in his throat. 'Come on! He hasn't got the bottle for that.'

Lindsay took a deep breath. Before she could say more, the doorbell rang insistently. 'That'll be Harry,' she said.

'You go. I'll get his stuff,' Alex muttered.

Lindsay returned moments later with an irritated Harry. They entered the room to find Alex pulling a plastic bag out from under his mattress. He turned to face them and gave Harry a grin. 'Hiya, Dirty Harry,' he said cheekily.

'You little shit!' Harry spat. 'You scumbag! How dare you steal my things.'

'Now, now, Harry, mind your language. There's a lady present. Don't give me a bad time or the deal might just be off.' Alex had clearly begun to enjoy himself.

'You . . .' Harry trailed off as Alex wagged an admonishing finger.

'All right, boys, let's cut the posturing. Harry, money on

the table. Alex, open the bag and let Harry have a look through it.'

Both men looked at her, Harry with astonished anger and Alex with amusement. 'You heard the lady,' Alex said.

'I should have known you were trouble the minute I clapped eyes on you,' Harry muttered as he put the bundle of tenners on the table.

Alex's eyes lit up at the sight of the money. It would be cocaine tonight instead of speed, Lindsay thought sadly. He moved towards it, but Lindsay swiftly interposed her body between him and the table. 'Aw, c'mon!' he complained.

'All in good time,' Lindsay said, keeping half an eye on Harry who was rifling through the bag's contents, an anxious look on his face. 'All present and correct, Harry?' she asked.

He nodded doubtfully. 'I think so. If you try and double-cross me, you little bastard . . .'

'You'll what, Harry? Give me a good spanking?' Alex asked sweetly.

Harry flushed purple. 'You . . .' he spluttered.

'I'll see you down at the car, Harry,' Lindsay said calmly. 'I just want to have a wee word with Alex here.'

Harry looked as if he was about to protest, but gave up without a fight. He edged out of the room, swearing under his breath.

'Don't vote, it only encourages them,' Alex giggled as Lindsay moved away and let him get to the money. He rifled the bundles of notes gleefully. 'Did you see his face? He was really shitting it, wasn't he?'

'Alex. About that other business. I was telling you a wee white lie when I said I was just nosy.'

Immediately, the wary look came back into his eyes. 'Oh aye?' he said.

Lindsay perched on the chair arm again. 'The woman they put away for Alison Maxwell's murder is a good friend of mine. Her girlfriend hired me to see if I could clear Jackie's name. So far, I've come up with plenty of suspects but no hard evidence. Now, what you told me this morning makes a big difference to me. I want you to help me. I want to see if you can identify the woman you saw that day.'

'You must be kidding. I told you before, I can't go to the police,' Alex objected.

'You won't have to go to the police,' Lindsay added, not caring whether it was the truth or not. 'You see, once I know who it is, I can easily find other evidence to corroborate it.'

'Oh aye. And once I've fingered the killer, what's to stop her killing me?'

'It's not you she's got to worry about. It's me. If anybody's taking a risk, it's me. I'm not talking about a one-to-one confrontation. I'm talking about a lot of witnesses. Will you help me, Alex?'

'Why should I? What's in it for me?' he demanded shrewdly.

'You won't lose by it. I can't say any more than that now. Think about it. If you come forward at this late stage, the first question the defence is going to ask you is whether you've been paid for giving evidence. Say yes and your evidence isn't worth a penny piece. So no talk about money now, eh? You'd have to take my word for it. But I saw you right this morning, didn't I?'

Reluctantly he nodded. 'I don't know, though,' he muttered, throwing himself petulantly into the armchair. 'I just don't want to get involved.'

'But you are involved, like it or not. And now I know, I intend to get you to help me to trap Alison's killer. With or without your co-operation,' she added with an edge to her voice.

'How do you mean, with or without my co-operation?' Alex challenged.

Lindsay reached over for her cigarettes and lit one. She'd tried being nice. Now it was time to put the pressure on. And she'd seen Alex under pressure. It shouldn't be too hard, she thought, already making excuses to herself for behaviour she was ashamed of. 'Look at it from my point of view for a minute,' she said. 'Jackie's my mate. I don't want to see her stuck in prison for a crime she didn't commit. But unlike Jackie, I don't owe you a damn thing. You're just a wee rent boy with a fondness for illegal chemicals and blackmail. I like you well enough, Alex, but it wouldn't honestly matter a toss to me if you were alive or dead. All I have to do is tell my suspects all about you, then sit back and wait to see what happens next.'

Alex paled. 'You wouldn't dare!' he gasped. 'You wouldn't set me up like that!'

'I don't want to, Alex. But if that's the only way I'm going to nail Alison Maxwell's killer, I'll do it. Like I said, Jackie matters to me. But you don't. So what's it to be? You going to help me? Or am I going to have to throw you to the wolves?'

'I've got no fucking choice, have I?' he said bitterly. 'Okay, okay, you win. I'll point the finger. But I'm not going to the police, is that clear?'

'As crystal, Alex.' She got to her feet. 'I'll be back here tomorrow to tell you about the arrangements.' Swiftly, before he could stop her, she moved to the table and scooped up his money.

'What the hell are you doing?' he shouted as he leapt out of the armchair and threw himself at her.

The struggle was brief, and Lindsay soon threw his slight frame off her. She stuffed the money into the inside pocket of her jacket. 'Think of it as insurance,' she said. 'In case you were tempted to try anything silly like doing a runner. I'll be back tomorrow, with your money.'

'You can't do this,' he howled, tears in his eyes.

'Who's going to stop me?' she asked calmly. 'Going to call the cops, Alex?'

He looked at her with pure hatred in his eyes. 'I thought you were okay,' he panted. 'But you're another bitch like the rest of them.'

'Afraid so, Alex. I'll see you tomorrow about twelve. I'll be back. I promise you. Here's my address and phone number, if you don't believe me.' She scribbled on her pad and tore off a sheet which she dropped on the bed, then walked out.

An hour later, Lindsay was driving down the motorway towards Stirling, and beyond that, to Dundee and Mrs

Maxwell. The morning's business had left her with a nasty taste in her mouth. She had hated being pressed into service on Harry's account, and she had hated even more having to play the bully to win Alex's co-operation. God alone knew what Claire would say when she told her he'd have to be paid eventually. But then, if Sophie's suspicions were right, it wouldn't be Claire who'd have to pay for her own nemesis.

Thinking of Sophie made Lindsay wish she were with her now. After dropping the still-complaining Harry at Rosalind's, she had driven back to the flat to ask Sophie if she wanted to come to Dundee with her for the ride. But Sophie had reluctantly declined, explaining she was on call. Lindsay thought wistfully that now she knew how Cordelia had felt all those times she'd been denied Lindsay's company because of the vagaries of a journalist's life. Lindsay put a Mathilde Santing tape into the cassette player and turned up the volume. It was all in the past now. Whatever she did to earn a living from now on would give her the freedom to spend time with Sophie. Or whoever, she thought to herself, refusing to count her chickens.

She wasn't entirely certain why she was still going through with her plan to collect Alison's papers, except that once she knew the killer's identity, there might be valuable corroborative evidence there. She still wasn't sure how she was going to persuade Mrs Maxwell to hand over the boxes that contained what was left of Alison's life. Somehow, she didn't think the truth would be very compelling. If Mrs Maxwell had convinced herself that Jackie was Alison's killer, it would take more than Lindsay to change her mind.

She had met Alison's widowed mother only once. But that had been enough. She had been staying with her daughter when Lindsay had popped in one afternoon to drop off a book she'd borrowed from Alison. Lindsay remembered a tall, ramrod-straight woman with iron grey hair carefully set like concrete who had peered disapprovingly at Lindsay's jeans through gold-rimmed glasses. Alison had told her how strict her mother had been with her as a child, and Lindsay found it easy to believe, having heard Mrs Maxwell pontificating about the appalling behaviour of the unions, the need for Mrs Thatcher's firm hand at the helm and the desirability of removing communism from the world. Remembering all that, Lindsay had taken time to change out of her jeans and sweatshirt and had borrowed a tweed suit and jade green silk shirt from Sophie. At least she now looked like the kind of woman Mrs Maxwell might allow across her threshold.

It was just after two when Lindsay pulled up in the quiet street where Mrs Maxwell lived. She'd found the address in the case papers Jim Carstairs had shown her, and had luckily taken a note of it at the time. The house was a large bungalow surrounded by a geometrically neat terraced garden, with dramatic views over the Firth of Tay to the Tentsmuir bird sanctuary in Fife. She climbed the steps leading to the bungalow's front door and rang the bell. In the distance, she could hear chimes ringing out.

Almost before the echoes died away, the door opened to reveal Mrs Maxwell. Grief had changed her outward appearance not one iota. She looked questioningly at Lindsay. 'Yes?' she said.

'Hello, Mrs Maxwell. I'm Lindsay Gordon. I don't know if you remember me, but we met once at Alison's flat.'

'I remember you perfectly well, Miss Gordon. I may be old, but I'm not senile yet,' she replied crisply. 'What can I do for you?'

'Well, I was in the area visiting friends, and I thought I ought to call and say how sorry I was about Alison. I was out of the country when it happened, you see, so I missed the funeral and everything,' Lindsay said.

'I see. Well, thank you very much for taking the trouble,' Mrs Maxwell said, showing no inclination to admit Lindsay.

'I also wondered . . . Well, Ruth Menzies told me you had all Alison's papers and correspondence. Before I went off to Italy, Alison and I had discussed a joint project. We were going to write a book together about Scots who had made their mark in the 1980s. Alison said she would carry out the preliminary research while I was away, then we could finish it together.'

'She said nothing about it to me,' Mrs Maxwell said. 'You'd better come in, I suppose.'

She ushered Lindsay into a lounge that looked as if no one had ever relaxed in it. Even the copies of the *Scots Magazine* and *Woman's Weekly* on the rack had their corners aligned. Lindsay sat on the edge of an armchair opposite Alison's mother. 'So, Miss Gordon, you and my daughter had planned to write a book together.'

'That's right. I thought that if Alison's notes were available, I might be able to complete the project as a sort of memorial to her.'

Mrs Maxwell compressed her lips. 'I see,' she said eventually. 'Judging by the kind of memorial most of her colleagues gave her in the columns of the papers, I'm not at all sure that I want anything more raked over.'

'I had nothing to do with that, Mrs Maxwell,' Lindsay remarked apologetically. 'I was very fond of Alison. I have no intention of besmirching your memories of her.'

'It's too late for that, Miss Gordon. My memories of my daughter have already been damaged beyond repair by the scurrilous lies of your colleagues.'

'I'm sorry about that. But what I had in mind was a genuine tribute to her journalistic skills. People should be able to remember her by what she was best at. I'm not interested in rehashing her private life. I'd hoped you'd be willing to help me.'

Mrs Maxwell got to her feet. 'My daughter is dead, Miss Gordon. Nothing can bring her back to me. But if her papers can be of any use to you, I suppose there is no harm in letting you go through them. But I insist that I have power of veto over anything you write using my daughter's work.'

Lindsay nodded vigorously. 'That's no problem, Mrs Maxwell. I'll happily let you have it in writing if that would make you happier.'

'It would,' Mrs Maxwell said. 'Have you pen and paper?'

Lindsay fished out her notebook and a pen and dashed off a note promising to give Mrs Maxwell complete control over the final product of her daughter's notes for the non-existent book.

She handed it to Mrs Maxwell, who scrutinised it carefully, then said, 'If you'll come with me, everything is in Alison's room.'

Lindsay followed her down the hall and into a pristine bedroom, a shrine to the teenage years of Alison Maxwell. It made Lindsay shiver inside as she surveyed the neat single bed with its hand-crocheted bedspread, the matching white wardrobe, chest of drawers and dressing table, and the framed photographs of Alison in the sixth form, Alison in Girl Guide uniform and Alison in cap and gown clutching her degree scroll from St Andrew's University. Mrs Maxwell opened the wardrobe and pointed to two large cardboard boxes.

'It's all in there,' she announced. 'I haven't had the heart to go through it.'

'Thank you,' Lindsay said. 'I'll bring it all back as soon as possible.'

'You mean you want to take it away?' Mrs Maxwell demanded, outrage in every line of her face.

'I'll have to. I'll need to be able to go through all her computer discs to see what they contain. And there could be documents in there that are referred to on the discs,' Lindsay explained. 'I'll be very careful with them, Mrs Maxwell.'

The elderly woman looked worried. 'I don't know,' she hesitated. 'I really don't know.'

'That way, I won't be under your feet. There's at least a few days work in there,' Lindsay said persuasively.

The thought of having Lindsay in her home for any length of time clearly tipped the balance. 'Very well,' Mrs Maxwell said, resuming her normal decisive manner. 'But I expect everything to be returned in the state in which you found it. Is that clear?'

'Perfectly,' said Lindsay. Half an hour later she was on her way back to Glasgow, feeling utterly triumphant. At last, everything was going her way.

18

Lindsay surveyed the living room with satisfaction. Everything was ready. Bottles and glasses were set out on a side table with mixers and a bucket of ice. The chairs were arranged so that she could see everyone if she stood in front of the fire. Very Hercule Poirot, she mocked herself as she went through to the study to check that there were no problems there either. She found Sophie sprawled across the divan reading the latest Jeanette Winterson, and Alex sitting at the computer, a fierce frown of concentration on his face.

'Glad to see you're making the best of it,' Lindsay remarked.

Alex looked up with a scowl. 'You didn't give me a lot of choice, did you? Huckling me off here to do your dirty work. When am I going to get my money back? You robbed me!'

'I didn't rob you,' Lindsay said mildly. 'Think of me as a kind of bank. You'll get your money back soon enough.'

Alex ignored her and said, 'Hey, Sophie, got any more games? I'm getting kind of fed up with Batman.'

Sophie dropped her book and got up. 'Sure, Alex, just a minute. No one here yet?' she asked as she rummaged in a drawer to emerge with another disc.

'They're due any minute,' Lindsay replied, nervously checking her watch.

'Good luck,' Sophie said.

'I'll come and get you when I'm ready,' Lindsay promised on her way out of the door. She paced up and down the hall, smoking continuously. Ten minutes passed before the doorbell pealed out.

Lindsay leapt for the door and opened it to reveal Claire and Cordelia. 'Come in, come in,' Lindsay invited them, ushering them into the lounge. They both looked striking. Lindsay felt like a scruff in her jeans and Levi shirt and wished she'd had the sense to raid Sophie's wardrobe again.

'This all looks very organised,' Claire commented coolly as Lindsay poured Scotch and water for her and Cordelia. 'Don't you think you should tell me exactly what is going on? After all, I am footing the bill.'

Lindsay bit back the angry retort that sprang to mind and smiled. 'The element of surprise is vital,' she said. 'I'm afraid you'll have to trust me. But I think I can promise you that by the end of the evening, we'll have a much clearer idea of who killed Alison Maxwell, and why.'

'Very mysterious,' Cordelia said sarcastically. 'You always did have a penchant for the dramatic, Lindsay. Let's just hope you don't pull your usual trick of accusing the wrong person.'

Lindsay flushed. Cordelia's raking up of the murder case that had brought them together was deeply unsettling. Lindsay fought to control herself and said, 'Only once, Cordelia, only once. And I didn't actually accuse the wrong person over the Derbyshire House murder. I can't help it if people take my questions the wrong way.'

'Well, let's hope you get it right this time,' Cordelia retorted.

The conversation was cut short by the sound of the doorbell. Lindsay returned moments later with Jim Carstairs, Jackie's lawyer. His only concession to being out of working hours was to swap his pinstripe suit for a sports jacket and cavalry twill trousers. He looked uncomfortable and slightly embarrassed.

'Thanks for coming on a Sunday evening, Jim,' Claire greeted him.

'This is all very irregular,' he complained. 'I hope you know what you're doing, Claire.'

'Me? I'm just a spectator like you, Jim. This is Lindsay's

show. And we're all waiting with bated breath to see what she has for us.' There was an edge of sarcasm in Claire's voice that grated on Lindsay, making her all the more determined to prove herself.

'I've never found orthodoxy a virtue in itself,' Lindsay muttered as she poured Jim a glass of red wine. 'Look, I know you're all as keen as I am to get Jackie out of prison. I'd thought of going straight to the police with the evidence I've got, but then I thought it would make much more sense to do it this way. After all, Claire, it was you yourself who warned me right at the beginning that my job was not so much to find the real killer as to cast enough doubt on Jackie's conviction to pave the way for an appeal. After tonight, I think we'll be able to do a little better than create reasonable doubt. You see, I've never thought it was enough just to get Jackie out of jail. If she's released on appeal, there will always be the wagging tongues who'll say she did it but she was lucky enough to get off. Ordeal by innocence, as Agatha Christie calls it. But I think I'd like to nail whoever did it. That settles all the doubts for good and all.'

Claire looked surprised and opened her mouth to speak, but before she could say anything Jim said sagely, 'Very commendable, I'm just not sure this is quite the right forum to do it in.'

'Well, I hope to prove you wrong,' Lindsay retorted.

'So what exactly is the plan?' Cordelia asked, strolling round the lounge with an expression of patronising superiority on her face.

'I'm just waiting for Ruth Menzies and her husband Antonis Makaronas to join us. You'll remember, Ruth gave evidence at the trial. She was the one who heard Jackie and Alison quarrelling. And where Ruth goes, Antonis follows. Once they are here, I want to outline what my enquiries have uncovered.' Lindsay checked her watch. 'They should be here any minute now,' she said abruptly, turning away and pouring herself a stiff Scotch and water.

'Have you uncovered new evidence since we last spoke?' Claire probed.

'I think so,' Lindsay confirmed. 'We'll see when everyone

else is here. I'm sorry, Claire, but I really want to be able to do this my way. Please trust me.'

'We don't seem to have a great deal of choice,' Cordelia cut in. 'May I have another drink?'

'Of course, please help yourself,' Lindsay said stiffly. Cordelia must be more worried about Claire then she was prepared to show, Lindsay thought with mild surprise as she watched her former lover pour herself a large whisky.

The doorbell rang again, and this time, Lindsay ushered in a mutinous-looking Antonis and Ruth, who looked as if she were about to burst into tears. Antonis opened his mouth to say something, but before he could speak, Lindsay offered them both drinks. As she poured their glasses of white wine, Antonis grumbled, 'I don't understand why you asked Ruth and me to come tonight. Jackie killing Alison had nothing to do with us.'

'I explained to Ruth on the phone,' Lindsay sighed. 'I have come up with some new evidence about Alison's murder, and I thought Ruth might be able to cast some light on it, with her having been in the building that afternoon. You know how it is – something that seems perfectly normal at the time can take on an entirely different significance in the light of new evidence. I really appreciate you both coming. Now, if you'd all like to sit down, I'll give you a brief resumé.'

Antonis frowned, but his curiosity got the better of him and he ushered Ruth towards the sofa. He sat next to her, and Jim joined them. Cordelia chose the armchair facing the door, and Claire sat opposite. Lindsay stationed herself in front of the fire and faced the audience.

'A week ago, Claire asked me to investigate the murder of Alison Maxwell. Ruth, Antonis, I'm sorry I was less than frank with you initially. But I didn't want to stir up too much attention in case people were put on their guard. I hope you'll forgive me.' She paused, and took in their reactions. Ruth looked terrified. Antonis was scowling, while a smile played round Cordelia's lips. Both lawyers gazed intently back at Lindsay.

'I don't think I need to rehash all the details of Alison's

murder. But I'd just like to remind you all of the timetable on that fatal afternoon. Jackie had been with Alison most of the afternoon. They'd had a row, then they'd kissed and made up in bed. Jackie left about quarter to six because Alison was expecting a visitor. On her way out of the building, she stopped and had a cigarette. She had a lot on her mind and she wanted to be clear about what she was going to say to Claire when she got home.

'At about five to six, Alison's mother saw Jackie leave the building. Mrs Maxwell was having problems getting into the building because she couldn't get any response from her daughter's entryphone. Eventually, after about ten minutes, someone let her into the block. Some time between five and ten past six, she discovered Alison's dead body.' Her audience shifted uncomfortably in their seats as she reminded them why they were there.

'Unless you subscribe to the official line that Jackie Mitchell killed her, someone else got into that flat in the crucial twenty minutes and strangled Alison Maxwell. The only clue to that person's identity was a glass with half of a thumbprint on it. It wasn't Jackie's thumbprint. And it was the only thing in the whole case that didn't point decisively at Jackie. But without a set of suspects, the print was in itself worthless. It could have belonged to anyone in Glasgow. The police had their killer, or so they thought. So they didn't have any incentive to pursue the point.

'Now, right from the start, Claire was convinced that Jackie had not murdered Alison, and I have to say I agreed with her the first time she explained her reasons to me. Everything I have learned since has only confirmed that opinion. Claire came to me because Alison and I were once lovers, and because with my contacts at the *Clarion* I could be expected to pick up gossip and information that was denied both to the police and to private detectives.

'What she didn't know when she hired me was that I knew where the bodies were buried. You see, I knew where Alison hid her secret diary.' She registered the momentary flash of fear that crossed Antonis' face and the trembling of Ruth's wine glass. That told her one of the things she wanted to know. The chances were that Ruth knew about her husband's affair, but that Antonis was unaware that she knew. Taking a deep breath, Lindsay continued.

'Her diary was an unsavoury and rather childish record of her sexual conquests. Alison made notes from the first time she decided she fancied someone. She catalogued the seduction and the subsequent affair, right through to its ending. I've got a copy of it right here.' Lindsay produced the diary pages from a folder sitting on the coffee table in front of her. 'The original is in a safe place,' she lied.

'I realised that the key to Alison's death probably lay in those diary pages. Initially, I eliminated anyone whose affair with Alison was over, as long as she hadn't taken any kind of revenge on them. I was left with a handful of suspects. A couple of them were quickly removed from the list when it turned out they had sound alibis for the time of the crime.

'I was left with a few possibilities. Firstly, there was a journalist whose career Alison had damaged. They'd had an affair, and when he cooled off, she spread a rumour that he had raped her. As a result, he lost his job. As long as Alison was alive, he lived with the constant fear that she might tell her lies to his wife. I checked out his alibi for the time of the crime and found it was very weak.' Lindsay looked around the room. Ruth was staring into her lap where her hands were shredding a tissue. Antonis was leaning back in his chair with a look of superiority on his handsome face. Claire and Cordelia were studying Lindsay with matching looks of concentration and interest. Jim Carstairs was busily making notes.

She took a deep breath and continued. 'Secondly, there was a surgeon whose career and marriage she could have wrecked. She started an affair with him shortly after he performed a minor operation on her, something which I'm sure the General Medical Council would have been interested to hear about, not to mention his wife. Again, when I made inquiries, it became clear that he could equally well have committed the crime.

'And thirdly, there was Antonis, who stood to lose everything if she turned on him . . .'

Before Lindsay could say more, Antonis had leapt to his feet. 'That is a filthy lie,' he shouted. 'How dare you suggest me! Alison was our friend. I would never betray my wife with her!' He took a step towards Lindsay. 'Take that back!' he roared.

To everyone's astonishment, Ruth piped up quietly but firmly. 'Sit down, Antonis. There's no need to make a fool of yourself. I know all about it. It's all right. I know you didn't kill Alison.'

Antonis turned to face her, dumbfounded. Ruth patted the seat next to her. 'Sit down, my love,' she said softly. Blindly, he obeyed and slumped into the sofa, head in his hands. Ruth put a hand on his shoulder and gazed hatred at Lindsay.

Lindsay discovered she'd been holding her breath and slowly let it out. She'd been right about one thing. Please God, she'd be right about the rest. 'There were, of course, other possibilities,' she continued. 'Even though Claire hired me, it was well within the bounds of possibility that she was engaged in a risky double bluff to mask the fact that she had in fact killed Alison.'

Claire shook her head wearily. 'You really can be most absurd, Lindsay,' she remarked. 'Trying to pin a murder on me simply because I'm living with your ex-girlfriend is very tacky. Not worthy of you at all.'

'Bear with me, please,' Lindsay said.

'I really don't see why we should,' Cordelia said belligerently.

'I think we should hear Lindsay out,' Jim commented, looking up from his notes. 'We've already got the makings of an appeal here, and as Jackie's lawyer, I want to hear what she has to say.'

'Thanks, Jim,' Lindsay replied. 'If I can pursue the idea of Claire for a moment. It's not unreasonable to suggest that Claire knew exactly how obsessed Jackie was with Alison and realised that while Alison was alive, their relationship had little chance of survival. She could easily have resolved to kill Alison. And she had no alibi for the crucial time. She could have gone to Alison's flat, waited in the rubbish chute cupboard till she saw Jackie leave, then slipped in and killed Alison. I'm not suggesting she was trying to frame Jackie, by the way. As far as she knew, Jackie was well clear of the building, and Claire had no way of knowing that Alison was expecting another visitor almost immediately. So, Claire could have had means and opportunity. And she certainly had motive.'

Claire shot a venomous look at Lindsay as Cordelia blurted, 'This is ridiculous. I've never heard anything so stupid in all my life. My God, Lindsay you really have excelled yourself this time.'

'Look, Cordelia. I was hired to do a job and quite frankly, I don't give a damn what you think of how I've done it,' Lindsay snapped angrily. 'But I intend to finish it in my own way whether you shut up and let me get on with it or not. Now, I'd like to return to Ruth and Antonis. Ruth too had a perfect motive for murder. Her best friend was sleeping with her husband, whom she loves with a blind passion. I think all her anger would have been directed at Alison, a woman who had betrayed her in such a cavalier fashion. I suspect she exonerated Antonis, because she knew only too well how good Alison was at getting what she wanted. Ruth was in the building on the afternoon of the murder. We have only her word for when she actually left. Haven't we, Ruth?'

Lindsay stared at Ruth, who was gazing at Lindsay with the horrified stare of the rabbit transfixed by the stoat. Relentlessly, Lindsay continued. 'You haven't really got an alibi, have you?'

Ruth swallowed hard then croaked, 'Yes, yes I have. I phoned one of my clients at six o'clock, and he rang me back ten minutes later. I was at my gallery, I was ... You've got to believe me!' Her voice broke on a note of rising hysteria.

'It's not much of an alibi, is it? It only takes five minutes to get from Caird House to your gallery, after all,' Lindsay said coldly. 'You could easily have killed Alison, phoned your client from her flat then raced off to the gallery to receive the phone call you hoped would give you an alibi.' Ruth stared at her in mute horror, her hands gripped so tight on her glass that her knuckles showed white.

Lindsay paused to light a cigarette then continued, aware that her audience was hanging tensely on her every word. 'Up until yesterday, this was all I had. A collection of suspects with no hard evidence against any of them. The only evidence that might tie any one of them to the murder was half a thumbprint on a glass. But short of secretly obtaining fingerprints from them all, I was stuck. Then, as a result of inquiries into a completely separate matter, I found someone who can crack this case wide open. I found a witness. I found the one person who saw Alison Maxwell's murderer leave the flat, a good ten minutes after Jackie Mitchell.' Lindsay looked round at her audience. Claire looked stunned, Cordelia sat up straight, and Ruth was frozen with fear.

Lindsay walked across the room to the door. 'His name is Alex and he's a rent boy. That's why he didn't go to the police at the time. He thought that no one would believe his story, because the police were convinced they already had the killer. He didn't want to get himself into trouble, so he kept his head down. But there's no doubt about it. Alex was in Caird House visiting a client on the afternoon of the murder. He left his lover's flat just after the six o'clock news started on the radio, and he saw Alison Maxwell's killer. If you'll all wait here, I'll just go and get him.'

She opened the door and called, 'Sophie? Can you bring Alex through?' Lindsay turned back to the room as Sophie walked in with Alex behind her. He looked slightly apprehensive, but excited.

Lindsay ushered him forward. 'Alex, I want you to look very carefully at the people in this room. If you can see the person whom you saw leaving Alison Maxwell's flat on the evening of the murder, I want you to point to him or her. Take your time, now. I want you to be sure. Okay?' Convinced that he was going to point to Ruth, Lindsay watched him carefully.

He nodded. Slowly, his eyes travelled from face to anxious face. Then, almost in slow motion, his arm came up and pointed to Cordelia. 'That's her,' he said. 'I'd swear it. I'd know her anywhere.'

19

A shocked silence greeted Alex's pronouncement. Lindsay stared at him in utter bewilderment, unable to believe her eyes. Then she turned wildly to look at everyone else. Ruth looked as if she would faint, and Claire's mouth fell open. Jim Carstairs had leapt to his feet, while Antonis finally lifted his head out of his hands. Cordelia went white, then scarlet. She broke the silence with a peal of laughter, which echoed round the room.

'Oh Lindsay,' she eventually gasped. 'You've really done it this time.'

Claire found her voice. 'This is the last straw,' she hissed. 'You're fired. You've turned this whole business into a circus.' She got to her feet. 'Come on, Cordelia. I've heard enough to know that this inquiry is a complete farce from start to finish.'

'No, wait a minute,' Cordelia protested, a laugh bubbling in her voice. 'I want to hear how Lindsay explains all this. Lindsay, come on. Tell me how your surprise witness identifies me as the murderer of a woman I'd never even met. I'm dying to hear this, Claire.'

Humiliated, Lindsay somehow found her voice. 'I can't explain it. There must be some mistake.'

Alex, unaware of the undercurrents in the scene before him, chose that moment to butt in. 'It was her, I'm telling you, she's the one I saw coming out of the flat that night. I swear it.'

Claire strode across the room and towered over his slight

frame. 'I don't know who the hell you are, you lying little shit. But if you say that once more, I'll sue you for defamation so fast your feet won't hit the ground.' She rounded on Lindsay. 'I don't know what you think you're playing at, but it had better stop right now. You've lost her, Lindsay, and no amount of ridiculous grandstanding will make an ounce of difference to that.' Lindsay listened in silence, wishing the ground would open up and swallow her. She couldn't understand what had gone wrong. All she knew was that she had made an utter fool of herself. She struggled for words, but before she could find anything suitable to say, Cordelia interjected.

'Calm down, Claire,' Cordelia said. 'Come on, let's go home.'

'I want her to apologise to you,' Claire replied obstinately. 'She's accused you of murder, for God's sake. Surely you're not going to calmly walk away as if nothing had happened?'

Cordelia shrugged. 'We all know how completely stupid Lindsay's accusations are. And we all know why she's making a fool of herself this way. I think we should feel pity rather than anger. Come on, Claire.' She crossed the room and took Claire's arm, steering her towards the door. Alex dodged out of her reach in a swift movement. On her way out, Cordelia turned to Sophie and said, 'You're a doctor, Sophie. Maybe you should get her some treatment.' Then they were gone. In the stunned silence following their departure, Jim Carstairs moved uncertainly towards the door.

'I'm sorry this has turned out so badly,' he said. 'I honestly don't know what can be salvaged, but I'd be obliged if you'd call at my office tomorrow morning. Perhaps you could bring the original of Alison's diary.'

Lindsay nodded dumbly. As Jim left the room, Antonis was suddenly galvanised into action. He jumped to his feet and followed him, calling, 'Wait, Mr Carstairs. I want your advice about these lies we have heard tonight.' He slammed the door behind him, and the muffled sound of their voices could be heard. Sophie put her arms round Lindsay and tried to hug her rigid form.

'What a fucking carry-on,' Alex complained. 'I need a drink.' He walked over to the tray and poured himself a brandy and dry ginger.

In her dazed state, Lindsay vaguely registered that Ruth was shaking with silent sobs on the sofa. She pulled away from Sophie and sat down beside Ruth. 'I'm really sorry,' she said. 'I didn't mean to hurt you.'

Ruth gulped and stammered, 'It . . . it's all right. I knew . . . I knew anyway. I've known for months. It's just . . .'

'Just what?' Lindsay asked gently.

Then it all poured out. 'I was so afraid when you brought that boy in. I was sure . . . I was so sure he'd point to me!' Ruth gasped brokenly.

'But why? Why would he point to you? You were in the gallery, weren't you?' Sophie cut in.

Ruth shook her head. 'No. I knew about Alison and Antonis, you see. I kept thinking it would stop, that she'd get rid of him when she'd had her fun. Like she usually did. But it kept on. I wanted to tell her to stop. So I waited till I knew she was on her own. After I heard her and Jackie quarrelling, I waited till I heard the door of her flat slam. Then I ran straight down and let myself in. I had a key, you see. And . . . I found her. Lying there.' A fresh burst of sobbing overtook Ruth.

Lindsay put her arm round her and stroked her back. 'She was dead already?'

Ruth nodded. She pulled herself together and carried on with her story. 'It must have been the murderer who slammed the door, not Jackie. Anyway, I panicked. I just ran. I didn't even close the door behind me. All I could think of was to get out of there as fast as I could. I knew that the police would think I'd done it. I . . . I had such a good motive, you see.'

'So you ran away? You went to the gallery?' Lindsay asked.

Ruth nodded. 'I took the lift to the underground garage. I stopped at the first phone box I came to and I called one of my clients. I pretended I had been interrupted and asked him to call me back in ten minutes. Then I drove to the gallery and got there in time to take the call.' As she reached the end of her tale, Ruth collapsed in a heap against Lindsay, as if telling the story had drained her of all her strength and energy.

Lindsay desperately wanted to ask Ruth more, but before she could, the door burst open and Antonis stalked in. 'Come on, Ruth,' he barked. 'Let's get out of here.' He pulled her to her feet and almost carried her out of the room. 'You lying bitch,' he called back at Lindsay. 'You will hear from my lawyers about this.'

Alex carried on leaning against the wall, shaking his head in silent amusement. 'You sure know how to lay on a good cabaret,' he said.

'Shut up,' said Sophie. 'You've made her look a complete fool. So just shut up.'

Alex looked hurt. 'Wait a minute,' he protested. 'I didn't ask to come here. She brought me here. I was doing her a favour.'

'Some favour,' Lindsay sighed, getting to her feet. 'I thought you said you'd know the woman again, anywhere?'

He nodded vigorously. 'It was her. Why would I make it up? Christ, all I had to do was say I didn't see the woman here,' he whined. 'It was her, I'm telling you. I was nearly shitting myself when I saw her. It's not my fault if you couldn't nail her.'

Lindsay walked over to the drinks table, feeling as if she were wading through treacle. She'd never felt worse in her entire life. 'Fuck off, Alex,' she stated blankly. 'Just fuck off.'

He shrugged away from the wall. 'Please yourself,' he muttered. 'Where's my money?'

'Give him his bloody money, would you, Sophie? It's in my briefcase under the bed in the spare room.'

'I'll be right back,' Sophie said, indicating to Alex that he should follow her. They left, and Lindsay slumped into an armchair.

She felt like she'd been hit on the back of the neck with a sandbag. How could she have been stupid enough to trust Alex? He'd assumed that anyone in the room apart from

Sophie must be a suspect and saw the prospect of earning himself a few quid by falsely testifying. Unfortunately for him, he'd picked the one person who had no reason at all for killing Alison Maxwell. Lindsay wished she were anywhere in the world but here.

A few minutes later, Sophie returned. She went straight to Lindsay and cradled her head in her arms. 'He's gone,' she whispered. 'Poor Lindsay.'

They sat in silence for what felt like an eternity, then Lindsay sighed. 'I feel such a complete jerk.'

'I know. There was no way you could have predicted that he'd do that. He seemed so plausible.'

'I know. I was so sure he was telling the truth. It crossed my mind that he might be blackmailing Harry over the murder, and that he was saying it was a woman so his little racket could carry on. But after I'd seen Harry's performance when he handed over the money, I gave up that idea. Neither of them behaved as if there was a hidden agenda. And I didn't think Alex was a good enough actor to con me like that. How wrong can you get?'

'But I was sure he was telling the truth, just like you. Then when he pointed to Cordelia like that, I didn't know whether to laugh or cry,' Sophie sympathised.

Lindsay got to her feet and started pacing the floor. 'I just can't believe it's all gone so wrong,' she said. 'I was positive that Alex would give us what we needed. How could I have been such a bloody fool?'

'Stop beating yourself up, Lindsay. You did what you thought was the right thing. It's not your fault that it went wrong.'

'Who's fault is it, then? I had to go for the grand gesture, instead of being sensible about it. I should just have taken him along to Jim Carstairs and let him loose on a pile of mug shots. But oh no, I had to be the big shot. And look at me now. Everybody thinks I did it to get even with Cordelia, and they couldn't be more wrong,' Lindsay ranted.

'I know that, and you know that. It doesn't matter what anyone else thinks, does it?' Sophie consoled her.

'In theory, no, but in practice, yes. But you know what

pisses me off almost as much as that?'

Sophie shook her head. 'Tell me,' she said.

'The fact that I won't be able to finish what I started. I desperately wanted to get Jackie off the hook. But you heard Claire. I'm fired. No one's going to give me an ounce of co-operation now, are they? And I was so close, Sophie,' Lindsay complained.

'Yes, but it's not all over,' Sophie said. 'You've got all the information you were ever going to get via official channels like Jim and Claire and Jackie and Mrs Maxwell. And there's nothing to stop you ferreting away at that. You can still find out the truth if you really want to.'

'Oh yes? And who's going to believe a word I say after that fiasco?' Lindsay objected.

'Well, Jim Carstairs seems to think that all is not lost,' Sophie replied. 'All he's really interested in is his client, you know. I don't think he's too bothered about whose toes you might have stepped on.'

'Maybe.'

'Look, I've got an idea. You brought all that stuff back from Mrs Maxwell's yesterday. Why don't you put everything that happened tonight on the back burner for now and go through all Alison's papers? You said yourself that if it hadn't been for the advent of Alex, the final solution might have been there. Why not give it a try? You could go through all the papers, and I'll have a look at what she's got stored on computer disc,' Sophie encouraged.

Lindsay shrugged. 'I don't know. I think I just want to forget all about it. I'd rather get pissed out of my brains.'

'It'll still be there in the morning,' Sophie said persuasively. She knew Lindsay well enough to realise that the best way to get her to forget the disaster of the evening was to give her something demanding to focus on. 'And it'll look much worse through the eyes of a hangover. Come on, humour me. Let's give it a go.'

'If you insist,' Lindsay agreed reluctantly.

Sophie got to her feet and grabbed Lindsay's hand. 'Come on, then, let's go.' She leaned over to kiss her. 'It's not the end of the world, you know. I still think you're very special.'

They settled down in the study, Lindsay with Alison's papers and correspondence, Sophie with her computer discs. 'Lucky you've got the same computer,' Lindsay commented as she watched her lover efficiently working her way through Alison's computer files.

'Not luck, really,' Sophie said. 'Half the world have got Amstrad PCWs. Cheap, cheerful and designed for techno-illiterates.'

After an hour, they stopped for a break. While Sophie defrosted a carton of chilli tomato sauce and Lindsay watched over a bubbling pan of tagliatelle, they compared notes.

'Those boxes are full of completely irrelevant shit,' Lindsay complained. 'Every letter she'd ever been sent from the office, from pay rises to herograms from the editor. Gas bills, electricity bills, deeply boring credit card bills.'

'What about the personal papers?' Sophie asked.

Lindsay shrugged. 'I'm only just getting to them. There's a couple of scribbled sheets of paper that seem to be the plot of a novel that she never wrote. There's a list of feature ideas that she was obviously planning to work on. Nothing contentious there, as far as I can see. Letters from her mother, letters from an old university friend in Canada. There are a load more letters and cards further down. Maybe they'll help. What about you?'

'Nothing you could describe as illuminating. She seems to have done quite a bit of freelance work on the side, mainly on the kind of arts features that the *Clarion* would never use. Letters to friends, mainly of the 'yesterday I went to the theatre and saw . . .' variety. A couple of the discs are virtually empty.'

'What about secret files? You know, hidden ones? Judging from her diary, she had a bit of a fetish about secrecy. Would you know if there were any like that?' Lindsay enquired.

'I don't know . . .' Sophie mused. 'I don't see any signs that she was a great computer expert, so if there were any I'd imagine they'd be easy enough to find.'

'So how would you hide something you didn't want anyone else to see?' Lindsay demanded, draining the tagliatelle and dividing it into two bowls.

Sophie poured sauce over the pasta while she thought. 'I suppose,' she started hesitantly. 'I suppose I'd make it into a limbo file.'

'What on earth is a limbo file?'

'It's a sort of failsafe in the Locoscript wordprocessing programme. Any file you erase goes into limbo – a sort of back-up memory. It doesn't appear in your file directory, but you can still get it back. It's supposed to stop you accidentally losing stuff, but it's a handy hiding place,' Sophie explained.

'So did you check Alison's discs for limbo files?' Lindsay asked through a mouthful of pasta.

Sophie shook her head. 'I didn't think of it. But I will.'

After they'd eaten, they headed back eagerly to the study. Lindsay perched on the edge of Sophie's desk and watched her as she called up all the limbo files on Alison's personal correspondence disc. 'Bingo,' Sophie breathed. There were four files, each identified by a year.

Sophie pressed the keys to restore the 1989 file to the main file directory, then tried to enter it. At once, a box appeared on the screen saying, 'Error in: Edit document. Not a Locoscript document. Cancel operation.'

'What the hell does that mean?' Lindsay demanded.

Sophie frowned. 'Well, it means that the document isn't accessible in this format. In other words, although I've brought it back from limbo, it's not actually a proper Locoscript file. It could have been written with different software, though that wouldn't make sense. Unless she's turned it into . . . Wait a minute. I think I know how to get into it.' Sophie's fingers flashed over the keyboard as she created a new document, then used the 'Insert text' command to feed the inaccessible file into the new document. Lindsay watched with a new respect as text quickly scrolled down the screen.

'Amazing,' Lindsay exclaimed. 'I had no idea you were a computer boffin.'

'I'm not,' Sophie said modestly. 'I just know my way round this machine. I've lost too many bits and pieces myself not to know how to get things back.' She pressed a couple of keys, and the cursor scrolled back to the top of the file.

Lindsay read the first few sentences incredulously. 'Good God,' she breathed. 'This is dynamite.'

Sophie nodded, scrolling slowly down the screen. 'The woman was poison,' she muttered as the full impact of Alison's secret file hit her. It was filled with nuggets of information about a wide variety of people in Alison's circle.

'If she'd been interested in money, she could have been the richest blackmailer in Glasgow,' Lindsay said bitterly. 'Jesus Christ! How did she find half of this stuff out? I can't believe . . .'

Whatever Lindsay intended to say disappeared from her mind as Sophie called up the last page of the file. The first name on the screen was Cordelia's.

20

The shock hit Lindsay with a sharp stab of physical pain. 'No,' she whispered. 'It can't be.'

Sophie gripped her hand tightly as they read the short entry under Cordelia's name. The glowing green letters spelt out on the black screen,

> *Cordelia Brown. What a story! I'd love to see the look on Splash Gordon's face when she finds out the love of her life has feet of clay. I've made some enquiries, and her new book is out in December. And surprise surprise, it's called* Ikhaya Lama-qhawe. *Very African! How could Cordelia believe she'd get away with it? I'm going to have some real fun with this, once I've worked out the best way to use it. Thank goodness Anisha's letter got through.*

'But what does it mean?' Sophie puzzled. 'Okay, it connects Cordelia to Alison, but what on earth is it all about?'

Lindsay sat staring at the screen, as if willing the words to disappear. Eventually, she slowly said, 'I guess we'd better find Anisha's letter.' But she made no move to return to the boxes of papers.

Sophie got to her feet and put her arms round Lindsay. 'Just because Alison thought she had something on Cordelia, it doesn't mean there's anything sinister in it. You said yourself that no one would ever believe Alex's evidence. So why are you placing so much importance on it? He probably saw Cordelia there on a completely separate occasion and just got confused.'

Lindsay shook her head. 'I don't know what to think, Sophie,' she said dully. 'A couple of hours ago, Cordelia said she'd never met Alison, and I saw no reason to doubt her. And now this! What am I supposed to make of it?'

'Lindsay, you can't draw any conclusions till you've read this mysterious letter from Anisha, whoever she is,' Sophie urged. 'Come on, I'll help you look.'

Lindsay moved like an automaton towards the piles of papers and sat on the floor. Sophie joined her and together they started working through the remaining letters and files from Alison's boxes. It was Sophie who struck gold. She stared at a slim blue airmail envelope with a Zimbabwean postmark. The sender's name and address were written on the back in a neat, flowing script. 'I've found Anisha's letter,' Sophie said, handing it over to Lindsay.

With a cold feeling of impending disaster, Lindsay pulled out the contents of the envelope. There were several sheets of thin airmail paper covered in the same hand. Lindsay closed her eyes and sighed. 'I don't know if I want to know what's in this,' she murmured. 'You know what I want to do? I want to burn it unread.'

'You can't stop now, Lindsay. You have to know,' Sophie said gently. 'Do you want me to read it first?'

Lindsay opened her eyes and shook her head. 'No. You're right. I do have to know.' She unfolded the pages and started to read. As she continued, her hands began to tremble and her eyes filled with tears. At the end, she dropped the letter to the floor, saying only, 'Dear God.'

Sophie picked up the scattered sheets. 'May I?' she asked.

Lindsay nodded. 'Go ahead,' she said bitterly, getting to her feet. 'I need a drink, Sophie.' She stumbled from the room, leaving Sophie alone with the letter. Filled with a mixture of anticipation and anxiety, Sophie began to read.

The letter was dated September of the previous year, weeks before Alison's murder. '*My dear Alison*,' it began.

*I don't know whether you will remember me, but in
August 1985 you interviewed me and three other South
African women. We were on tour with a protest
cabaret, and when we came to Glasgow, you came to
see the show and talked to us afterwards. I am writing
to you because of all the newspaper and magazine
articles that were written about us, yours was the best.
You painted an honest picture without being sentimental, and the memory I have of you is a journalist
eager to tell the truth.*

*We need your help now. In all honesty, I do not know
if you can help us, but I can think of no one else. Some
time ago, Joshua Shabala, a good friend of mine
disappeared. No one knew what had happened to him,
but we all had our suspicions that he had been taken
away by the secret police. As you will know, finding out
information about the actions of officials in South
Africa is virtually impossible if you are black, but his
girlfriend, a young teacher in the townships called
Mary Nkobo, determined that she would discover what
had happened to Joshua.*

*Mary was a talented writer. She had already written
a play for us to perform. She decided that she would
write down the story of her search, which she did
in all its details. She called her story 'Black Hope'.
After a few weeks, it became clear to her that
Joshua had been murdered by the secret police in South
Africa, and she wrote all she could find out about this
too.*

*But in our country, asking too many questions is a
dangerous path to take, and Mary too was arrested.
Her manuscript was smuggled out to Zimbabwe by the
same friend who is taking this letter. Mary had left
instructions that if anything was to happen to her, the
manuscript should be sent to an English writer,
Cordelia Brown. She chose this woman because she
had enjoyed her work, and when she had written her a
letter to express her admiration, this Cordelia Brown
had written back a very encouraging letter to her.*

Mary felt she could trust her. Now Mary too has disappeared without trace and we fear that she has been murdered by the police.

Now this Black Hope manuscript appears to have gone missing. We have written to Cordelia Brown several times but we have had no reply. A white sympathiser in Johannesburg has tried to telephone, but all she ever gets is an answering machine, and her messages have not been returned. I am turning to you in the hope that you can help us trace Mary's book, for hers is a story that must be told to the world. She was very reluctant to show her work to anyone over here, for our protection, she said. But I had read a little of the book, and I know that its dramatic power and force will strike a blow against the white supremacists who keep my people in chains.

I know you lead a busy life, but I beg you to help us make sure that Mary and Joshua have not died in vain.

The rest of the letter consisted of instructions to Alison on how to make contact with Anisha and her friends to report any progress.

Sophie could hardly believe her eyes. She turned back to the first page and hastily read the letter again. Then she picked up her copy of *Ikhaya Lamaqhawe*. No wonder Cordelia had caught so authentically the flavour of life in South Africa, she thought bitterly. Hastily, she got to her feet and dashed out of the study. Lindsay would never need her more than she needed her now.

Sophie found Lindsay in the lounge, carefully sliding a glass into a paper bag. 'What are you doing?' she asked, bemused by the seemingly bizarre behaviour.

'This is Cordelia's glass,' Lindsay explained calmly. 'Jim will need to compare her prints with the thumbprint on the glass in Alison's flat.'

Sophie almost panicked at Lindsay's coolness. She had expected rage, hurt, tears and recriminations. Not this studied calm. She struggled to find words that would give

Lindsay the support she needed. 'You think Alex was right?' she asked cautiously.

'Looks like it, doesn't it?' Lindsay said bitterly. 'There's only one explanation for that letter, isn't there? Cordelia was so desperate to have another literary success that she stole a dead woman's work. She must have thought that she was the only person who knew about Mary Nkobo's manuscript. You've read Anisha's letter – Mary hadn't shown anything other than small excerpts to anyone over there. And when Cordelia found out that somehow Alison had uncovered her deception, she panicked.' Lindsay let out a long, shuddering sigh. 'I can't take it in, Sophie. Cordelia as Alison's killer? It had never even crossed my mind. I was so convinced it was either Claire or Ruth.' She carefully put the bag down on the table then threw herself down on the sofa.

Sophie crossed the room and joined her, but Lindsay shrugged out of her embrace. 'Please, Sophie. Just leave me alone. I know it's daft, but I really don't want to be touched right now.'

Sophie let her go immediately, but stayed on the sofa next to her. 'You couldn't be expected to guess,' she tried. 'There was no reason on earth why you should connect Cordelia to Alison's murder.'

'No reason on earth except for her guilt, you mean?' Lindsay raged. 'Jesus, doesn't everything just fall into place when you get the key to it? The entry in Alison's diary about the political hot potato, you remember? She was hoping for some originality between the sheets! No wonder Cordelia wanted to 'help' me investigate the murder! No wonder she wanted to get me into bed to distract me, then drag me back to London. And I stupidly thought she was doing it to protect Claire!'

'There was still no reason for you to suspect her,' Sophie argued, desperately wanting to help Lindsay but not being certain how to do it.

'Of course I should! I was the one person who knew damn well that she hadn't written a word of that book when I left last May. The time scale was all wrong. I should have known there was something fishy going on. And if I hadn't run off to Italy in the first place, none of this could ever have happened.' Lindsay's face was like stone, her eyes cold and dead, her voice dull and flat.

'You really can't take responsibility for everything,' Sophie protested, trying to control the anger she felt towards Cordelia. 'Anyway, you didn't give in to her attempts to distract you. You stuck with it.'

'I wish now I hadn't,' Lindsay retorted. 'How do you think it feels to know that the woman I loved and lived with for three years is a plagiarist and a killer? Jesus, where did she think it was going to end? Did she really think that killing Alison was any kind of answer?'

'Like you said, she probably panicked. She didn't expect any doubts to surface about the book's authenticity, she didn't have her answers off pat. Besides, you've told me yourself how twisted and provocative Alison could be,' Sophie replied.

'Don't make excuses for her, Sophie,' Lindsay said angrily. 'She killed someone just to protect her reputation. Alison might have been a complete shit, but that's no excuse for what Cordelia did.' She got up and restlessly paced the floor.

'What are you going to do about it?' Sophie asked.

'I'm going to finish the job that Claire paid me to do,' Lindsay said. 'My personal feelings don't enter into it. Tomorrow morning, I'm going to see Jim Carstairs with a print-out of that file, Anisha's letter and a set of Cordelia's prints. Then I'm going to report to my employer that I have completed my assignment. Do you have a problem with that?' she asked belligerently.

Sophie shook her head. She was desperate now to break Lindsay's calm to force her to release the emotions that were tormenting her. She struggled to find the words that would do the trick. 'No, I don't,' she said emphatically. 'And frankly, I don't give a shit what happens to Cordelia. But I do care very much about you. And I won't sit quietly by while you go through this pointless self-flagellation. You've done nothing wrong. Cordelia's the one who's done wrong. So stop blaming yourself. By all means, let out your feelings of hurt and anger and disappointment. But stop behaving like you're the one person in the universe who has to carry the can. Blame Cordelia as much as you like, but don't blame yourself.'

Lindsay stopped pacing as Sophie's words hit home. Then, like an animal in pain, she let out a roar of anguish and fell to her knees, sobbing like a child. Sophie leapt up from the sofa and cradled Lindsay in her arms till exhaustion finally stilled her tears.

At last, Sophie said, 'Let's go to bed, Lindsay. Today's gone on long enough.'

Lindsay got to her feet and allowed herself to be led through to the bedroom, where Sophie quickly undressed her and put her to bed with a hot water bottle. Then she too climbed under the duvet and held Lindsay's cold, rigid body till sleep finally released her from her pain.

At nine the following morning, Lindsay was waiting in Jim Carstairs' secretary's office, the damning evidence in her hands. While she waited for him to arrive, she persuaded his secretary to let her make photocopies of Anisha's letter. When he bustled in looking harried with a briefcase and an armful of files, he gave Lindsay a friendly grin. 'Come on through,' he invited her.

She hovered nervously in front of his desk while he deposited his papers, then looked up at her. 'Sit down then,' he said. 'It's all right. I'm not going to eat you. Though after yesterday evening's little farce, don't be surprised if Antonis Makaronas does.'

'I'm sorry I wasted your time,' Lindsay sighed. 'I should just have brought Alex straight to you and we could have taken it from there.'

'I can't deny that would have been the more sensible course,' Jim admitted. 'But what's done is done. And you've uncovered some very significant material. I think in Alison Maxwell's diary alone we have the basis of an appeal.'

Lindsay nodded miserably. 'I've brought that with me. But I'm afraid I've got some more information for you. It should be enough to get Jackie a Queen's Pardon, never mind to win an appeal.'

His eyebrows rose. 'I hope it's a bit more convincing than that young lad last night. Bit of a blunder, that was, eh?'

'Not really, as it turns out.' Lindsay handed over Anisha's letter and a print-out from Alison's computer file. She sat in silence while Jim Carstairs read the letter, looking more and more disturbed as he neared the end.

Lindsay deposited the paper bag on his desk, saying, 'This is Cordelia's glass from last night. Maybe you can get the prints checked against the thumbprint that was found in Alison's flat.'

He sat bolt upright in his chair and for the first time, Lindsay was aware of his acute intelligence as he stared fixedly at her. 'Let me get this perfectly clear,' he said slowly. 'You are making an accusation against Cordelia Brown in the matter of Alison Maxwell's murder?'

Lindsay nodded. 'That's right. As you've probably gathered, Cordelia and I used to be lovers. We lived together till May last year, when I had to leave the country for a while. At the point when I left, she hadn't written a word of *Ikhaya Lamaqhawe*. Yet that book was published in December. Even if her publishers had worked like hell to get it out, it can only have taken her eight weeks to write. Now that's a nonsense when you look at the quality of the book and the research it must have entailed.'

Jim nodded encouragingly. 'Go on,' he urged.

'Looking at Anisha's letter, it appears that Cordelia stole this Mary Nkobo's manuscript and published it as hers. Oh, she probably made a few changes here and there, but I suspect that the bulk of it is Mary Nkobo's work. Unfortunately for everyone, Anisha chose the wrong woman. She only knew Alison Maxwell the journalist. She had no way of knowing she was handing her information to a woman who preferred the pleasures of blackmail to getting a stunning exclusive in the paper. But the very qualities that made Alison such a good journalist also made her a serious threat as a blackmailer.

'Faced with Anisha's letter, Alison of course put two and

two together. I suspect she was holding the threat of exposure over Cordelia, and in doing that, she signed her own death warrant. Cordelia was spending time in Glasgow then, supposedly looking for me. I would imagine it won't be too difficult to put her in the right place at the right time.' She stopped abruptly.

'I see,' he said pensively. 'And it's your contention that the boy you produced last night actually did see Cordelia leaving the flat?'

'That's right. I know that on the surface he might not seem the most reliable of witnesses, but I think he's telling the truth. He had no reason to lie, and he was so accurate about his timings. The reason I met him was nothing whatsoever to do with the murder. It was he who volunteered the information to me, and he said spontaneously that it was just after six because he heard the radio news starting as he left his client's flat. I believe him, Jim, I really do,' she said persuasively.

He nodded slowly, and sat silent for a moment, as if he were carefully weighing what she had said in some private balance. Then he said, 'You've done a good job, Lindsay. It can't have been easy for you to come here with this evidence.'

Lindsay said nothing of her temptation to destroy the letter, merely saying, 'How soon will Jackie be in the clear?'

'I can't be certain,' he replied. 'But I'll be placing this new evidence in the hands of the Procurator Fiscal just as soon as I've had this fingerprint checked. Then it will simply be a matter of deciding what procedure to adopt. The Fiscal may decide at once to re-open the case. If he does, I'll immediately apply to the court for Jackie to be released on bail pending appeal, and I'll apply to the Secretary of State for a pardon. It could be days, it could be weeks. But either way, she'll soon be free again. And I know she'll never be able to thank you enough for what you've done.'

Lindsay shrugged. 'She might thank me. But there are others who won't. And I've got to face one of them right now.'

21

Lindsay eyed the receptionist coldly. 'You're seriously trying to tell me that Miss Ogilvie is completely tied up in meetings for every minute of the day?'

The receptionist gave Lindsay the frozen stare of her breed. 'All I can do is pass on what her secretary has just told me. Miss Ogilvie's diary is full today and she cannot see you.'

'Doesn't she eat lunch? Doesn't she take a coffee break?' Lindsay persisted.

'I really have no idea what Miss Ogilvie's nutritional arrangements are,' the receptionist retaliated, pointedly opening a file and reading its contents.

'I'll wait, then,' Lindsay said defiantly, throwing herself into a chair.

'Please yourself,' the receptionist shrugged. She picked up her phone and punched in a number. 'Mrs Cox? Miss Gordon is waiting in reception on the off-chance of seeing Miss Ogilvie . . . I see . . . Yes, I'll tell her.' She looked up at Lindsay. 'Miss Ogilvie's secretary says you'll be wasting your time. She really does have a very busy schedule today and there's no chance of her seeing you.'

'I told you, it's vital that I see her,' Lindsay said. 'If only for five minutes. I'll wait, if it's all the same to you.'

The receptionist went back to her work, and Lindsay settled down to wait. She pulled a paperback out of her bag and tried with little success to concentrate on its convoluted plot. All she could think about was Cordelia. They had lived together for three years, and yet she felt as though Cordelia was a total stranger to her. The woman she had loved had far too much respect for the talent of others to steal someone else's work and pass it off as her own. The woman she had loved was not the sort to give in to intimidation, but she would never have chosen murder as the way to escape it. What had happened to Cordelia to change all that? Or had she, Lindsay, simply been blind to her lover's real character? And if she had, how could she ever trust her judgment again?

The minutes ticked slowly by. Lindsay checked her watch. Half past twelve. It was obvious that her former employer was avoiding her. Claire would be going to lunch soon, she felt sure. But if she knew Lindsay was still sitting in reception, she'd either stay holed up in her office or sneak out another way. Lindsay gave a deep sigh to attract the receptionist's attention and got to her feet. 'I've not got all day,' she complained and walked out.

She took the lift down to the ground floor and cast a quick glance round the lobby. There were a few chairs scattered round, but none that offered a vantage point where she could see without being seen. And she didn't want to accost Claire on company property. It would be too easy to get herself thrown out while Claire retreated to the safety of her office. Muttering under her breath, Lindsay stepped out of the warm building into the knife edge of a freezing north-easterly wind. She walked to the corner of the building and tried unsuccessfully to shelter in its lee while keeping an eye on the door.

She thought her ears would drop off by the time Claire emerged from the building. She turned in the opposite direction and walked briskly up the street. Lindsay followed her, breaking into a run to catch up. Claire stopped on the corner, waiting for the lights to change, and Lindsay grabbed her arm.

'What the . . .?' Claire demanded, wheeling round to face Lindsay. 'How dare you! I thought I made it perfectly clear that I never want to see you again! Let go of my arm!'

'We need to talk,' Lindsay informed her.

'We have nothing to say to each other,' Claire retorted, shaking loose and heading across the street at a brisk pace.

Lindsay hurried after her. 'Look, you hired me to do a job. Last night, you marched off before I could finish that job. But I've got solid evidence that will prove that Jackie didn't kill Alison Maxwell. If you care a damn about her, you'll listen to me.'

When she reached the other pavement, Claire stopped. 'All right,' she snapped. 'I'll give you five minutes. No more.'

'Can we get out of this wind?' Lindsay asked, gesturing towards a nearby café bar.

Claire nodded and followed her in. They found a table near the door and sat down, not bothering to order drinks. 'All right, Lindsay,' Claire said. 'What have you got? And let me tell you that after last night, it had better be good.'

Without saying a word, Lindsay handed her the print-out and a photocopy of the letter. As Claire read them, all colour drained from her face, leaving her an ugly shade of grey, with patches of blusher standing out on her cheeks like clown's make-up. 'The originals are with Jim Carstairs. What he's doing now is checking Cordelia's prints against the thumb-print on the glass from Alison's flat. Alex was right, you see. It was Cordelia he saw leaving the flat that day.'

'I don't believe you,' Claire croaked. 'Cordelia isn't a plagiarist, or a murderer. You of all people must know that. You've set her up. You've done all this just to frame her. What a cheap trick, Lindsay. My God, are there no lengths you won't go to, to get your own back on Cordelia?'

'Claire, stop it! You're kidding yourself. I don't blame you, I couldn't believe it either. But how on earth could I have done this? How could I forge a letter with a September postmark from Zimbabwe? The handwriting on the envelope is identical to this. I know you don't want to believe she's a killer. But at the very least, she's got some questions to answer. She lied to all of us about Alison.'

Claire pushed her glasses up and rubbed her eyes. She looked very tired and vulnerable. No bloody wonder, thought Lindsay. 'Where is Cordelia now?' Lindsay asked. 'I think we both owe it to her to ask her face to face about this.'

Claire got to her feet. 'She's at my flat. I'm surprised you've got the nerve to face her with this. And I hope you've got the good grace to accept her explanation when she gives it.' Claire swept out of the bar, Lindsay following.

'My car's just round the corner,' Lindsay said.

Claire nodded. She followed Lindsay in silence, and didn't open her mouth again till they were on the threshold of her flat. 'No accusations, Lindsay. No performances like last night. We'll just show her what you've shown me then ask her in a civilised manner for an explanation.'

Claire's injunctions were wasted. They entered the flat to find it empty. 'That's funny,' Claire said, half to herself. 'She said she'd be in all day. She had some work to do.' She hurried through to the bedroom, followed by Lindsay. One wardrobe door stood open, revealing a row of empty hangers. 'Oh no,' Claire breathed. She turned to a tall pine chest of drawers and pulled the bottom two open. They too were empty.

'Looks like she's done a runner,' Lindsay commented. 'I think that tells us all we need to know.'

Claire turned on her. 'Are you happy now?' she screamed.

Unable to cope with Claire, Lindsay walked out of the room and through to the kitchen. There, on top of the dishwasher, was a note. Unashamed, Lindsay picked it up and read it.

Dearest Claire, I'm sorry. I can't stay here waiting for Lindsay to weave a net around me. Going to jail would kill me, and Lindsay can be very efficient when she's got the bit between her teeth. I never meant to hurt you, and I'm sorry it turned out that way. I know you'll doubt this in the light of what has happened, but my love for you was and is genuine. I didn't make you love me out of expediency, please believe that. Once again, I'm truly sorry. Love, C.

Very clever, thought Lindsay. A long way short of a confession, yet managing to cast doubt on anything Lindsay herself might turn up. She dropped the note and turned to find Claire standing in the doorway.

'I think you've done enough snooping,' Claire said, her

voice shaking. 'You've outstayed your welcome, Lindsay.'

'I'm sorry too, Claire,' Lindsay said.

'Spare me the crocodile tears,' Claire retorted bitterly. 'Just get out.'

Lindsay let herself into the flat, wishing Sophie was home. As she closed the door behind her, she sensed another presence in the flat. Warily, she took her Swiss Army knife out of her bag and opened a blade. Not exactly the world's most effective weapon, but better than nothing, she thought as she tiptoed down the hall. She cautiously walked into the living room and nearly dropped her knife in shock.

Sitting in the armchair opposite the door was Cordelia. She looked as if she hadn't slept, and her clothes were uncharacteristically crumpled. 'How the hell did you get in?' Lindsay demanded.

'You can put the knife away, Lindsay. I'm not about to attack you. I'm sorry about the surprise, but I needed to talk to you,' Cordelia remarked calmly.

Feeling a mixture of apprehension and foolishness, Lindsay folded the blade away. 'You didn't answer me,' she said. 'How did you get in?'

'I took the precaution of helping myself to Sophie's spare keys last night. It didn't exactly require the skills of a master cracksman. They were hanging on the hook by the phone as usual. I had a feeling they'd come in handy,' Cordelia replied.

'It's all over, you know. I found the evidence that Alison had on you. Coupled with Alex's identification, and your fingerprints on the glass in Alison's flat, I'd say they've got an open and shut case against you,' Lindsay said, fighting to control the surge of emotions that Cordelia's cool presence was provoking. As she looked at her sitting there, Lindsay found it impossible to believe the evidence she herself had uncovered. Surely she must have got it wrong somehow?

But Cordelia made no attempt to argue. 'Once you started to consider the idea that the identification might be correct, I knew you wouldn't rest till you'd nailed me,' she acknowledged. 'I mean, what chance would an ex-lover stand against that finely honed sense of justice of yours?' she added in a tone of heavy irony.

Lindsay found her legs were too weak to support her and she collapsed into the chair opposite Cordelia. 'I still don't understand. What in God's name made you do it?'

Cordelia ran a hand through her thick dark hair. 'That makes two of us. I still don't understand either. I suppose it was a sort of temporary insanity.'

'I can't see a court believing that. Stealing Mary Nkobo's book was hardly something you did in the wink of an eye. How could you, Cordelia? You had it all. How could you throw it away? You must have known it would come out one day!' Lindsay wailed.

'I was in despair,' Cordelia replied defensively. 'You'd walked out on me. I didn't know where you were, or even if you were still alive, for God's sake. My work had come to an abrupt full stop. When Mary's manuscript arrived, it was like manna from heaven. Her covering letter emphasised how secret it was, and that I'd have to change the names to protect people. So I changed the title as well, as extra insurance.'

'I don't think she meant you to change the name of the author to Cordelia Brown,' Lindsay said savagely.

'I know what I did was wrong. But I thought I was safe. If anyone had ever got any solid information and questioned me, I would have admitted that I had based *Ikhaya Lamaqhawe* on Mary's Nkobo's story, but that I had rewritten her prose completely. No one could prove otherwise.'

'Or so you thought. Jesus, Cordelia, how on earth could you have believed you'd get away with it?'

Cordelia shrugged wearily. 'I don't know. By the time I saw how stupid I'd been, I'd gone too far. The book was already with the publishers.'

'And then Anisha's letter turned up. It couldn't have gone to a worse person, from your point of view, could it?'

'You have no idea what it was like,' Cordelia complained. 'Alison was such a bitch.'

'Oh, I know exactly what a bitch Alison could be. The

difference is that I didn't kill her for it. Why in God's name didn't you call her bluff? Why was it necessary to strangle the life out of her?' Lindsay pursued.

Cordelia got to her feet and poured herself a drink from the decanter left out from the previous evening. 'I didn't set out to kill her,' she defended herself. 'I'd already had one meeting with her and she'd played with me like a cat with a mouse. She threatened that if I didn't do as she told me, she'd expose me. Not just expose me, but, as she put it, 'give Splash Gordon the story of her life'. She was going to wait until you reappeared then pass all the information on to you and let you deliver the *coup de grâce*.'

'She always did have a good line in poetic justice,' Lindsay said cynically, to cover the feelings of sympathy that, in spite of herself, she found rising for Cordelia. 'So what exactly were her demands?'

'She wanted all the money from the book. I could just about have lived with that if she'd been going to donate it to some charity, but she wanted it all for herself.'

'Your charitable impulses are very commendable, if lacking in credibility,' said Lindsay sarcastically. 'And that was all?'

'Oh no. She wanted me to go to bed with her.'

'What a terrible price to have to pay. You'd probably have enjoyed it, you know. She was a stunning lover,' Lindsay replied, determined to wound Cordelia in return for the pain she was causing her.

For the first time, Cordelia's calm was disturbed. 'Sorry I could never come up to her high standards,' she retorted.

'Never mind the self-pity, just tell me how it happened.'

Cordelia flinched as if Lindsay's words had been a physical blow. Then she swallowed hard and said, 'I went to the flat that afternoon. I was supposed to be there in the morning, but I missed the plane. There was no reply when I rang the bell, but I followed someone else into the block and went up to her floor. The door wasn't locked, so I slipped inside. I could hear Alison in the bedroom, having a row with someone. I know now that it was Jackie, of course, but I didn't then. I decided I'd wait for Alison, maybe snoop on her the way she'd snooped on me. I even thought I might be able to find the original of Anisha's letter and get myself off the hook. I couldn't help overhearing what she was saying to Jackie, and it made my blood boil.' Cordelia sat down heavily in the chair, her hands nervously fiddling with her glass.

'I fixed myself a drink and searched Alison's desk,' Cordelia continued. 'I couldn't find what I was looking for. By then, they were making love. It wasn't the most pleasant of experiences, listening to that. Eventually, they finished and Alison threw Jackie out, adding a few nasty threats and taunts on the way. I felt angry and upset on Jackie's account as well as on my own, and I was furious when I went through to Alison's bedroom. She was just getting out of bed, but she didn't let that bother her.'

Lindsay's blood ran cold at the matter-of-fact way in which Cordelia told her story. 'Go on,' she insisted. 'Don't feel you've got to spare me. I don't want to be left with any doubts, Cordelia.'

'For God's sake, Lindsay. She started in on me in the same vein she'd been giving Jackie. She was ranting that I was late and she wouldn't be kept waiting, and she'd make me pay for it. She was like a madwoman. She moved towards me and I panicked. I grabbed the scarf and I throttled her. She . . . she wouldn't die, Lindsay, it was horrible. But once I'd started, I couldn't stop, could I? I had to go on.' Cordelia covered her face with her hands and rocked back and forwards.

Lindsay, feeling equally shattered by her ex-lover's revelations, could find nothing to say. At last, Cordelia looked up. 'I can't face going to prison, Lindsay. You know what it would do to me. I'd kill myself before I'd spend years in prison.'

Lindsay knew it was no bluff. Cordelia's hatred of confined spaces had been a familiar consideration for Lindsay in their relationship. Hotel rooms had to be spacious, and Cordelia had once flatly refused to even enter a cabin they'd booked for a long ferry crossing. Being locked in a cell would be her idea of hell, and even though part of Lindsay was convinced she deserved to suffer, another part of her still felt too much for Cordelia to condemn her to that. She swallowed hard and said, 'Do you see me calling the police?'

'I need to get away. To get out of the country,' she said desperately. 'Give me your car. No one will be looking for that. I'll get a boat somewhere, I can disappear like you did.'

Lindsay shook her head. 'I can't do that. If I let you take my car, that makes me an accessory. And I don't fancy the idea of prison any more than you do.'

'Please, Lindsay,' Cordelia pleaded. 'You're the only person I can trust. We loved each other for a long time. Please don't turn your back on me now!'

Lindsay was buffeted by a series of contradictory emotions. The love she still felt for Cordelia battled with her new knowledge of what she was capable of. Her anger and sorrow at what had been done to Jackie and Alison was no longer any match for the pity she felt for what Cordelia had done to herself in the pursuit of reputation. Eventually she opened her handbag and took out her driving licence.

'Here you are,' she said, tossing it over to Cordelia. 'No one will be looking for you yet. Go and hire a car and get out. And if you do get caught, tell them you stole it from my bag.'

Cordelia got to her feet and moved towards Lindsay as if to embrace her. 'Don't you dare touch me,' Lindsay snapped. 'Just go.'

Cordelia halted abruptly as if Lindsay had slapped her. From her pocket, she pulled the keys to her Mercedes coupé, and the car's registration documents. 'It's parked round the corner. I've filled in the change of ownership section. I backdated it to last week. It's about time you had a decent car.'

'I don't want your bloody car,' Lindsay said. 'What do you take me for? You think I can be bought and sold, just like that?'

'No,' Cordelia said. 'I don't. It's one of the reasons why I still love you. But I know you're broke. I can't use the car. You might as well have it. No ulterior motive, I promise you.'

Lindsay marvelled that Cordelia still had the power to

make her feel ashamed. 'Okay. But please, just go.' She stood up and watched Cordelia cross the room, knowing that it would be the last time they shared the same space.

Cordelia turned in the doorway. 'Thanks,' she said.

'Goodbye, Cordelia,' Lindsay said. She listened to the front door closing, then walked over to the window. From above, she watched the foreshortened figure emerge from the tenement block and hurry down towards the main thoroughfare. Discovering the truth about Cordelia was going to change her life in ways she couldn't even imagine yet. Her trust in her own judgment was only the latest casualty of Cordelia's monstrous course of action. To preserve Cordelia's good name, Alison Maxwell had had to die and Jackie Mitchell's life had been destroyed. But in spite of her 'finely honed sense of justice', Lindsay prayed that Cordelia would escape.

Epilogue

Lindsay picked up her briefcase and slammed the car door shut. She collected a bundle of letters and a newspaper from the mailbox and sniffed the salty air appreciatively. She walked down the path to the house overlooking the beach, taking her time in the late afternoon sun.

She juggled her burdens till she had a free hand then let herself into the newly-painted timber house. Kicking her shoes off, she headed for the long verandah that stretched the length of the house. There, she dropped everything on the table and went to the kitchen where she took a bottle of Stolichnaya out of the freezer and mixed herself a vodka and freshly-squeezed orange juice. Then she returned to the balcony and opened her mail. A letter from her mother, a resistible invitation to join a book club, a note from a fellow faculty member inviting her and her partner to a barbecue brunch on Sunday.

Lindsay grinned happily. Just another day in paradise, she thought. It was the best thing she'd ever done, moving out here to California. Though it was early days, the job was everything it had promised and more. Teaching journalism at the local university was a dream compared with doing the real thing. And San Francisco was a peach of a place to live.

She ripped the wrapper open on her copy of the *Sunday Times* and settled back to enjoy her weekly taste of home. At the end of the news section, she refreshed her drink, then settled down with the arts pages. Her eye was instantly caught by a headline which read, 'FROM SCANDAL TO BOOKER'.

Lindsay read on eagerly.

Mary Nkobo's masterpiece, *Ikhaya Lamaqhawe*, this week became the most controversial Booker Prize winner in the history of the award.

Ikhaya Lamaqhawe (Home of the Heroes) was first published under the name of feminist author Cordelia Brown.

But following the issue of a warrant for Brown's arrest for the murder of Scottish journalist Alison Maxwell, the truth about *Ikhaya Lamaqhawe*'s authorship came to light.

It was the work of African teacher Mary Nkobo, who has disappeared in South Africa after her arrest last year by the secret police. Friends fear that she has been killed.

Like a previous Booker winner, *Schindler's Ark*, the book is a fictionalised version of real events. *Ikhaya Lamaqhawe* is the thinly disguised story of Mary Nkobo's struggle to uncover the truth about her fiancé Joshua Shabala who was murdered by South African security forces. When she finally uncovered the truth, she too vanished.

Mary had the manuscript smuggled out via Zimbabwe prior to her disappearance. She sent it to Cordelia Brown, because they had been in correspondence about Brown's work.

Believing that she was the only person who had actually seen the manuscript, Brown presented it to her publishers as her own work. *Ikhaya Lamaqhawe* was published under her name last December.

But her secret was not safe. Police sources say that Alison Maxwell uncovered the truth, and Brown killed her to maintain the fiction of her authorship of *Ikhaya Lamaqhawe*.

Another journalist, Jackie Mitchell, was found guilty of the murder, and had served some months in prison when the real sequence of events was uncovered by a private investigator working for Miss Mitchell's lawyers.

By the time Brown's imposture was discovered, she had fled the country, becoming the literary world's Lord Lucan.

Ikhaya Lamaqhawe was recalled and reissued under Mary Nkobo's name, and the Booker judges rewarded the undoubted power and clarity of the book on Thursday night.

The book's publisher, Jonas Milner, said, 'It has been a very difficult and embarrassing experience for us. No one likes to be conned. We had no reason to be suspicious, because we knew Cordelia Brown was a very talented and versatile writer.

'But I'm glad to say that it has all been sorted out now. *Ikhaya Lamaqhawe* was a very worthy winner.

'Mary Nkobo's mother, who accepted the award on her behalf, has announced that the money will go into a trust to award bursaries to black writers.'

Justice may have been done to Mary Nkobo. But it awaits Cordelia Brown, still on the missing list.

Lindsay folded up the paper with a smile on her face. She glanced at her watch. Sophie would be home any minute now, crises permitting. Her AIDS specialisation had paid off handsomely, and she was now a senior consultant at the city's maternity hospital. The offer of the job had come less than a week after Cordelia's escape, and Lindsay had been more than glad to accept Sophie's suggestion that they go to California together.

After some wrangling with the police, she'd been allowed to remove her belongings from Cordelia's London house. It had been a sad and depressing experience, for the discovery of Cordelia's crime had made it impossible for Lindsay to enjoy the good memories. The house had seemed oppressive and threatening, not the home where she had once been happy. Selling the Mercedes and donating the proceeds to an AIDS charity had felt like the last act in a long tragedy.

But California had banished the shadows from her life. And the job had been the icing on the cake. Lindsay padded through to the kitchen and opened a bottle of the local sparkling Chardonnay. Mary Nkobo's Booker prize deserved a celebration. As she topped her glass up with orange juice, she heard the front door slam. Hastily, she poured another glass for Sophie, and greeted her as she strolled cheerfully in.

'Good day?' Lindsay enquired, kissing her lightly.

'Not bad. And you? Are we celebrating something?'

'In a way. The end of a story. Or at least, the end of a chapter. Come and see.' Lindsay took Sophie's hand and led her out on to the sun deck. 'Read that,' she said, pointing to the article.

Curious, Sophie picked up the paper and sat down with her glass of Buck's Fizz. She read through to the end with a smile on her face. 'I'm glad it won,' she said. 'You're right, it is the end of the chapter. Strangely enough, I have a surprise for you too.' She opened her bag and fished out a postcard which she handed to Lindsay.

Lindsay picked it up and glanced at the front, an artistic photograph of two cats on the doorstep of a Greek village house. She flipped it over and immediately recognised the handwriting. The card had been forwarded from Sophie's flat in Glasgow to the hospital. The message was brief but curiously final.

'*Dear Lindsay: Weather wonderful. Life very simple here. It's good to get away from it all. A wonderful place to set a thriller, don't you think? Hope everything is fine with you and Sophie.*' There was no signature, but it needed none. She looked up at Sophie's concerned face and managed a wan smile.

Relieved that the card hadn't upset Lindsay, Sophie smiled back and said, 'I know you haven't wanted to talk about it, but how are you feeling now?'

Lindsay sat down. 'I think I've finally managed to let it go. I read that article and I didn't feel a single pang of regret for Cordelia. Even that postcard didn't churn up any unwanted feelings. I'm not sorry that she seems to have escaped, but I don't think I care very much about what happens to her now. The woman who committed those crimes feels like a stranger. She must have existed inside the person I loved, but I never saw any clue to that side of her. She's lost all power to hurt me. A lot of that's to do with you. And California. And the new job.'

'In reverse order, eh?' Sophie grinned. 'Aren't you bored with our quiet life? No chasing fire engines? No murders to solve?'

'If I never hear about another murder as long as I live, I'll die a happy woman,' Lindsay vowed.

'Funny you should say that,' Sophie said nonchalantly. 'A patient I saw today told me this long story about how she was convinced that her room-mate had been murdered . . .'

Val McDermid
Report for Murder
The first Lindsay Gordon crime thriller

Freelance journalist Lindsay Gordon is strapped
for cash. Why else would she agree to cover a
fund-raising gala at a girls' public school? But
when the star attraction is found garrotted with
her own cello string instants before she is due
on stage, Lindsay finds herself investigating a
vicious murder. Who would have wanted Lorna
Smith Cooper dead? Who had the key to the
locked room in which her body was found? And
who could have slipped out of the hall at just
the right time to commit this calculated and
cold-blooded crime?

**'Fresh and funny with a spanking sense of time
and place.'** *Literary Review*

**'McDermid cannot write an uninteresting
sentence.'** *Women's Review of Books*

Crime Fiction £5.99
ISBN 0 7043 4591 9

Val McDermid
Common Murder
The second Lindsay Gordon crime thriller

A protest group hits the headlines when unrest
explodes into murder. Already on the scene,
journalist Lindsay Gordon desperately tries to
strike a balance between personal and professional
responsibilities. As she peels back the layers of
deception surrounding the protest and its opponents,
she finds that no one – ratepayer or reporter,
policeman or peace woman – seems wholly above
suspicion. Then Lindsay uncovers a truth that
even she can scarcely believe . . .

'Pacey and wittily written . . . bound to make
McDermid one of Britain's favourite detective
writers.' *Options*

'Val McDermid is an inspiration.' *Herald*

Crime Fiction £5.99
ISBN 0 7043 4592 7

Val McDermid
Booked for Murder
The fifth Lindsay Gordon crime thriller

The freak 'accident' that killed bestselling author
Penny Varnavides takes on a more sinister
aspect when police discover that her latest
unpublished novel featured murder by the same
means. Of the handful of people who knew the
plot, the prime suspect is wise enough to call in
her old friend, journalist Lindsay Gordon, to
uncover the truth that lies behind the seething
rivalries and desperate power games that infect
the publishing world . . .

'Has the reader gripped from the first page . . .
both moody and hilarious and thoroughly
unpredictable.' *Tribune*

'The writing is tough and colourful, the scene
setting excellent.' *Times Literary Supplement*

Crime Fiction £5.99
ISBN 0 7043 4595 1

The Women's Press is Britain's leading women's publishing house. Established in 1978, we publish high-quality fiction and non-fiction from outstanding women writers worldwide. Our exciting and diverse list includes literary fiction, detective novels, biography and autobiography, health, women's studies, handbooks, literary criticism, psychology and self-help, the arts, our popular Livewire Books series for young women and the bestselling annual *Women Artists Diary* featuring beautiful colour and black-and-white illustrations from the best in contemporary women's art.

If you would like more information about our books or about our mail order book club, please send an A5 sae for our latest catalogue and complete list to:

The Sales Department
The Women's Press Ltd
34 Great Sutton Street
London EC1V 0DX
Tel: 0171 251 3007
Fax: 0171 608 1938